Praise for #1 New

KR

and the first two no

THE MASTER

"Kresley Cole is getting hotter—sexy hot!"

"This combination of humor, heart, and heat is absolute perfection."

"The hottest, most sensually erotic scenes I've ever read! The chemistry is beyond explosive. . . . I can't tell you how many times I blushed, fanned myself, or squirmed in my seat while reading."

"The suspense is addictive, the characters likeable, and the drama palpable. I found my new addiction, and it comes in the shape of a hot and sexy Siberian."

"The book crackled with sensuality. . . . The only thing I hated? That it ended."

"Full of beautiful descriptions, vivid imagery, great characters and humor. This isn't a run of the mill, slapped together erotica. This is engrossing, well written literature that happens to be sexy as hell."

"Intriguing, smart, super hot, and just plain well written have come to be hallmarks of Cole's writing, and it comes out full force in this new series."

"Five sexy CAN'T-WAIT-TIL-THE-NEXT-ONE, WHAT-AM-I-SUPPOSED-TO-DO-WITH-MYSELF-TIL-THEN stars."

—*Kayla the Bibliophile*

"Intense, ridiculously sexy, and thrilling the entire way through. . . . One of the HOTTEST series I have ever read!"

—*Shayna Renee's Spicy Reads*

"Absolutely intoxicating! . . . The perfect balance of intrigue, chemistry, raw sexuality, and supreme storytelling!"

—*Hesperia Loves Books*

"Can someone please hand me a chainsaw to cut this sexual tension?"

—*Guilty Pleasures Book Reviews*

"A riveting story that you won't want to put down."

—*Fiction Vixen*

"Scrumptious, scandalous, and scorching. . . . Natalie and Sevastyan's gloriously descriptive and deliciously detailed stolen and wildly illicit moments demanded an immediate re-read."

—*The Lusty Literate*

"Turns up the heat—the hot, molten lava kind! Cole delivers erotica on a platter of orgasmic proportions."

—*Readaholics Anonymous*

Also by Kresley Cole

THE
PLAYER

KRESLEY COLE

VALKYRIE PRESS

New York   Rothkalina   Dacia   Abaddon   New Orleans

Valkyrie Press
228 Park Ave S #11599
New York, NY 10003

ISBN 978-0-9972151-1-3
ISBN 978-0-9972151-0-6 (ebook)

Published in the United States of America.

"Desire is like chess.
Do whatever you must to achieve your endgame."

—DMITRI SEVASTYAN,
COMPUTER PRODIGY, SELF-MADE BILLIONAIRE

✦

"Cardinal rule of the con:
never, never, never fall for your mark."

—VICTORIA VALENTINE, A.K.A. VICE,
PROUD PRACTITIONER OF CONFIDENCE ARTS

Steps of the Long Con (for experts only)

1. Identify your mark. Target for greed, dishonesty, criminality.

2. Foundation work. Investigate background, eliminate impediments, and assemble team.

3. The Meet. Orchestrate for a memorable first impression.

4. Integration. Insinuate yourself into the mark's life.

5. The Pitch. Gradually make a desire known to the mark.

6. The Sacrifice. Surrender something of value, to deepen the mark's trust.

7. The Crisis. Create a sense of urgency through an ultimatum. The mark must act now or lose the possibility forever.

8. The Snare. Manipulate the mark toward an irrevocable commitment.

CHAPTER 1

"I know my fairy tales," I told my cousin. "And there's a beast up in that lair." Pete and I stood on the spacious terrace of the Calydon Casino's penthouse, peering at an even higher observation deck.

We were already so elevated, I felt as if we could reach up and graze the full moon.

"You're calling Dmitri Sevastyan a beast now?" Pete's expression was amused, the dark blue of his smiling eyes a contrast to his light blond hair. Like my sister and me, he got his coloring from my dad's side of the family. "Even though you've never met him?"

"Yep." The Sevastyans' lavish party was in full swing—music boomed and hundreds of revelers crowded inside the enormous four-suite penthouse—yet Dmitri had sequestered himself up on that deck, apparently on his worst behavior. "And just like in the fairy tales, you plan to sacrifice this maiden." Pete wanted me to go scope out the combative man.

"That's crazy talk. Everybody knows you're not a maiden."

I punched his arm. "Funny guy." I might as well be a maiden. My three notches hadn't been worth it.

"And Dmitri isn't *a beast*," he said, adding, "Much. Hardly at all."

Pete knew everything there was to know about the Sevastyan family. Well, everything a grifter could find out with choice sources. As the casino's VIP host, he catered to the whims of his rich high rollers—our very own inside man.

I didn't know how much juice he'd had to use to snag his plum position, but for weeks, we'd targeted the Calydon's degenerate whales, mainly for blackmail.

A curl escaped my up-do, and the warm August breeze made it flit around my face. "Since I started casing the deck, Dmitri's chewed out a dozen women, sending them packing."

Another group of hopefuls had ascended a few moments ago. Every female on the Strip seemed to have heard about this party—free food, free booze, and an eligible billionaire in attendance.

Pete shrugged his buff shoulders. I swore he was still growing at twenty-nine. "I'm not asking you to run game"—work a con—"on Dmitri. Just give me your take before we cut the Sevastyan crew loose for good."

Half talent manager, half con coach, Pete had positioned me and my sister in the VIP lounge as cocktail servers/honey traps.

Toe the line, boys, or you'll feel the sting.

Unfortunately, the three brothers, two wives, and one tagalong friend *were* toeing the line.

They didn't ask for drugs, and their tastes didn't run toward the illegal or immoral. Both of the married couples were devoted. In fact, the middle brother and his wife were here to celebrate their four-year wedding anniversary.

No dirt, no dinero; no sins, no in.

"Besides, you gotta get a looksee at Dmitri," Pete said. "He'll be the most beautiful man you've ever laid eyes on." My sister Karin had said the same. She'd served the group drinks in the lounge last night.

"Even finer than his brothers?" I'd passed them in the penthouse, two built, black-haired hotties who'd been glued to their lovely wives.

"Much finer." Pete made his eyes look guileless as he said, "Trust me."

"Trust you?" Despite our circumstances, we had to share a chuckle. I could make my eyes guileless too, had learned that trick before I could even read with them.

Grated words sounded from the deck above as Dmitri chewed out the latest females who'd dared to breach his lair.

Not long after, a bevy of babes in vagina-length dresses flounced down the steps. They all talked at once. "What a prick!" "I don't care how gorgeous he is; who says shit like that?" "Could he have been hotter? *Or* more insulting?"

I recognized Sharon, a bottle-service girl who lived in my apartment complex. The buxom brunette was no stranger to the grifter life herself.

Champagne flute in hand, she waved her friends onward toward the bar, then sashayed over to us; with her every step, her strapless red dress valiantly struggled to contain her rack.

She rose on her toes to kiss my cousin's cheek and murmured with affection, "Petey Three Times."

Grifter nicknames might be cliché, but Pete's was spot-on. He was so good he could con you twice more, even if you caught him the first time. Also known as Re-Pete.

I'd gotten the nickname Vice as a baby. I'd earned my Cold-as-Ice designation from my family's stock-investment schemes.

For years, we'd found men who wanted something for nothing, so we'd sold them nothing for something.

But those days were over. . . .

Pete smoothly said, "Sharon, you're looking fabulous as ever."

"Charmer." She smoothed her hair, giving me a once-over. "Great dress, Vice. All classy."

"Thanks, doll." I'd made this white, one-shoulder drape a few months ago for a job. Tonight, my look was *sexy good-girl*, a change from my usual *racy/alternative*. My black nails were now nude, my glam makeup neutral. I'd exchanged my spike earrings for diamond—read cubic zirconia—studs and secured my long hair into an elegant knot. Instead of platform heels, I wore ankle-strap d'Orsay pumps.

Sharon sipped her flute. "You dress up for that Sebastian *gull*?" A gullible, anyone outside the grift.

"It's actually with a V," Pete said. "Suh-vast-yun." Details were our job.

Sharon shrugged, her dress hanging on precariously. Her enhanced boobs dwarfed my 32Cs; she could legit carry drinks without a tray.

I always pictured her balancing martinis on her mammaries with circus music teed up. "No, not for him. I had a high roller on the line." Wardrobe was critical in cons, and this look played to rich guys. My mark, Nigel, had approved. Until he'd inexplicably abandoned me in the

Caly lobby a little while ago. "My con went south, so Pete invited me here." To dig. These days, I wasn't good for much else.

This honey trap might be stingerless.

"Looks like you're having a shit week," Sharon said. "I saw an eviction notice on your door."

I lowered my voice to say, "I forgot my neck brace *one* freaking time."

Pete's blond brows rose. I hadn't told him about my eviction, not with all my other recent failures.

"Happens to the best of us." Sharon finished her champagne. "Two tears in a bucket; motherfuck it."

I grinned. "I will never stop saying that saying."

"How'd you hear about this party?" Pete asked her.

"Some crazy chick named Alicia or Jessica or something invited the entire Strip, telling everyone about a whale she's trying to hook up. I came here to harpoon said whale. No dice. He actually told me, 'I have a woman in mind for myself, and you are not her.' Russians suck."

Pete and I shared a look. We had a Russian KA, a known associate, who was like our grandfather.

"I'm gonna go find some real action. *Ciao*, babies." Sharon blew air kisses as she rejoined her friends. Just before they headed inside, she yelled over her shoulder to Dmitri, "Go fuck yourself, Russki!"

When a tirade of Russian boomed out from above, I raised my brows at Pete. "Maybe he's not interested in women. If Karin bombed with this guy . . ." Last night, he'd ignored my breathtaking sister as if she were invisible. "Maybe Dmitri's gay."

"I should be so lucky," Pete said, a wistful note to his

voice. "For a guy like that, I would turn honey trap in a heartbeat."

"It's not as easy as it looks, chief." I would know. I was supposed to have run my first badger game tonight. In a badger, a honey trap would maneuver a married mark into a compromising position while an accomplice snapped photos and took video. Voilà, blackmail.

Nigel had been my ideal man—a hitched skirt-chaser with a cheating clause in his prenup, wandering hands, and a tan line on his ring finger. Tonight the older man's watery gaze had beamed at the sight of me—right up until the moment he'd checked his phone, sputtered at whatever he'd read, then all but fled the casino.

My fifth busted con in a row. I was as superstitious as the next grifter and knew what this streak meant. "Pete, I'm pretty sure I'm jinxed." And yet I would drag myself back to the VIP lounge tomorrow to troll for yet another sleazebag. It'd taken me three double-backs—sixteen-hour stints in stilettos—to scare up Nigel.

Pete said, "It could be the badger that's giving you trouble, since it's your first and all."

"You're making me sound like a noob." Sure, every grifter had a specialty—mine had been those pump-and-dump stock cons—but a skilled confidence artist was versatile.

"Until you get your footing, you should help out with Karin's kid another night or two a week, so she can close more. Just till we settle the debt."

I blinked in disbelief. "We're in the middle of a crisis, and you want me to babysit?" Not to mention that Mom and Dad would cage-fight me if I tried to limit their grandbaby time.

Pete scrubbed a palm over his handsome face. "Nigel should've been ... well, he should've been low-hanging fruit." In a grudging tone, he broke it to me straight: "Karin could've run him in her sleep."

Ouch. Though one could definitely tell we were sisters, I was like a short, less-endowed indie version of her. At twenty-eight, she was all long-legged grace, confidence, and effortless sex-appeal; around men, if I didn't concentrate, I could come across as standoffish—a kiss of death for a honey trap.

Pete rushed to say, "You're an ace at cards, and your grift sense is the most honed of anybody I know. Your instincts in those stock schemes kept the lights on for the entire family. But stocks are out forever."

We'd conned the wrong people, and they wanted their money back—plus interest. "Our deadline is only twenty days away, and you're benching me?" No wonder everyone had texted me encouragement tonight! Yet I'd failed to pluck the low-hanging fruit.

"It's *because* the deadline's on us." He exhaled. "You're wasting marks that Karin could close." Over the last several weeks, she'd run a ton of lechers. She even had a two-timing congressman in the pipeline for tomorrow.

I hadn't gotten a mark anywhere near our hidden-camera prop house.

Karin was my best friend, but sometimes I felt like screaming, "Marcia, Marcia, Marcia!"

In a softer tone, Pete said, "All you need is a little brushing up on your, you know, sexual manipulation skills, but we don't have time right now."

Sexual manipulation skills? Really? How did he think I got all those lowlifes to invest in our bogus stock deals?

By making sure they read my cleavage instead of the writing on the wall!

"When you're not so exhausted, you'll see where I'm coming from," Pete said. "Why don't you skip Dmitri and rest up?"

My eyes widened with realization. "You've already decided to cut the Sevastyans! My 'assignment' to dig . . . it's *busy work*, isn't it?" To make me feel better about Nigel!

After a moment, Pete raised his palms.

Busy work and babysitting. If he sidelined me, I'd go crazy in the next three weeks. How could I *not* be out fighting for my loved ones?

I burned to prove my value and contribute when they needed me most. My gaze darted up, landing on a beast's lair. Words started leaving my mouth: "You know what? You're not going to bench me. Because I'm gonna run game on the juiciest mark of them all—*Dmitri Sevastyan.*"

CHAPTER 2

*P*ete laughed—until he saw I was serious. "Karin couldn't get a word out of him."

Last night, when Pete had heard the Sevastyans were heading down to the VIP lounge, he'd sent me home and called in the family's MVP for a milk-cow con—one of the most difficult of the long cons.

In a milk-cow, a temptress would whip a mark into a sexual frenzy, teasingly withholding intercourse to maneuver him into buying jewelry, cars, even real estate.

"Not a single word." Pete shook his head. "Even though Dmitri was dateless, and she was *on*."

If Karin couldn't get the Russian to engage, then he wasn't engage-able. But I'd talked a big game. "Then I won't be wasting a potential mark, will I?"

"Don't be pissed."

I handed Pete my purse. "Pissed? Me? Haven't you heard?" I started toward the stairs, saying over my shoulder, "I'm cold as ice."

In reality, I was so pissed I almost stomped up the steps.

But I controlled my temper, keeping my heels from striking the tile surface. Maybe I could sneak up on Dmitri and observe him unawares.

I knew the basics about him from Pete's copious notes. Thirty-two years old, a resident of Russia, raised in Siberia. Youngest of the three brothers. A computer and math prodigy.

He'd graduated at the top of his class from Oxford, then founded a company that revolutionized aspects of business computing. He'd cashed out with a couple of patents, retiring a billionaire. Yet there were few mentions of him online—and zero pictures.

As I stepped onto the deck, I raised my brows at the beast's extravagant lair. Fire pits lit the area. A hot tub steamed under a wisteria-covered trellis, and a mosaic-tiled fountain sloshed against the back wall. A fully stocked bar stood off to the side, unmanned.

I spotted Dmitri at the railing, taking in the city's vista. Not another soul was up here.

I silently approached, noting details about him. He had a muscular build and stood well over six feet, even taller than my ex's six foot three.

My grandmother would call Dmitri Sevastyan *a mountain of a man*. He'd tower over my five feet four.

His expensive clothes were so well made, I nearly salivated. He wore tailored gray slacks that highlighted his narrow hips and tight ass. His charcoal-colored shirt clung to his back and arm muscles.

Beneath the thin material, I could see his triceps bulging as he white-knuckled that railing. Like Bruce Banner warding off the Hulk.

Pete had told me he'd picked up intermittent tension in

Dmitri and Aleks, the oldest Sevastyan brother. Perhaps they'd fought and Dmitri was taking out his frustration on others?

If Dmitri was so angry, why not go back to his room? Why not take his fortune and fly somewhere else?

In the next second, everything I speculated got turned upside down—because Dmitri's head tipped back, and his broad shoulders rose and fell on a breath. Even from this angle I could tell he was gazing at the full moon.

People didn't normally do that when stewing; they did it when they felt regret, or even longing.

A flare of pity arose. His family was right downstairs, but he remained here all by himself.

That was the thing about the beast from fairy tales; he didn't *want* to be a beast. He didn't *want* to be alone.

Dmitri finally released his grip to rub his temples.

Curiosity to see his face won out, so I headed toward the opposite end of the railing, letting my heels click.

He dropped his hands, and his muscles tensed even more. "How many times do I have to fucking say this?" he bit out, his accent thick. As he turned toward me, he snapped, "I—AM—NOT—GODDAMNED—INTER ..." He trailed off, looking staggered.

I knew the feeling. Dmitri Sevastyan was ... magnificent.

His flawless, masculine face swindled your breath and left your lungs holding the bag.

Thick black hair, chiseled cheekbones. Proud, slim nose and a rugged jaw. His eyes were blazing amber.

Beautiful, beautiful beast. I nearly reeled on my feet. I *never* did that, except as a ruse for pick-pocketing.

Once the angry set of his jaw eased, his lips went from thinned to oh-so-kissable. That vivid gaze of his roamed over my body from my heels to the top of my head. "You . . ." he breathed.

Make the talk, Vice. "Me?" I knew we hadn't met. Because his face would've been seared into my brain forever.

". . . are stunning. The sight of you has defeated my wits."

Huh? Guys thought I was pretty, but in the land of long-legged showgirls and surgically enhanced models, it took a lot to stand out. (I'd always told myself I would *crush* it in Reno.)

And what about Karin? Maybe he'd forgotten his contacts last night.

Instead of chasing me away, the beast strode over to join me. I had to crane my head up to meet his gaze. *Well, hello there, big guy.*

He stood so close I could feel the heat coming off his body. I caught a hint of his aftershave—evergreen and something mysterious—and I wanted to purr. No, not a hint—a *hit*. His scent was a drug spiking the air.

"I am Dmitri Sevastyan," he said in a deep voice. "You must tell me your name." With way too much familiarity, he lifted that loose lock of my hair, the color stark against his tanned skin.

Engagement! What if I actually *could* run this guy?

"I'm Victoria Valentine." My steady tone was impressive.

"Victoryaa." The way he drew out the end of my name, rumbling the last syllable, made my cheeks burn.

I'd never been able to control my blushing, no matter how much grief my family gave me over a tell. "It's nice to meet you. But I believe you were about to yell at me that you weren't goddamned interested?"

Color tinged his own cheekbones, and he dropped my hair. "The women here have been . . . persistent."

"Most guys would consider that a good problem to have."

"The women weren't the only irritation," he said. "I had the sense that tonight would be different in some way. I was disappointed."

"I figured."

"Why?" His gaze skimmed my face, lingering on each of my features, as if committing them to memory.

"People who sigh at the moon are usually filled with regret or longing." Now that I'd snagged his attention, it was time to be elusive. "I'll leave you to it, big guy." I turned toward the stairs. *Chase me, chase me. . . .*

Dmitri rushed to cut me off. "*However*, I am no longer disappointed since this curvy little blonde appeared, because in the moonlight, she looks like an angel. And I happen to be in great need of one."

Angel? To save my family, I'd cut his nuts with a hangnail if I had to. "What if I'm not an angel? What if I'm a she-demon? Would you lock horns with me?"

He nodded solemnly. "I would very much like to lock *anything* with you."

He was serious, but I caught myself fighting a grin. "Locking horns can be very meaningful, Mr. Sevastyan, and we've only just met."

One corner of his lips quirked. "Call me Dmitri. Or Dima." He stood between me and the stairs.

"You've been bellowing at women all night, yet you're preventing me from leaving? I don't know whether to be flattered or alarmed."

"You heard that?" Another flush over those cheekbones.

"I was out on the terrace. I remarked that you were like a beast from a fairy tale, alone in his lair."

Holding my gaze, he said, "I've found Beauty."

My toes curled. I'd been prepared for anger and blustering, not charm. My eyes dipped to his full bottom lip. I had the urge to suck on it.

Though I'd had every intention of doing the deed with someone since my ex, no guy had tempted me enough. What would it be like to kiss this Russian? To sleep with him?

"I won't prevent you from leaving," he said, "but I invite you to stay." His hair was close-cut at the sides, yet longer on top. A breeze tousled those thick locks.

"How do I know you won't lose your temper again, Dmitri?"

His lids grew heavy—as if he enjoyed the way I said his name. "I believe I can behave, if motivated by a sweet enough treat."

"You believe? You don't know?"

"This is foreign territory for me. But I like my new guide very much."

Did he, then? My good-girl disguise was paying off! What if I pulled my first ever milk-cow—with a billionaire? That would show everyone! And more importantly . . .

That would *save* everyone.

The con was *on*. "Perhaps you're using me to keep other women away."

"Perhaps I drove the others away so you would appear in front of me."

I tilted my head at him. "You could be using me to make someone else jealous." Which would explain a lot of this unexpected attention.

"Twice you've accused me of using you. Are *you* using *me*?"

Clever man. I'd have to be careful with this one. "I came up to check out the view. You're the tourist chatting up the local girl." In the timeline of a con, we'd just had "the meet."

I glanced over my shoulder, wishing Pete could see this. *Dmitri's got a little change in his pocket goin' jingle lingle ling!* I would so fake-flirt with this Russian, in order to manipulate him into fake near-sex situations.

I would be perfect for a milk-cow, because I didn't lose control sexually, even when I was supposed to.

"Do you want to get back to someone?" Dmitri asked. "Are you here with another man?"

Surely I misheard the jealousy in his tone. "Your VIP host invited me. Peter Valentine's my cousin."

"Ah, yes. He helped smooth over the near arrest of my sister-in-law's friend."

Jessica, the tagalong, was best friends with Natalie Sevastyan, the PhD redhead.

We'd been stoked about Jessica's trouble with the law, thinking *dirt!* But Pete had heard the woman begging for a "pic with the po-po." For her blog. "You guys must've been having a ton of fun for the LVPD to step in." The five-o seemed to have given up on my family and our KAs.

"Jessica attracts trouble wherever she goes." Sounding mystified, Dmitri said, "And yet she is invited everywhere with the group."

"I think she's funny. As I passed her downstairs, she was wondering aloud if a local plant-eater would be a 'vegan Las Vegan.' Then she did a spot-on Lady Gaga impression."

"Funny?" Dmitri seemed to be processing this information.

"Yep." Pete had told me he'd walked in on Jessica in the *men's* bathroom, voguing and primping her hair. Upon seeing him, she'd lifted a leg and plopped her heel on the counter to vogue her junk. "My bush stylist talked me into this natural look," she'd told him, "but I'm not convinced. What say you, Peter Pumpkin Eater?" And she thought he was straight.

Dmitri gave a curt nod. "Jessica is around your age. You would want to socialize with her. I will take you inside."

"Wait, I don't want to intrude." He sounded as if he wanted to formally introduce me. "Pete said you're here to celebrate something." I worried my bottom lip.

His eyes clocked the little movement. "*Da.* Natalie, my oldest brother's wife, completed her doctorate. And my middle brother and his wife just had their four-year anniversary." Maksimilian, the retired politician, and his hot Latina heiress, Lucía.

Pete had learned the pair owned half of Miami and were refurbishing it while they acquired the other half. "Those are some great accomplishments. Most people come here to celebrate getting a paycheck on Friday."

He raised his gaze from my mouth. "You do sound like a local."

"Third generation." My mom came from a long line of serial brides, and my dad descended from carnies. They'd never leave this city.

"What do you do here?"

"I sling drinks downstairs. Like my sister." I had to find out why he was talking to me over her. Grifters around town had nicknamed her "the Woman," because she was everything a man could ever want in one. Even my mom, the infamous Diamond Jill, hadn't landed as many marks in her badger days. "Karin served you guys last night at the tables."

"Had you been there, we could have met a day sooner," he said, as if he regretted the loss.

I'd been substituted out by Coach Grift.

Dmitri frowned. "I hope we tipped your sister enough."

"Plenty." A family record for tips, in fact. And it'd all gone toward the debt. Always the freaking debt. Which brought my mind back to the con. Time for more elusiveness. "I better be going. Maybe I'll see you around."

He clasped my elbow with a warm, strong hand.

My back shot straight as if I'd been jolted, and unfamiliar sensations radiated through my body. A rush of heat mixed with shivers? Before I turned back to him, I masked my look of bewilderment.

He didn't mask his. His eyes had narrowed, his lips parting. "I had no idea skin could be so soft." He released me to run the backs of his fingers along my bare arm.

I watched in confusion as my skin prickled in the wake of his caress. Cold-as-Ice Vice was feeling very, very hot. I peered up at him, as if I could find the answer in his expression.

His eyes really were glorious. This close, I could see his amber pupils were awash with brighter flecks; they made his eyes gleam gold.

I could get lost in them. If he were a grifter, he'd be a *thrall*, the type of con artist whose sex appeal was so strong he or she could manipulate a mark's behavior with just a look.

He eased in even closer, raising a hand to brush his knuckles over my jawline, then a cheekbone. "So incredibly beautiful, *moy ángel*."

Was this billionaire going to kiss me? I murmured, "You're a player, aren't you?"

Still caressing my face, he said, "Give me your definition of 'player.'"

"A guy who finds women interchangeable, and goes

through a lot of them. He plays games with their heads." The only thing worse than a player? A tourist player.

Dmitri lowered his hand to curl his forefinger under my chin. "There are two things you should know about me, Victoria. One, I *will* play games with you."

Warmth flooded my body, centering between my thighs. I swallowed. "What's the other thing, big guy?"

He palmed the back of my head, drawing me close. Yet then he hesitated, as if relishing that he was *about* to kiss me. "You will like my games." He leaned down and trailed his warm, firm lips along the side of my neck.

My lids slid shut, all of my senses heightening. His scent had been enticing; now irresistible. His body heat had been magnetic; now he felt hot as flames.

My thoughts tried to scatter, but I struggled for control. *Potential mark. Keep your head. What're you doing?*

I perceived his light breaths against my mouth. His lips grazed mine with such tenderness—almost . . . reverence. He was seducing me.

And it was *delicious*.

For all my sexual life, I'd longed for the wild passion other people talked about, wrote about, sang about. I'd enjoyed sex, but I'd easily lived without it for a year. Sometimes I feared I would never find the key to unlock my passion.

When I parted my lips for him, he slanted his mouth and our tongues touched. My breath hitched at the contact, my neglected libido sizzling to life. Could a single, solitary man be my key?

With a groan, he cradled my face and slowly twined his tongue with mine.

I shivered with wonder, grasping his broad shoulders,

savoring his muscles. My nipples stiffened against the cups of my strapless bra, and my thong grew damp.

Though tension stole through his body, he kept up his measured seduction.

I got the impression he struggled to be gentle with me; I didn't want gentle. I inwardly begged, *More* . . .

But he kept up his slow-burn, seething pace.

More! My fingernails bit into his shoulders; as if I'd flipped a switch in him, ferocity overpowered his tenderness. With a growl against my lips, his hands landed on my ass, yanking me against him.

I gasped into our kiss—his cock was huge! Was he moving us? My back met a wall.

He pressed his body against mine and rocked his hips, grinding his erection.

I shuddered with want, moaning for the thick length trapped between us. I grew even wetter, my pussy aching for it. My head swam. I couldn't get close enough to him. Rolling my hips against him, I sucked on his tongue—

"Vice?"

CHAPTER 3

————————————————————————

$\mathscr{I}$ broke away from that dream kiss. When I pushed against Dmitri's chest, his muscles flexed to my touch. My greedy fingers decided to clutch at his rigid pecs, and I was about to dip right back into the dream—

Pete cleared his throat.

I dropped my hands and shimmied around Dmitri, trying to catch my breath.

The Russian refused to let go, turning to pull my back against his front so we both faced Pete. I blushed again when I felt Dmitri's cock between us.

He draped his arms over me possessively. "Peter, how could you hide a cousin this beautiful from me?"

Pete must be thinking: *But I threw our best and brightest at your feet.* With my little purse in his hands, he said, "I had no idea you would hit it off . . . with her." Obviously. He'd been so shocked to find us kissing, he'd used my family nickname in front of a gull.

Dmitri made a sound of disbelief. "How could I *not*?"

I made a mental note to ask my cousin how smug I looked at this moment.

"Maksimilian is looking for you," Pete said. "They're about to start the toasts."

Dmitri tugged me even closer. "We will be down soon."

"Actually"—I twisted in his arms to peer up at him—"can I meet you downstairs? I need to talk to Pete about something."

Dmitri glanced at my cousin. He shuttered his reaction, but I read faces like a pro, even micro expressions. And right now, Dmitri's was micro-irritated. "Before I go . . ." He dug in his shirt pocket and handed me his miniscule phone. "I would like you to call yourself."

I accepted the high-tech looking thing, but playfully said, "Hmm. Maybe I shouldn't give you my number." *I am desperate for you to have my number.*

"I will simply hound Peter for it. Maksim paid ten thousand dollars for Lucía's; do you think I'll do less?" He peered down at me. He was using the thrall on me!

But then, I *did* want to comply. In a way, he was assisting in his own conning. As I dialed myself, he strode to a nearby table and collected his jacket. With his back to us, he drew it on and fastened a button.

Because he was still hard?

When music sounded from my purse, Dmitri returned, raising a brow at my unusual ringtone.

"It's 'Let's Go Crazy' by Prince and the Revolution." Zero recognition. Apparently he didn't share my love of eighties hits. I returned his phone.

He took my hand to press a kiss into my palm. "Don't keep me waiting too long, Victoria." He descended the stairs.

My cousin and I stared after him until we were alone. "What the hell did you do to him?"

I examined my nails. "I used some good, old-fashioned sexual manipulation skills," I said, as if I'd done more than hold on for dear life.

Four aces couldn't beat Dmitri's kiss.

Pete handed me my purse. "You're thinking a milk-cow, aren't you? Even though you've never done one before? That is a completely different animal from stock cons, with full-on emotion and entanglement. You've never even done a one-night badger game!" More to himself, he said, "We could still bring in Karin to close this. Maybe Dmitri didn't have his contacts in last night."

Though I'd had the exact same thought, I snapped, "Oh, come on!" *Marcia, Marcia, Marcia!* "He likes *me*."

"You're right, you're right. But are you ready for a sexual con?"

After that kiss? Deal me in! "I'm ready."

"You've only been with three men," Pete pointed out. "And one of those guys lasted five seconds!"

I should never have told my cousin about one-thrust Ronny.

"Can you tease Dmitri to sexual insanity and then deny him? Get him so crazed he'll promise you anything?"

As if I had a choice? I lifted my chin. "I'm going down to that party—as primary." The lead player in a con. "I'm gonna do my job, so why don't you do yours?" I wasn't entering the room blind—I'd read Pete's notes on the Sevastyans—but I'd take any more information he could give me. "How many bodyguards?" The bane of a grifter's existence.

"Several. Dmitri and Aleks have two each. Maksim's head

of security is the bald one, Vasili. He could be trouble, so keep a lookout for him."

"Will we stand up to a billionaire's kind of background scrutiny?" Though no one in my immediate family had an arrest record, we were KAs of people who'd done time.

"We couldn't beat the investigation three months ago, but Benji's made adjustments since then. So maybe." My adopted brother, Ben Valentine—a.k.a. Benji the Eye—was our tech guy. "We'll have to roll the dice on that."

"Any last-minute tips?"

"This crew likes ribald—and I mean filthy—humor. The girls do tequila; the guys don't drink that much. Jessica will make you do shooters. Don't waste energy resisting her. Just try to keep eating. If she likes you, life will be a lot easier. She'll probably be attracted to you."

"Let's hope." I'd read she liked both guys and dolls.

"If the opportunity arises, impress Lucía with your Spanish. She's an influencer with Dmitri. Oh, and if the group hits the tables, don't give poker advice. Besides, I think he calculates pot odds as well as you do."

Did he, then? To a girl like me, that was sexy as hell. "Speaking of poker"—I tapped my chin—"what if I could get him to stake me?"

"Forget it. You're a grinder at the tables. We need a huge score."

He was right. I had all the tools to make a living, but not to make a killing. Not unless I could get my hands on the deck. "So you aren't coming with?" I didn't expect him to. A mark couldn't relax fully with a male family member around.

"I'll hang on the periphery and work the environment." Keeping the atmosphere conducive to romance.

I'd seen him do everything from bribing DJs to wild-dog removal.

"Vice, these people might be gulls, but they're still brilliant. Listen to your grift sense."

Grift sense was like the Force for a con artist. Maybe there was some mystical basis; maybe a grifter's subconscious picked up on behavioral clues and channeled them into intuition.

One thing I knew for certain: to trust mine. I cracked my knuckles. "I've got this. Clear eyes, full hearts, can't lose, right?"

He gave a long-suffering sigh, and we turned toward the stairs. On the way down, he said, "Quiet in there."

The DJ had stopped playing. "They've probably already started the toasts."

Pete and I entered the living room together. No toasts. Every eye was focused . . . on *me*. No one spoke.

On a stretch sectional couch, Maksim sat with Lucía, Aleks with Natalie. Jessica too. All five stared wordlessly, and the other party-goers seemed to follow their lead.

Standing nearby, Dmitri proudly announced, "Meet Victoria Valentine. *She* is my date."

CHAPTER 4

*P*ete murmured, *"All yours, primary."* Then he abandoned me. Fucker.

Lucía popped up from the couch so fast she nearly tripped. The brunette wore a bronze slipdress that matched her widened eyes. She hurried over to me and put out a hand, her diamond-studded watch catching my notice. *"Encantada,* Victoria. I can't tell you how wonderful it is to meet you," she said with a marked accent. "Really, really wonderful."

What was up with the over-the-top welcome? You'd think Dmitri had never introduced a date before. "Pleasure's mine." I shook her hand.

Natalie, a curvaceous redhead in a slate-blue wrap dress, followed right behind her. "I'm Natalie. Welcome to the party! Why don't you have a drink? You need a drink. Lemme get you something." Her green gaze bounced around the room for a server.

"Um . . ." Most of the party-goers were still watching this awkward scene.

Black-haired, ballsy Jessica traipsed over, rocking a garnet catsuit, clearly designer couture. The girl shoved a champagne flute into my hand. "I'm Jess. Now that we've met, the course of your life just altered. Smoking bod, by the way. I'm an admirer. Are those colored contacts?"

My face heated. "Uh, no."

To Lucía, Jessica said, "My hot *mamí*, I'm going to have to throw you over for this stone-cold fox."

Fox? How fitting. And the henhouse door was opening before me.

Lucía chuckled. "I will try to soldier on, Jessabel."

A nervous laugh escaped me, and I darted a glance in Dmitri's direction.

His brothers had waylaid him, speaking in low Russian. But they didn't look unhappy—just the opposite.

And Dmitri? His shoulders were squared, his eyes smoldering as he openly stared at me.

I inhaled, then asked bluntly, "What's going on?"

Natalie recovered first. "Right. You don't know anything about us, so this would be overwhelming and weird, huh?"

"A scoch."

Jessica explained, "Over the last year, I have thrown myself and every other available woman at that man. But he turned this"—she waved at her spectacular figure—"down. Repeatedly. Pickiest guy ever. Yet now he can't take his eyes off his new 'date'. You've beaten out millions. Tell me, was it as simple as swallowing?"

I snapped my gaze to her. "I met him fifteen minutes ago."

Jessica nodded. "In those fifteen minutes, did you happen to swallow?"

She had to be kidding. Ribald humor, right?

"Don't mind Jess," Natalie said. "I'd blame it on the alcohol, but she's always like this."

As Dmitri strode over with his brothers, Lucía murmured to me, "*Ay*, they make quite a picture, no?" She sighed. *"Tan guapo."* So very handsome.

"Sí que lo son," I replied. That they are. All three were closing in on six and a half feet with cut bodies, though Dmitri was a touch leaner—and the most handsome.

"Tú hablas español?" she asked, seeming overjoyed.

Everyone in my family spoke at least two languages. Each tongue opened up new mark pools. I answered, *"Sólo lo suficiente para ser peligroso."* Just enough to be dangerous.

Dmitri crossed to stand beside me, introducing his brothers. Aleks, the oldest, had amber eyes like Dmitri's, while Maksim's were piercing blue.

"We are very pleased to meet you, Victoria," Maksim said. He put his arm around Lucía, holding her close, as if they were about to burst from happiness.

Dmitri and I had had *one* kiss!

Aleks had gravitated to Natalie's side, taking her hand in his big one. "Yes, Victoria. A genuine pleasure."

I eked out a smile. "Likewise." Though I didn't sense any acute tension between Aleks and his youngest brother, body language told me Dmitri was closer to Maksim.

Lucía asked me, "Where did you get that dazzling dress?"

"I made it."

Jessica circled me, assessing. "Get the fuck out. I know clothes. That's serious clothes."

"Thanks."

Dmitri moved closer, draping an arm over my shoulders. "She is beautiful *and* talented."

Natalie and Lucía shared an *awww* look.

Was this some kind of punking? Where was the camera? Why was I tempted to relax back against Dmitri and enjoy the ride?

My gaze darted to Pete, standing across the room. He looked as dumbstruck as I felt.

I told the group, "Peter's my cousin." *Hint-hint: I'm related to "the help."* I lifted my flute for a sip.

Jessica said, "I see the resemblance. I plan to fuck him too. So now it all makes sense."

I coughed champagne, then laughed at the absurdity of all this; they thought I was laughing at Jessica, and everyone relaxed. *So, okay, this is happening.*

Dmitri said, "Let's hear from the toastmaster, then."

Maksim nodded. "Have a seat."

As the others returned to the sectional, Lucía said, "We can scoot closer."

Dmitri said, "No need." He took the remaining plush chair, then pulled me down to sit across his lap, all casual possessiveness.

Near the bar, Pete texted the family faster than I'd ever seen him type.

Maybe I wasn't jinxed! Hell, if Nigel hadn't bailed, I wouldn't have been at this party.

A man like Dmitri Sevastyan wouldn't be signaling a server for another glass of champagne for me.

I hated to drink on a con, but for fuck's sake . . . I traded out my empty flute. "Thank you."

Dmitri took one himself. We met gazes. His spellbinding eyes seemed to hold a thousand secrets.

And could I be a bigger idiot? I knew better than to moon over a mark. I knew all the lines—

"I want you to be comfortable and enjoy yourself," he told me.

Huh. A line I'd never heard.

He adjusted me closer to his chest until I could feel the steady drum of his heart. He inhaled the scent of my hair, and his heartbeat sped up.

At my ear, he murmured, "Our first kiss made me burn. I'm eager for our second."

I melted from his voice, as if the sound had been hot-wired to my pussy.

"You should not make me wait too much longer, *moy ángel.*"

Did that mean my angel? When I shivered, his cock stirred beneath my ass, but he controlled himself.

I whispered, "You assume you get a second?"

"If I have to move heaven and earth . . ."

Guh. Heart thud. My con had a glaring weakness; how the hell could *anyone* deny him?

With an enviable social ease, Maksim began a speech about accomplishments and marriage, happiness and love. He'd entranced everyone else—were Lucía's eyes glinting?—but Dmitri overloaded my senses until I hardly registered a word.

Get cold, Vice. Work. The. Con.

After a couple of toasts, Maksim raised his glass to Dmitri and to . . . me. "A toast to new friends. May they always feel our family's welcome."

I raised my glass and drank, nearly coughing when I spied the bald Vasili in the background. He crossed his beefy arms, his gaze locked on me.

It's his job to be an asshole, I assured myself. *Nature of the beast.*

Everyone clapped for the charismatic Maksim, and the music resumed. Servers made their way through the crowd with platters and more drinks. One delivered a tequila bottle service with shot glasses and accompaniments, setting it on the coffee table.

Jessica slid off the couch, kneeling on the fluffy rug to begin pouring. "Let's get this party rolling!" Lucía and Natalie dropped down beside her. "Come sit with us, Blondie."

And so it begins.

Dmitri said, "You can remain here."

If he wanted something, then my job was to *not quite* give it to him. "I'll just be a minute." I wriggled out of his grasp to join the girls.

Micro scowl.

Jessica asked, "What do people call you? Vicky or Tori? I think we should go with Tori—"

"Vice," I rushed to say. Only my ex had ever called me Tori. Besides, Pete had already spilled my nickname. "My friends call me Vice."

"I want to know why." Dmitri leaned forward with his elbows on his knees. "The word is slang for *police*." He sounded as if he'd given this matter a lot of thought and was frustrated to have no answer.

Again, I wouldn't give him what he wanted. "Hmmm. Maybe I'll tell you later."

Full on scowl.

Lucía said, "Will Peter come sit and drink with us?"

My cousin milled around on the periphery, ever ready to make an assist. "I think he's still working for a bit longer."

Natalie asked me, "So what do you do?"

"I used to help out with my parents' financial planning business until about three months ago. But it's a tough"— lethal—"market."

"Your investment background interests me," Dmitri said. "Perhaps you can help me make a determination about a few prospects."

Doubtful. My skill set involved selling dummy stocks like they were snake oil—not evaluating them. "Those days are over for me, I'm afraid. Now I'm a cocktail waitress here at the casino."

"How are you liking the service industry?" Lucía asked.

In Vegas? Why, I just love when customers drunkenly grope me. And married men do it best!

As I tried to formulate an answer, Natalie groaned. "My server gigs sucked. Note to self: If a restaurant supplies sporks, tips there will be nil."

She'd had server jobs? According to Pete's intel, she'd grown up on a huge farm in Nebraska and had inherited a fortune five years ago.

Lucía said, "I enjoyed cleaning houses better than I did slinging wings at a Hooters-type establishment. Scrubbing toilets was . . . purer."

Even as I laughed, I wondered why she had done either. Her mega-rich family had controlled one of the largest coastline tracts in Florida for generations.

Maybe their parents had made them work minimum-wage jobs to try to keep them grounded. Or perhaps the Sevastyans controlled their public information, putting their best face forward. I glanced at Dmitri, finding his gaze on me.

A tech genius with unlimited resources could hide a lot of dirt. Hmm . . .

"Customers can be so bizarre," Natalie said, drawing my attention. "Have you ever had a guy ask for a cosmopolitan, but he wanted it in a 'manly glass'?"

"Yes! Then there's always the guy who says, 'No, *you*'re cut off!'"

Natalie laughed. "I've had dudes say that to me too!"

Dmitri wasn't laughing, but one corner of his lips curled, the barest hint of a coming smile. His amused expression? It looked so . . . out of practice.

Jessica handed out shots, only to the girls. Once we'd geared up with salt and lemon, she said, "Okay, ladies, start your livers. Now it's our turn to make roast toasts."

Come again?

Natalie raised her glass and winked at Lucía. "To the three types of orgasms. To the holy kind: 'Oh God, oh God, oh God.' To the affirmative kind: 'Oh yes, oh yes, oh yes.' And to the fake kind: 'Oh Maks, oh Maks, oh Maks.'"

Lucía and Maksim laughed with such ease I figured their sex life must be stratospheric. With a sly grin, Lucía said, "To Natalie. She doesn't have a cherry, but that's no sin, since she's still got the box that the cherry came in."

I chuckled until I realized they might expect me to come up with one. In past toasts, I'd paid tribute to Lady Luck, but if these people expected a *roast toast* . . . I loved limericks, had even won a contest once, so I cobbled one together.

"Here's to my Vice-Vice Baby"—Jessica gazed meaning-fully at me—"for being single, seeing double, sleeping triple . . . and having multiple."

I was still laughing when, sure enough, everyone turned to me. I raised my glass to Jessica. Feigning an Irish burr, I said, "There once was a looker named Jess, who always knew just how to dress. At a party like this, she'd land more than one kiss; who she'd fuck was anyone's guess. Sláinte!"

Jessica guffawed. Natalie and Lucía howled. Aleks and Maksim cracked up.

Dmitri hadn't laughed, but his lips curled again, and his eyes were lively, crinkling a touch at the sides.

Everyone seemed delighted—and surprised—by even that mere response.

Jessica commanded, "Lick, shoot, suck, my bitches!"

After that shot, the night sped by too fast. Despite an occasional glare from Vasili, I ended up having a great time. I'd had to remind myself I was working, a career first.

Dmitri was unfailingly attentive, asking if I was comfortable or if I needed anything. Once he found out my favorite cocktail, a fresh rum and Coke was always in front of me.

Jess was one of a kind, and Lucía and Nat were seriously cool. I admired how tight those two had their husbands locked up. *Devoted* didn't really cover it.

Whenever Nat left Aleks' side, his gaze would clock her, as if he counted the seconds until she returned to him. Maksim couldn't seem to touch Lucía enough, and he often whispered things to her that made her eyes shimmer.

My sister and I had a theory that three percent of the masculine population was good. How else could we reconcile all the scrotes we met in our business with the great guys in our family and among our KAs?

Were the Sevastyan brothers in that tiny percentage?

Maksim was the most charming of the three, confident and friendly. Aleks seemed more introspective and intense. He laughed with the group, but he didn't talk much.

Dmitri was quiet too, seeming to catalog like a computer any information I divulged. . . .

The Caly's midnight light show had just concluded when

Maksim pressed a kiss to Lucía's head and rose. "I think it's time for a cigar with my brothers." Aleks stood, but Dmitri didn't.

"Come, Dima, let them do another round without us," Maksim said, then added something in Russian.

Seeming resigned, Dmitri rose. But he told the girls, "Do not scare her away."

Though they laughed, I didn't think his tone was playful. I thought his tone said, *Do not motherfucking scare her away.*

As soon as the brothers had stepped outside, questions from the girls came rapid-fire. "What do you think so far? Will you go on another date with him? What are your intentions and can we do a threesome?" That one came from Jess.

I answered, "I think he seems . . . nice. He hasn't asked, but I'd probably go out with him again. I'm not into threesomes, and I have no intentions."

Natalie frowned. "But you like him, right?"

I get high on his scent. His body makes mine feverish. I could suck on his tongue for hours.

I kept it noncommittal: "I'm local. I know better than to get involved with a tourist." This was true. No matter what they told you, they would always leave. *Men and their promises.*

Lucía smoothed her long, glossy hair over one shoulder. "Dmitri really likes you. A party this rowdy is a special kind of hell for him, but he's staying because you're having fun."

"He doesn't enjoy parties?"

"He's more of a lone-wolf type. This crowd must be trying for him." Almost to herself, she said, "I was so surprised he recommended we celebrate in Vegas."

I sipped my drink, logging info. "I can't believe he's single."

Jess snorted. "Despite my best efforts." She poured another round of shots. "But now I can rest."

As if he were no longer single? "It's all very sudden."

"You wanna know a secret?" Natalie asked with a hiccup. *Only always, Dr. Nat.* "That's how the men in this family are. Aleks told me he knew I'd be his wife after one look."

Wait, had she just said *wife* in a sentence even remotely associated with me?

Lucía nodded. "*Máxim* told me that as soon as he got close enough to see I had freckles, he knew he was 'fucked.' Clearly, we had some things to work out. But the point is, he knew within half an hour that I'd be his."

Jess was even more direct. "Dmitri's looking at you like he's been drowning for years, and you're a lifeline. Another Sevastyan brother gone at first sight. Dibs on wedding coordination services!" She started singing "Tale as Old as Time."

Could a gorgeous billionaire like Dmitri truly . . . *want me* want me? Or, more likely, were all these rich people crazy?

Silly, Vice. Every grifter knew that when you took your eyes off the immediate prize and your hands out of play, Lady Luck would frown upon you.

The lesson?

Never reach for the stars.

CHAPTER 5

*J*n the hallway, Pete and I argued in whispers, sounding like two hissing cats.

"Are they fucking with you?" he demanded. "Playing games or something? Rich gulls *are* weird."

"Yes! They have to be." Once Dmitri had returned from the terrace—a mere ten minutes later—he'd seemed even more determined to make me enjoy the night, plying me with drinks and fancy foods.

The servers began treating me as if *I* were one of the people staying in that fantastical penthouse!

"This is the Sevastyans' idea of a joke," I whispered/hissed. "Amusing themselves with the peasants and shit." Rich people and con artists were like cats and dogs. No love lost between them. "I need to bail."

"What if it's not a joke? Do you understand what this could mean?"

I adjusted my purse strap on my shoulder. "That I maybe shouldn't have lifted Lucía's watch." We weren't usually straight-up thieves, much. And I'd never stolen from someone so nice.

No sins, still *in?*

"Vice!"

"I want to contribute, and even at fence value, the watch is a legit two-fifty." I'd stowed it in the false bottom of my purse. "Gotta be insured, right? They're so hammered, she'll think she lost it." The beauty of Vegas. Fresh marks flooded in every day, wearing their chum-pants as they dove into the shark tank. And they always left the city, which meant we never had to.

"You're drinking too," Pete pointed out. "Someone might've seen you lift it."

"The bodyguards don't even look at me anymore." And Vasili had disappeared. *Good riddance.* I could've strolled right into any of the bedrooms, and no one would've stopped me. "Besides, you try telling Jess you don't want a sixth tequila shooter."

"So now she's Jess? And Natalie is Nat? And you're regular old Vice, the plucky cocktail waitress with a heart of gold?" He swore under his breath. "Do I have to remind you? We're not like them. We're a different breed. . . ."

In a monotone, I repeated lines I'd heard all my life: "We're the last of the long-conners, the aristocrats of grifters. Living by our wits, smiled upon by Lady Luck. The only thing we can't cheat is fate. . . ."

"Yet you're melding with them? We do *not* meld with gulls." Feigning a look of realization, he said, "Oh wait, you already did once."

My ex-fiancé. The one who'd betrayed me. The one who was still attempting to win me back. "Low blow, Pete."

"I'm trying to get your head in the game. I caught you looking at Dmitri with something like infatuation. You have to be cold to maneuver a guy like that."

"You're right. What am I doing?" I wobbled in my heels, the alcohol starting to hit hard.

"It's not too late to get it together. Vice, we might have a live one on the line. The Moby Dick of whales."

But nobody ever landed Moby Dick! "Pull the plug on this, man! We'll figure out a way to get Karin in here as primary. She's a lock. It's too big a score to blow, and I'm jinxed!" Pete was right; stock cons were way easier than this. Give me a greedy money-launderer or hard-up tax-evader any day!

Pete shook his head. "I've seen the way this guy looks at you. I can't describe it, but he seems addicted to you already. He won't accept anyone else. Trust me." We shared another laugh over that.

In reality, I did halfway trust my extended family of scoundrels. "So you're backing my play here?" I asked. "Backing me?"

"All in. Damn, you've already had the meet." He rubbed his chin. "I would've liked you to be in better lighting and not so tired from the week—"

"Come on!"

"I should've made sure you had the phone cloner." Which would've enabled us to see Dmitri's every text, e-mail, and online visit. "He handed you his telephone and turned his back." Pete looked disgusted. "That's on me." My cousin could give us all grief, but never more than he gave himself.

"The window was too short," I assured him. "Even with misdirection, I wouldn't have had enough time."

"Speaking of time . . . Where'd you tell Dmitri you were going?"

"I used my emergency-phone-ring app and said I needed to take the call. I should get back." And I really needed to pee.

"My host duties are done for the night." The party was winding down. "If I'm still here, it'll be weird not to join you guys. Can you handle this on your own?"

I raised my chin. "I've got it. All good." *Please, Lady Luck, don't let me botch this!*

"I'm a text away. Just watch yourself in there, Vice. And remember—we're a world apart from them."

So why had I felt so at home with that crew?

As I made my way back inside, Jess, Nat, and Lucía were talking to Dmitri. He looked antsy, his leg jogging.

Jess slurred, "Ever since you decided to mend fences with the big bro, I've been trying to set you up. Even though you were my last chance to go to Cirque du Cock."

Mend fences? Cirque du Cock? I ducked back into the foyer, listening in.

"Kuh-learly, I have now succeeded in setting you up, because I brilliantly invited *every* vegan here to our little party."

Nat hiccupped again. "The tribe has spoken, Dmitri. You are keeping Vice."

Lucía added, "We like her so much."

Jess said, "She's got these knowing eyes—you can tell she's seen things that leave a mark—but she *blushes*. Driving me fugging crazy! If you don't keep her, I will."

"Perhaps that is not at issue," Dmitri said. "Perhaps the crux is whether she will keep me."

My chest squeezed with panic. They weren't fucking with me. They thought I was a great gal who got their humor and matched their drinking. I fit in seamlessly and was hitting it off with one of their own.

How could they be so trusting? They had no idea what I was, yet they were letting me into their lives? I'd stolen a watch our fence would convert for a quarter of a million dollars, and I'd do it again. And dear God, the identity theft opportunities in those bedrooms . . .

I wanted to shake them. *Stupid rich people.*

Couldn't they see I was false gold?

I stared at the ceiling, my mind zooming to a memory from my early childhood. I'd been pensive and confused as I'd told my mom, "Gulls always say, 'If something seems too good to be true, it is.' That's supposed to be *our* secret, but it's out there, right in the open. Why don't they listen?"

"They get greedy and ignore what they know deep down," my beautiful mother had said. "Vice, never forget that we sell fairy tales. And fairy tales don't exist."

CHAPTER 6

When I opened the door to exit one of the guest bathrooms, Dmitri was striding down the hallway, heading for me with an intent look on his face.

Intent on what?

My God, he was huge. I instinctively backed up, which only trapped me with him. But when he shut and locked the door behind him, I wasn't anxious; I felt excitement . . . expectancy.

What would he do? We certainly wouldn't be the first strangers to get busy in a Vegas bathroom. Should I go along with the scenario?

Maybe, but a show of resistance wouldn't go amiss. "Dmitri, I'm not the type of girl who hooks up in bathrooms."

"I know."

"But you still want us to?"

He reached for my purse, setting it aside.

I guess he does. "I'm not going to have sex with you."

"Understood. Let down all that lovely hair of yours."

After a hesitation, I removed my hair stick, and the length tumbled over my shoulders. My hair was platinum, courtesy of some distant Norwegian ancestors, and had a little curl to it.

Dmitri appeared captivated as he ran his fingers through it. "Like silk," he said absently, seeming not to realize he'd spoken aloud. "I want to see all this blond hair fanning out in my bed."

Could be in your future.

He wrapped the ends around his fist, then leaned down to graze his lips along my neck. His tongue flicked me, and the pleasure was so intense, I couldn't bite back a soft moan. I clutched his chest to keep my balance.

"I want my second kiss." He brushed his lips against mine. Once, twice . . . His tongue swept in.

I met it with my own, and heat shot through me.

He groaned against my lips, deepening the contact. As our tongues twined, my breasts began to ache, my thong getting damp. I was panting by the time he drew back.

His golden eyes looked darker with lust, now full amber. "So many things I want to do to you." His voice was husky. Releasing my hair, he said, "Turn to face the mirror."

"Pardon?" He'd muddled my thoughts.

"I'm going to give you commands. If you obey me, you'll be rewarded."

He'd warned me he would play games. "I don't know," I murmured, another show of hesitation before I played along. For my con, I was supposed to make his dreams come true—almost. Teasingly, and short of sex.

"Turn around." The seething need in his eyes made me do it.

When I faced the mirror, I thought I'd see bewilderment in my reflection. I was confronted by my own excitement. Did I *like* being bossed around?

"Lift your dress for me."

I wore only a white lacy thong. I nibbled my lip.

"You want to show your body to me."

I did. I really did.

No, the tequila must be making me loopy! All I could think over and over: *Give him whatever he needs.*

"Do it. *Now.*" This control he wielded unnerved me—even as it aroused me.

Heart racing, I pinched the hem of my dress and started to raise it. Any shyness I'd expected—along with the impulse to cover myself—faded.

For some reason, I craved his gaze on my ass and my wet panties. But I took my time pulling my dress up to my waist.

He sucked in a breath, ogling my curves.

My face was on fire. Things were getting confused in my head until even my embarrassment was making me wet. And happy. Giddy, even. My lips curled.

"Is that a victory smile, Victoria? It should be. I'm coming undone. If you ever discover the extent of my attraction to you, I will be doomed."

"Doomed to what?" In the mirror, I gazed down his body.

His big cock surged against his pants. "To whatever it is my Victoria desires."

It's a material world, Russian.

"Keep your dress raised." He reached for me, using both hands to cup my cheeks, to knead them, to spread them. This wasn't a mere seduction. He was exploring me, his eyes lit with curiosity. A boy with a new toy.

He gripped my hips, head tilted down as he watched himself thrust against me. Low masculine sounds broke from his chest.

I inhaled sharply. His excitement and need were fueling the

same in me, but I still said, "No sex, right?" I didn't think I physically *could* take that dick in me. Not without some prep time.

We met gazes in the mirror. "I'm not going to fuck you yet." Wait, *yet*? "Take off your dress. I must see more of you."

While he remained clothed? "Why should I?"

He gave me his thrall look. "Because, beautiful girl, this is the most pleasurable thing I have ever done, and I'll give anything for it to continue."

He wasn't . . . he wasn't lying?

I found myself unzipping the side of my dress. I drew it off, leaving only my bra, thong, and heels.

"*Victoria,*" he growled. He dipped his gaze, then checked out my front in the mirror. "The treasures you've been hiding, woman." His control seemed to be slipping.

So what would happen if he lost it?

He ghosted his fingertips down my back, drawing a tremor. "Your back is sensitive?"

I'd never known. What was this guy doing to me? He continued down, fingers brushing over my ass. Without thinking, I raised it to follow his touch.

"Responsive."

He was making me sound like some kind of wanton sexpot; I wasn't. Not normally.

What if this man had the key? The key to me?

He bent to one knee, his hands roving over my legs, as if my body was a prize and he intended to worship every inch of it. He massaged my thighs, kissing the sides of them. On his way back to his feet, he pressed his lips to one cheek, then the other.

In the mirror, I watched my fight to keep my eyes open—

He nipped me with his teeth!

I squealed, but I kind of liked it.

Then he kissed his way up my back. "I will never get enough of this body." As he nuzzled my ear, he unsnapped my bra.

I caught it against my breasts, surprised by how swollen they'd become. "I don't know about wearing only a thong while you're still dressed." Honey traps tantalized. They didn't roll over at the mark's every whim.

Instead of ordering me to let my bra go, he piled up my hair and traced his lips across my nape, drawing a shiver from me. His heated breaths and firm lips undermined my resistance. His reaction to the rest of my body had been so thrilling. With each of his touches, I yearned to show this strange man more, to jut my aching tits and raise my ass for him.

"Victoria, you must show me all your treasures while I've still enough control to enjoy them fully." He turned me to face him.

I let his spell take me over. I dropped the bra.

He didn't glance down. Not yet. He gave my mouth a brief kiss—praise?—*then* he lowered his gaze.

His response was worth my flush of embarrassment. He closed his eyes tight, then opened them, as if he'd expected me—or my tits—to disappear. In a gravelly voice, he said, "You have the most exquisite breasts I've ever seen." He stared at them with lust, but also with an eager curiosity, as if he'd been *dying* to know what I looked like beneath my clothes.

Without warning, he lifted me up on the marble counter, easing his hips between my knees. His Adam's apple bobbed as he reached for my chest with both hands. . . .

Contact.

A breath shuddered out of his lungs; I moaned, arching into his palms.

"I could come in my pants just from the feel of you." His huge dick strained against the material to get free.

I reached for it, needing to fondle him, to learn what made him groan—

"Ah-ah. Not yet. Hands on the counter."

When I reluctantly obeyed, he circled one puckered nipple with a forefinger. Again. And again. Never varying his maddening speed.

My clit began to throb along with my nipples. I whispered, "Oh, my God." When my head lolled, he cupped my nape, holding me steady. "Dmitri . . ." This was something like, like *adoration.*

He placed his other hand on my back, forcing me to arch even more to him. He bent to rub the side of his face against my chest.

I *felt* his low, guttural groan. Panting, I watched him nuzzle my breasts, looking as if he'd lost himself.

His hot exhalations whispered across one nipple, then . . . his tongue.

"Oh, *yes!*" I threaded my fingers into his thick black hair, gripping his head. I heard myself repeatedly whispering his name.

"You like what I do to you." I could have sworn he was grinning against my breast.

I wanted to see his grin! The thought vanished when he sucked the peak between his lips.

I was *levitating!* His mouth was so hot, his tongue strong as he teased my nipple. A graze of teeth made me whimper.

Then he lavished the same care on my other breast. Could I come from this?

When he suckled with hungry pulls, my eyes flashed wide, then slid closed. Sounds bombarded me. The music from the penthouse. My desperate moans. His blissed-out groans. The wet suction of his mouth . . .

Too soon, he drew back. "Pull your panties aside."

Between breaths, I asked, "Why am I the only one baring it all?" I'd had a half Brazilian, leaving a small thatch of hair on my mons. Would he like that?

He arched a brow. "You want me to have skin in the game?"

Wordplay? Ah, delicious!

"Perhaps you'll like being naked next to a fully dressed man."

The idea felt wicked; I'd be so vulnerable to him. Could I really do this with someone I'd just met?

"Show me how wet you are, Victoria."

I swallowed with nervousness, but I did tug aside my thong. Cool air hit my lips.

Grating something harsh in Russian, he stared at my pussy like it was a revelation, the highlight of his entire life. His riveted gaze made me tremble. With his brows drawn, he tenderly caressed the backs of his fingers over my lips. "Beautiful girl. You're fucking mouthwatering."

Beautiful. Mouthwatering.

"Look at this light hair. I'm glad you left some." Then he parted me. "Ah! You're *drenched.*"

My face burned. I'd never felt more exposed.

And that only made me wetter.

His hands were shaking, his words ragged as he said, "I

never knew my cock could ache this much." He started kissing down my body.

A flick of his tongue along my cleavage. Another above my navel.

"Whoa. What are you going to do?" I barely recognized my own voice.

He tugged my soaked panties down to my knees. "Need to eat you."

I pressed his head back. "Wait, let's don't. Not that much of a fan actually." I never could come from it, and guys seemed to think they'd failed if they couldn't bring me off. The pressure spoiled it for me.

But I didn't want to put Dmitri off totally, so I said, "I make up for that with my love of head."

He narrowed his eyes. "We'll address this soon." He cupped me, massaging my pussy.

What did *that* mean? I couldn't think when he was stroking me—like he owned me. "It's just . . . not my favorite."

"It will be when *I* do it." His confidence could almost make me believe. He released me, raising his glistening fingers between us. "A taste of what will come." Then he licked them.

Another play on words! What will *come*.

As he tasted my wetness, his eyes rolled back in his head. "So—fucking—luscious!" He sucked his fingers as if he couldn't get enough.

I moaned, just from the sight. *"Dmitri."*

With a growl, he tore his fingers away. "If you deny me that, then I will have to punish you."

"Punish?"

He pulled me to my feet and turned me to face the mirror again. "Spread your legs and put your hands on the counter.

Do not move them from there."

I hesitated, partly because of the con, partly from trepidation. With my panties around my knees and my legs parted, I rested my palms on the marble—

His palm cracked against my ass.

Comprehension came slowly. He'd . . . *spanked* me? I'd just been freaking spanked! I wasn't into this *at all.*

But my job was to send him ever closer to sexual insanity; if a whipping lit his wick, then I'd be forced to go along with this.

Another slap. The sound was ridiculously loud.

I gritted my teeth and accepted my fate.

Slap! He collared my throat with his other hand, holding me steady. *Slap!*

Heat from my ass radiated to my back, my legs, my . . . pussy. This weird interplay started getting to me. My internal resistance dwindled.

He must've sensed it. "That's it," he said, his tone filled with dark praise. "Submit to me."

Submit . . . My core clenched at the word. With each spank, my tits shook, and I loved the way he watched them in the mirror. My nipples were harder than I'd ever seen them, my clit throbbing.

"Look at you meeting my strikes."

I'd been raising my ass for more! What was happening to me? Unknown circuits in my brain seemed to be firing for the first time.

Because of this man. *The key* . . .

"Do you want more?" His voice *was* hot-wired to my pussy.

I had to know what he'd do next! He'd said he wouldn't fuck me. Anything else was working the con—with a freaking billionaire as my mark! "Yes!"

With his free hand, he gripped me firmly between my thighs. "So wet! It feels like my beautiful girl needs to come."

I sucked in a breath at the shocking contact. "Dmitri, I can't take much more of this!"

His body thrummed, muscles bulging beneath his clothes. "Can you take *this*?" He shook that hand, vibrating all of my pussy.

"Oh, my *GOD*." My back bowed, my nipples straining painfully. My spread legs twitched, my ass quivering.

He slapped it again. The force shoved my clit against his vibrating palm.

Pleasure mounted. I was going to come in his hand if he kept spanking me. *"More."*

He whipped me again, sending me into his waiting grip.

I stared into his eyes as my orgasm neared. "Please . . ."

Another slap.

"What are you *doing* to me?" I sounded awed.

"I want to make you feel good so you'll keep coming back to me for more."

Good? I was about to climb the walls! "Please let me come!"

"Show me how badly you need it. Use my hand." The hand he'd stilled. The one I was all but resting on.

He'd taken me to the very edge, then upped the ante. Could I call his bet? It would be so shameful to work my clit against him. To soak his palm with my cum.

"Submit to me." He released the hand gripping my ass. Because he wanted me to do this all on my own?

I'd never felt so out of control. Why was I fighting the overwhelming urge to obey him? I needed to grind my orgasm out right in his hand!

"You want to do it for me, beautiful." His amber eyes mesmerized me.

Did I? Could I? My face flamed as I accepted the truth.

I let the spell come over me, and I started to move my hips.

"That's it," he hissed. "That's what I want to see."

My toes curled. "It's so good . . . so good . . . so good." As I rocked to his palm, my heavy-lidded gaze dipped. When I saw his big cock threatening to rip free, all thoughts of restraint dissolved. "I changed my mind! Do you have a condom?"

He groaned. "I would kill to fuck you. Never been so hard." He rubbed the heel of his free hand over the ridge in his pants. A circle of precum dampened the material.

It should've wet my tongue.

"But I told you I wouldn't." That mattered to him right now?

"I *need* you to fuck me, Dmitri—I feel out of my mind!"

His lips drew back from his white teeth, his expression fierce. "*That* is how crazed you've made me every moment since I first saw you!" He stood behind me to thrust his cock against my burning ass.

When the material of his pants abraded my skin, I cried out.

"Are you going to come for me, Vika?" He gave another thrust as I continued to grind his hand.

"I'm so close!" What had he called me? Vika? "So *close* . . ." My lids slid shut.

"Ah-ah. You look at me when you come."

I opened my eyes. Panting, I stared into the mirror, losing myself in his penetrating gaze. My hips rocked frantically, my body drawing tight, preparing to climax. *"Oh, God . . ."*

"Now say please, beautiful." His dick swelled even more between us.

I would've done anything. "Please!"

"Come *hard*." He vibrated his grip and thrust against my abused ass.

I screamed as I hurtled over the edge, helplessly grinding my pussy into his hot palm. My vision blurred. My body writhed, tits shaking.

Pleasure overpowered me as I came and came for this man. . . .

He and I worked together to draw out my orgasm—the strongest I'd ever experienced. Finally, I leveled out, boneless against him.

He removed his hand. "The pressure . . . about to spill!" His zipper sounded.

I whirled around and nearly lost my footing as he worked his erection free. I gasped at the jaw-dropping sight.

Dmitri was pierced!

He had a silver ring through the crown, a Prince Albert piercing. "Oh, my God, your cock is so sexy!" Veins protruded over his thick shaft, the head stretched taut. My tongue swirled in my mouth for the precum wetting that pierced slit.

He rocked his hips, fucking the air between us. "Can *feel* your gaze on my cock!"

"I need to suck it, Dmitri." I dropped to my knees on the rug to worship it.

"Woman! Drive me madder than I already am!"

When I gripped his shaft, it jerked against my palm. I leaned in to kiss him, but he pinched my chin.

"Can't hold my cum! Look at me, *ángel*. Keep me here."

Keep him? Entranced by this man, I nodded and pumped his length.

His hooded gaze bored into mine. He never glanced away.

Not even when he emptied his lungs on a bellow. Not even when I felt the first lash of his scorching semen across my chest.

His massive body quaked uncontrollably, a prisoner to my hand. Eyes gone wide, I milked his cum over and over, till my tits were drenched and it dripped from my swollen nipples.

Next time it'd go between my lips.

Once his yells died down, he repeatedly grated something in Russian. *Prosto rai?* He shuddered, stilling my hand.

Reality returned by degrees. *Dmitri Sevastyan came on my tits.* Cold-as-Ice Vice had humped a strange guy's palm and got a very filthy cum shot. I released his dick and quickly tugged up my panties, as if that would lessen what I'd done.

When he helped me stand, I whispered, "I can't believe I just did that." I nearly buried my face in my hands. How had I lost control like that? Toward the end, I hadn't had a single thought about the con.

He hissed in a breath when he tucked his semihard cock back in his pants. I expected a player's disdain, the zip-up and the casual, "Yeah, I'll call you."

I deserved nothing less.

Yet Dmitri seemed even more interested in me. "Let me help you, *moy ángel.*" He wetted a cloth and reached for my chest, then hesitated. "I never want to forget this sight."

I gasped when he rubbed the cloth over my sensitive nipples, cleaning his warm cream. Voice rumbling, he said, "This will get us right back to where we were."

To me frantic for sex? I took the cloth from him. "I can do it. I'll be right out."

Out. With everyone else. After what I'd just let happen?

The entire penthouse had to have heard us.

His brows drew together. "You want me to ... I'm to *leave?*"

What a confusing man. He'd been all blistering need and steely command in the throes, but now he seemed unsure. In a quiet rasp, he said, "I don't want to let you out of my sight."

I bit my lip. "I'm kind of wearing your DNA right now, so do me a solid, huh?"

He canted his head, as if trying to gauge my reaction. "With reluctance."

CHAPTER 7

After washing, redressing, and twisting my hair up again, I checked my appearance in the mirror. Other than my flushed cheeks, I didn't see any outward evidence of what we'd done. But I was still feeling my jackpot of an orgasm—and those shooters.

I drew a steadying breath, looped my purse over my shoulder, then opened the door.

Dmitri stood directly outside. A hank of jet-black hair fell over his forehead as he stared down at me.

My cousin had tried to describe this very look; I realized why he'd had so much trouble.

Dmitri Sevastyan's expression was half longing, half dark possessiveness, as intense as everything else about the Russian. "Was that too much? I want you to be comfortable with me."

"I'm just a little . . . overwhelmed. I'm gonna slip out." I really didn't want to say *good-bye* and *how nice to meet you* to all of them right now.

"I understand. I will see you home at once." He fished his phone from his pocket, texting even faster than Pete.

"We can leave through the doorway at the end of the hall."

Minutes later, we'd arrived downstairs and a sleek Mercedes limo was pulling up to the VIP entrance. This private drive was shielded behind the Calydon's gate—so barbarians like my family couldn't get in.

A nondescript brown-haired bodyguard opened the door for me, asking for my address. I muttered it, and Dmitri helped me in.

Then he sat beside me.

I blinked. "I thought you'd just see me off." Good God, this was going to be the longest fifteen-minute ride of my life.

In reply, he reached for me, pulling me across his lap—as if he couldn't get close enough to me. So much for a player's disdain.

His body heat and scent lit me right back up again. My ass still tingled from my spanking. *Blush.* "You keep putting me on your lap."

"Why should I not?" The question wasn't rhetorical. He was genuinely curious.

I didn't have an answer for him, so I just sighed.

In a low tone, he said, "I have . . . difficulty reading others. Did I do too much?"

"Of what?"

"Are you angry that I came on you?"

My eyes widened. *Okay, then, let's talk sex.* I dragged my mind back to business. I needed to ignite his desire for a future encounter, while planting some good-girl seeds. "When I felt your cum, I loved it. My first thought was that it would go between my lips next time."

His lips parted on a breath. *"Victoria . . ."*

"But I've only known you for a few hours. I worry I gave

you the wrong idea. I don't behave like this. Ever. I made it to twenty-four with only three notches in my belt, and those experiences were vanilla." I'd enjoyed my ex's linebacker physique and had gotten off with him more times than I hadn't. But, yeah, sex with Brett had been relatively tame.

"Did anything else make you uncomfortable?" Dmitri asked.

"I don't know about being spanked. About . . . BDSM." I liked things simple. From what I'd seen online, BDSM seemed to be all about props and wardrobe and power dynamics. As if I didn't have to deal with those three things enough when conning.

Too much work; too much prep.

"It made you come hard, no? What if we agree to stop as soon as it fails to do so?" He assumed we'd be spending that much time together?

"Do you want to tie me up?" What did my future hold?

"Yes. I want to control the pace of what happens between us."

"When did you get interested in this stuff?" Had I put off a *spank me* vibe to Dmitri? Was that why he'd engaged with me instead of Karin? The thought made me uneasy.

"A year ago. My brothers have those leanings. I got the idea from Maksim."

"Do Lucía and Natalie share those leanings?"

"Proudly."

The PhD and the heiress? Mind blown. "Is that why you got your piercing done?"

"I suppose it's all related."

"You just woke up and thought, *I could pierce my dick today*?" Maybe for a lover?

He shrugged. "I considered the decision for a while. I wanted to make myself different than I'd been, and I thought it would alter the . . . sensations."

Different. Altered. What was wrong with how he'd been?

"I had it done a few months ago." He paused. "You don't mind it?"

"I'll probably dream about your dick tonight."

"I could stay over and ensure that." Oh, he could be so charming.

Dmitri was a conundrum. At times tonight, I could sense him struggling socially—hesitating before he spoke, gazing away, seeming to have more in common with quiet Aleks. Yet then Dmitri could turn around and demonstrate as much charm as Maksim.

"Why have you slept with so few men?" he asked.

"I wasn't exactly intent on preserving my virtue, sirrah."

The corner of his lips almost tilted up. A micro-smile. "Then why?"

Residual tequila made me reveal my superpowers: "I can always tell two things. When someone is lying to my face, and when someone is selling me. The words sound like nails down a chalkboard to me. It's always been that way." A handy talent. "When I was a teenager, the guys I fooled around with pulled out all the stops to close one deal in particular. It turned me off like a bucket of ice water."

I remembered all their ploys.

My parents are out of town—but only *for this weekend.* (This deal won't last long!)

If you don't wanna be with me like this, maybe I'll find a girl who will. (Act now or lose this opportunity forever!)

We don't have to go all the way; I'll only put the tip in. (Sign and drive! No cash down!)

Dmitri tucked a stray curl behind my ear. "I will never lie to you." Eventually he would. They always did.

But I didn't care—because I was running game on him. "When do you return to Russia?"

"That depends. I have an opportunity I'm investigating here." He made *me* sound like the opportunity.

Was he almost on the hook? If so, then I would need to be elusive. Give and take, ebb and flow. "I might have to work tomorrow night."

"Why?"

"Is work such a foreign concept?"

"I *know* work. For over a decade, I sequestered myself in a research lab seventeen hours a day, seven days a week."

"Really?" According to Pete's notes, Dmitri owned two of the fifty highest-grossing tech patents.

He nodded. "I've already completed a lifetime of work. Literally. I did the math."

"Then what were you asking?"

"Are you working toward something? Saving up?"

"Oh. I wouldn't mind replacing A2B. That's my ancient truck's nickname." Because getting me from point A to point B was the only thing noteworthy about the junker. Lately, point B was a stretch. When I'd left Brett, I'd also left behind the car he'd been paying for. "By the sound of its engine, I'm pretty sure my truck's trying to tell me, 'Go on . . . without me . . . save yourself.'"

The corner of Dmitri's lips curled again. I hadn't seen him smile fully, but his micro-smile was still a heart-stopper.

"A vehicle is all you want?"

Was he angling for big gifts already? I was an ace at milk-cowing! It seemed a little early for step five of the long con—the pitch—but if he was receptive . . . "And I'm getting evicted soon." *So buy me a pony—and a condo!*

"We can't have you getting evicted, *moy ángel.*"

Step five was best done gradually over several meetings; having planted the seed, I changed the subject. "What did you mean when you said you have difficulty reading others?"

"I can claim no talent for it. I know science and math and technology, but I am repeatedly thrown by people."

His admission softened me even more toward him. Any hints of vulnerability made this larger-than-life man more relatable—*he's actually a mortal*—but he shouldn't tell people stuff like that, or they'd fleece him blind.

People like me. My pang of guilt hit me like a sucker punch. "Then how do you know who to trust?"

His eyes dimmed. "We always find out in the long run, do we not?"

Whoa, I wasn't the only one whose trust had been betrayed. And this man was still suffering from it. Had a former friend inflicted that damage? A family member?

A lover?

The idea of him scorned by a woman and possibly still in love with her made me so jealous, I grew anxious. Developing feelings for him would be disastrous.

And how would a man like him react if he found out what I was? His security might flag something on us, sooner or later.

I was betraying Dmitri's trust right now. "Sounds like you got burned somewhere along the line."

He gazed out the window. "Early along the line."

"By someone you were involved with?"

He shrugged.

A pall seemed to have fallen over us. "Dmitri?" I laid my hand on his cheek, and his lids grew heavy. He leaned into my palm, and my heart twisted. He'd needed that tiny show of comfort from me.

Realization struck. He hadn't been burned—he'd been *hurt*. A sense of protectiveness surged, startling me. I'd only ever felt this way about family.

Our motto was "To the grave," because our loyalty to one another would never die.

Dmitri was revisiting some kind of pain; I wanted him to stay in the present with me. "Okay, big guy"—I skimmed the back of my fingers along his rugged jawline—"you ready to find out how I got my nickname?"

His eyes lit up with interest. "Yes. It does not make sense." He was obviously a man who liked things to add up.

"When I was little, I was fascinated with vices. A mobile spinning above my crib would make me cry, but the sound of shuffled cards and clinking poker chips soothed me. I laughed and clapped if someone popped a bottle of bubbly, and I smothered other toddlers with kisses. *All* of them." I grinned. "I was very inconstant."

"I could listen to you talk about yourself for . . ." He trailed off. "There is no quantifiable limit of time."

His compliment made me smile. Such a computer guy.

"I want more of this with you, Victoria. Be forewarned: I will have it."

Had I made myself seem like a sure thing? Or was he thinking like a typical male in Vegas? "People have weird ideas about cocktail waitresses, Dmitri. You know that I'm not for sale, right?"

"I know. Or I would have already bought you."

I grinned, thinking he was kidding, but he just stared into my eyes.

Too intense! So I tried a playful turn. "And what would you do if you owned me?" I tweaked his strong chin. "Would I be your slave?"

He shook his head. "I would free you, Victoria. And then I would buy you the entire goddamned world."

My grin faded, my grift sense taking over. "Dmitri, are you . . . crazy?"

His chest stilled as he held his breath. Never looking away, he gave me a slow nod.

Oh, yeah, this family had some secrets. What *kind* of crazy? Eccentric billionaire? Or "I keep ladies' ears as trophies"?

No, my grift sense told me he wasn't the type of man who'd harm a woman, a spanking aside. Just to be sure, I asked, "Have you ever hurt anyone?"

He exhaled a gust of air that heated my ear. "Never a woman, never anyone weaker than myself."

Not a lie. I suspected Dmitri's damage was turned inward; he'd *been* hurt. I had no idea what to say.

He cupped my nape and pulled me in until our foreheads met. All of a sudden, we were the only two people in the world. "Are my chances blown?" he rasped.

In real life? Yes. I would end this tonight. With my family in survival mode, I didn't have time for a damaged man. Hell, I didn't have time for any guy. "I'm surprised you'll admit it."

"I will never lie to you. And you asked me a very direct question."

As I considered his admission, my mind hurtled to that last

night with Brett—when I'd found him naked in our bed with a showgirl, his fingers deep inside her.

I'd known men were dogs, yet for some reason I'd let down my guard with the big, affable high-school football coach.

Now as I gazed at the Russian, I realized where my preferences lay. I looked Dmitri in the eyes and told him the truth: "I'd rather have an honest madman than a sane liar."

He squeezed me to him so tightly I thought I would bruise, but I didn't want it to stop. . . .

CHAPTER 8

"Tell us what happened!" Karin called from my bedroom before I'd even shut my apartment door.

Had Dmitri heard that? He'd walked me from the limo, taken my key, and opened the lock for me. His kiss goodnight had been brief but tender. "Until tomorrow," he'd said.

I peered out the peephole. He stood at my doorstep with his brows drawn. He'd made no secret that he wanted to come in, but I had grift gear out in the open: wigs, ID maker, props, etc. Besides, I needed to be elusive at this point.

With clear reluctance, he finally headed toward the limo.

I put my back against the door and exhaled, as if I were catching my breath for the first time tonight. . . .

Still buzzed, I veered toward my bedroom, passing the tiny living area I used as a sewing studio. My mom had taught Karin and me how to make our own clothes because many of our cons required us to look like money; retail couture would eat into profits.

As I passed my dress dummies, garment racks, and my old

busted-up Singer, I tried to remember when I'd last had time to use them.

Karin, Pete, and Benji were camped out on my oversize bed, flipping through textbooks from my stint at design school.

"What are you guys doing here?" Hanging out in my lame one-bedroom unit? I had barely any furniture, zero decorations, and no TV. Boxes filled with posters of eighties bands and movie memorabilia lined the walls, unopened since I'd moved from Brett's last year.

I'd meant to do a POP—pratfall on property—at a better apartment complex, but hadn't gotten around to it.

Karin sat up against the headboard, beaming. "We could hardly wait for you to divvy what happened!" She wore shorts and a broken-in T-shirt that read: *It was me. I let the dogs out.* Our grandmother had given that to her. Out of love, Karin wore it constantly.

My pink cellphone had been a present from Gram, which meant I cherished it—no matter how much I hated the color pink. Not to mention that "dialing the pink telephone" was a euphemism for masturbation. I told myself it was better than the Snuggie she'd gotten Pete or Benji's hobbit-feet socks.

"Holy shit, sis." Benji's coffee-brown eyes lit up. "What a difference a day makes, huh?"

To see my brother today, you'd never guess how much he'd suffered on the streets as a little boy. He'd grown up to be lava-hot, tall and built, with a quiet strength that drew people.

Eighteen years ago, he'd been a seven-year-old street urchin trying to hustle my dad. A scrawny thing with huge eyes, he'd had a talent at cards that rivaled mine and little memory of how he got to the States. He'd called himself Benji because he'd probably been born in Bengal, India.

Dad had seen potential. With no parents to be found, he'd brought Benji home, and we'd adopted him.

"Did you really tangle with a billionaire?" he asked.

I hiccupped and grinned.

"You didn't sleep with the Russian, did you?" Pete asked, seeming to brace himself for my answer.

I made a chopping motion. "Sex—*nyet*."

Relieved looks all around.

I tossed my keys and my purse onto my dime-store desk. Lucía's watch rattled inside that secret compartment. "But we did hook up." I sat in my fold-up chair and took off my heels, wincing from my aching feet.

"Tell us, hon!" Karin said. "What's he like?"

"He's . . . he's . . ." I tried to put him into words. "With him, it's . . ." I gave up. "Lemme go take a shower."

Under the paltry water pressure, I considered and discarded descriptions. How to explain someone like Dmitri Sevastyan?

Once I padded back out in my robe, Benji said, "Well?"

I hopped up on a free corner of my bed. "Dmitri is magnetic and fascinating and . . . unconventional."

Karin studied my expression. "Then the con won't be such a chore. Everybody's so excited, Vice. I've been bragging about my boss of a little sister." She would; she didn't have a jealous bone in her body. "Pete said he's never seen a mark respond like this."

He chuckled. "Not fifteen minutes after I told Vice she needed to practice sexual manipulation, she had the Russian shoving her up against a wall, groaning into her mouth, and hard as rock."

I blushed. "I wondered if you'd seen that detail."

"As if I could *miss* that huge . . . detail."

Karin laughed. "The student has become the teacher! I tried every trick in the book to get that man's attention—even a noob move like the toppled tray."

She'd dropped a tray filled with plastic cups of ice, enabling her to spend lots of time on all fours in a miniskirt hunting for each cube.

The idea of my sister doing that in front of Dmitri . . . Jealousy hit me. Again.

Benji said, "Start from the beginning and tell us everything that happened."

I did—because this was my first sex con and I needed their input. But I omitted the finer points of each orgasm, and I found myself leaving out details that made Dmitri sound even more . . . eccentric.

I finished with: "He walked me to my door, all gentlemanlike, which blew my mind after the way he'd been sexually."

"He spanked you?" Pete raised his brows. "I did not see that one coming. Pun intended."

"Yep." My ass still burned. I'd gotten a glimpse of what sex would be like with Sevastyan.

Earth-shattering. Filthy. Baffling.

Pete snapped his fingers. "Now that I think of it, I've overheard some jokes and innuendo about BDSM from the Sevastyan couples."

Natalie and Lucía just didn't seem like the type.

"Did you like it?" Karin asked. "I didn't think your tastes ran that way."

"It's not my bag," I said, even though I'd gotten off on being whipped.

Karin tilted her head. "Luckily, you won't have to deal with his penchant for very long."

Because I only had so much time to fleece the man.

I'd once been asked if I felt guilty conning people. Nope. *You have to play to pay. Behave yourself, and you'll never know my family exists.* We targeted those who could never report a con to the police—because of their own dirty deeds.

So what had Dmitri done to deserve me? What if he was a little crazy—and a lot vulnerable? I kept replaying how he'd leaned into my touch for comfort. He'd already been burned in his life and still bore the scars.

Maybe Pete's initial instinct to cut that family had been right on. "I've been thinking about tomorrow night," I said to no one in particular. "About the congressman."

Blackmailing him could be the family's largest score yet. Badger games were like grifter annuities; they paid for life, and sometimes even appreciated if the mark made it big.

The congressman could be a presidential hopeful. We wished him all the best in his future campaigns.

Unfortunately, Karin would have to turn over the big payout from that asshole to service our debt.

Her blond brows drew together. "What about him?"

Benji perked up too. He was instrumental in badgers. He'd earned his nickname "the Eye" from his remarkable camera work.

"My string of bad luck, or whatever, seems to be over." I got up, knocked on the wood of my desk, then returned. "If I start roping guys and you bag the congressman, maybe we . . . shouldn't run Dmitri."

"What?" the three exclaimed in unison.

I played with the sash on my robe. "We might be able to

scrounge up enough if Mom and Dad make good on their art scam. And Nigel could reconnect. Plus there's the watch I lifted." From a genuinely nice woman. If I felt this shitty about that, I couldn't imagine what playing with Dmitri's feelings would do to me.

In a scandalized tone, Karin said, "You *like* him."

"Or maybe I'm thinking about our own rules? No sins, no in. We have a code, remember?" In all my life, we'd never broken it. "What has the Russian done to merit a financial punishment and a helping of pain? We prey on vulnerabilities, not the vulnerable."

Benji scratched his head. "Why would you consider a brilliant and handsome BDSM billionaire vulnerable?"

"Call it grift sense."

"He simply hasn't shown you his sins *yet*," Karin said, disturbingly confident. "Give him time. Sins always out. I guarantee he's part of the ninety-seven percent."

Like the father of her kid?

She was right. I knew better. You'd think I would've learned after all the lying, two-timing scrotes I'd encountered in the grift. Hell, my own ex-fiancé should've taught me.

"The point is moot anyway." Karin sighed. "Dmitri could be pure as driven snow, and we'd still have to target him. Hon, think of the alternative."

Three months ago, we'd swindled a drug-trafficking couple from overseas for a cool million, our largest take to date. We'd spent ages doing foundation work, yet no amount of research would've revealed that the woman was an untouchable. The lovechild of a cartel kingpin.

In lieu of an outright execution, the man had allowed us to repay the score in full—while owing six million in interest.

Karin had banked one and a half of it with her nonstop badgers. My parents' art scheme might net us five hundred. I would contribute two fifty. We had less than three weeks left to pull together the rest.

If we failed . . . That kingpin enjoyed *necklacing*: shoving a gasoline-soaked tire around a victim's chest and arms, then lighting it on fire. He'd threatened to do that to the primary on the con—my dad.

Pete said, "Vice, it's life or death. You have to break the code."

Dad was the bighearted rock of the family, nicknamed Gentleman Joe because he could mingle with the upper crust—but also because he had a kind smile and was a softie for a grifter.

My mom and dad were freaking symbiotic. If anything happened to him, I'd lose both parents.

Our only other option was to rabbit. The problem with that? We had dozens of people at Sunday dinner. Would everyone in our extended family go into hiding? What if someone wanted to remain?

To the grave. "You're right. When the Russian calls tomorrow, I'll do what I need to do."

CHAPTER 9

*A*s I skulked in platform high-heeled boots and a party dress through the dark, I could have sworn I was being watched.

I narrowed my eyes and surveyed the murky brush around our prop house, a.k.a. the badger den. I strained to hear, but A2B continued to wheeze and rattle long after I'd turned off the ignition.

For months, I'd been feeling paranoid like this. Probably because I *was* jinxed.

Dmitri hadn't called today, had written me only one cold line of text.

DSevastyan: I will contact you tomorrow.

My *sixth* busted mark.

At the back door, I glanced over my shoulder again, unable to shake the feeling that I wasn't alone. Maybe one of the cartel's henchmen was following me until we paid.

Surely it couldn't be Brett. . . .

I slipped inside and headed toward the camera room. Recording equipment crowded the small area. Benji was already here, manning a desk with a mic and several monitors. The screens played streams from video cameras all around the exterior—and interior—of the house, but I didn't spot anyone outside.

Benji swiveled around in his chair. "I thought you were meeting us later." Like me, he was dressed up to go out afterward. His stovepipe pants and fitted jacket accentuated his tall frame. He'd shaved his lean face.

"Got stir-crazy." I couldn't stand my lonely apartment any longer.

Earlier, Pete had texted me not to come in, that the VIP lounge was dead.

Vice: I can still take a shift.

P3X: We'll celebrate tonight and let off steam. Tomorrow huge group of Canadian high rollers.

Trying not to appear desperate for news on Dmitri, I'd asked about Nigel.

P3X: He checked out.

Seriously?? Vice: Dmitri? How could a one-word text be so pathetic?

P3X: No one's come down from the penthouse. Not a peep from them. But I know he'll call you.

Vice: Two tears in a bucket, motherfuck it.

I dropped my false-bottomed purse on the couch, then plopped down beside it. I would've gone biking in Red Rock Canyon today to burn off some energy, but A2B might not have made it back, and I'd worried about spotty telephone reception. Not that I'd needed to.

One sentence, Dmitri? After he'd spanked me so much I still felt it? I didn't know if I should be pissed or worried, so I'd settled on pissed.

Benji said, "Well, you're just in time. Karin's ten minutes out."

Like clockwork. In less than an hour, I'd be on a dance floor. Vegas was the capital of electronic dance music; even our local club had EDM Saturdays. After so much work, I craved one wild night out—and I'd dressed accordingly.

I pulled my Bee deck of playing cards from my purse, then mindlessly cut and shuffled for comfort, warming up with basics. Pinky cut, false cut, double cut, the false riffle shuffle.

"Bad day?" My brother knew me all too well.

"It was fine." *It was shit.* Though I should've caught up on sleep, I kept replaying what the Russian had done to me.

When I'd pictured the look in Dmitri's smoldering eyes— and the glint of his piercing—I'd gotten so horny I'd had to take the edge off. Repeatedly.

Then I'd broken down and looked up *Vika.* It was a Russian diminutive of Victoria, an endearment. I'd sighed like a sap.

Yet all that had been *before* I'd known he wouldn't call me the entire day. I flashed cards from my right palm to my left, lifting a king of hearts.

Benji asked, "You never heard from him?"

Everyone in the family now knew I'd fooled around with the richest mark we could ever imagine—but hadn't set my claws. Why had I even expected him to call? Talk about reaching for the stars! I'd reached for a different galaxy!

Roughly eighteen hundred male billionaires existed in the world. Only one out of every four million people was that rich.

My suggestion that we cut him loose now embarrassed me. "He texted that one time." I gave Benji a breezy nod that would convince anyone but a fellow grifter. "He'll call tomorrow." Long cons had taught me to be patient. I drew on that inner well.

"Hey, that's a big mark for anyone."

The unspoken words hung in the air: *But especially for you, Vice.* With my six busted cons. Everyone was so focused on my recent failures, they seemed to have forgotten my years of success.

I'd had such a great start, and all the support I could ever need.

My mom loved to tell our friends: "I remember when Vice pulled her first card hustle at four." Her voice would grow thick with emotion. "Her hands were so tiny, she could barely palm-deal. And don't get me started on her first three-card monte."

In a monte, the dealer would shuffle around three cards, two black and a queen of hearts, using misdirection to obscure the queen. Dealers of montes were called *broad tossers* because of the queen card.

Mom had home movies of me hustling tourists, lisping, "Can you keep your eyeth on the queen, thsir?"

Benji whirled back around toward the desk. "Here comes the congressman's limo."

The Midwestern lawmaker was a married father of four—who'd told Karin he was a childless movie producer from California, a widower since his wife had passed away in a "fiery car crash." So Karin had told him she was a divorced, childless waitress and aspiring actress.

Benji tossed me his phone. "Check out the texts he sent right before he met up with Karin." Benji had cloned the congressman's phone while Karin had distracted the man.

If we'd gotten a clone of Dmitri's phone, maybe I would have a better understanding of what was going on up in that penthouse villa.

I scanned the politician's exchange from an hour ago as he'd played up his day of meetings and told his (strangely alive) wife, Sheila, that he was about to pass out for the night and he'd call in the morning. The woman had responded that he was working too hard and that she and the kids couldn't love him more. Then, his cherry-on-top text: There's nothing I wouldn't do for my family.

I wanted to vomit.

As Karin and her "date" laughingly strolled up the walk, Benji murmured into the mic, "Earpiece check. Check."

Behind the mark's back, she gave a thumbs-up sign.

Benji said, "Get me a sound bite about his 'dead' wife, luv, and I'll buy drinks all night."

Another secret thumbs-up.

I'd seen Karin do this dozens of times. She was so sexy and skilled, she never even had to touch a bare dick. After her customary striptease, she'd tell the mark to lie back in bed and show her how badly he wanted her. He'd sprawl and grip his junk, then she'd kneel over it. Taking her time, seeming about to slide down, she'd say smutty things while the guy gawked with utter desperation on his face.

Boo-yah. Money shot. Oftentimes, from one angle, it'd look like he was inside her.

As soon as Benji had collected enough evidence to hold up in a potential divorce, he would go bang on the door, acting like a murderous ex-husband. On cue, Karin would hurry the mark out the back door.

Damn it, I could do this—if I could ever lure a guy back

here. Did I want to kiss a man I *knew* was a lowlife? No. But that didn't matter. . . .

As Karin poured a round of drinks, beginning to tighten the noose, I stowed my cards and pulled out my phone, hoping I'd missed a text chime.

Nope.

My unread e-mail number blinked. I found offers from my former design school, a downloadable "hot fireman" calendar from Gram, and a seamstress forum newsletter.

I knew I'd get another message from Brett tomorrow. Initially, his fight to win me back had consisted of long, remorseful voice messages, with him swearing he wouldn't have gone all the way with that bombshell.

Then he'd started a weekly e-mail campaign, recounting some memory from our history. He'd written every Sunday without fail for several months.

Last week's:

On our second date, you tangled with Jack Daniels and Jack won. I held back your hair as you got sick. You told me to leave you and go back to the party. I realized I'd rather hang out with you over a toilet than be around anyone else. The next day you made me feel like a hero and gave me a helluva thank-you.

I'll always love you, B

Regardless of his betrayal, I felt guilty that he couldn't move on. I mean, yeah, we'd been about to join our lives together forever and all, but a year had passed. Maybe my persistent singlehood spurred his hopes.

"Whoa," Benji said. "You sew that up for her?"

I glanced at the monitor. Karin was already on the striptease portion of tonight's program?

She wore my newest lingerie creation, a system of red bands

that resembled a merry widow. "Yep." I'd designed it to be nearly impossible for a guy to rip off. To undo each snap would be like a puzzle for a patient man—or a tease for a honey trap.

She'd had her son, Cash, six months ago, but Karin had bounced back with a vengeance. The only lasting effect from her pregnancy: her boobs were now bigger than mine.

At the sight of her in lingerie, tension stole through Benji's shoulders and his respiration accelerated—even though he'd never want me to note those signs. Alas, some reactions couldn't be masked. "Don't bother trying to hide it. Grifter here, remember?" Details were my job.

Without looking away, he said, "You're an annoying kid sister, you know that?"

"I'm not technically your sister, which means Karin isn't either."

"Which means your parents aren't my parents. And I quite like our parents."

They were babysitting Cash tonight. "Mom and Dad could be in-law parents. Or you could just be family with no labels." Like Russian Al, our favorite fence.

"I've got enough weird stuff going on in my head. Falling for Karin is the last thing I need to do."

When he'd first come to live with us, he'd had horrific nightmares, screaming in the middle of the night. I'd started sneaking into his room to sleep on the floor, standing guard against whatever kept scaring him. I'd been too young to realize I couldn't protect him from his own memories.

He'd gotten so much better, but yeah, I could see why he'd be gun-shy.

"Here we go," Benji said. "She's getting him to talk. . . ."

Some highlights from the congressman's audio reel:

—"I've never felt this way about anyone. Not even Sheila, God rest her soul." *(BINGO!)*

—"My late wife was the only one I've ever been with." *(Except for the escort orgy last night.)*

—"I've had a vasectomy. We can skip the condom." *(Sheila would not appreciate this, Congressman.)*

And people wondered why I thought men sucked? Even Karin seemed to be losing patience.

Once she had the mark naked in bed, holding his needle dick, Benji murmured into the mic, "Not much longer now."

She slinked over in heels to straddle the guy, starting her dirty talk, a script she'd tweaked and polished over the years. *You can't improve on a classic.*

Benji directed her. "Move a little to your left. A bit more. Almost got it—*there*. That shot is worth at least a million. And the video will show his hands shaking. Would you like to see your 'irate ex-husband' now?"

Another thumbs-up.

Benji rose and winked at me. "Showtime."

CHAPTER 10

*M*usic thumped, laser lights pierced the dimly lit club, and scantily clad twentysomethings ground their crotches all around me on the dance floor.

My head was spinning, my body moving to the house tunes.

I loved showing off my tiny black dress. I'd designed the micro-length sheath with a zipper down the front for easy access. The material had hidden writing—"go hard" translated into a half a dozen different languages—that glowed under the black light. My platform high-heeled boots stretched up to the middle of my thighs. I wore glam eye makeup, spike earrings, and a neon choker some random guy had given me.

My hair was free and wild, my good-girl disguise long gone.

I'd had Jell-O shots for dinner—who said they weren't a food group?—and a vat's worth of rum and Cokes. Apparently, I was hammered. I'd asked Karin in all seriousness, "If we're honey traps doing badger games, are we really honey badgers?"

For now, my dance partner was a brown-haired Dane with nice muscles and a Rolex on his beefy wrist.

I already had two other watches in my purse, lifted from a pair of guys who'd negged me, earning their punishment.

I rubbed my nape again. I kept getting that sense of being watched. Maybe a grifter had me in his sights. Ha!

Pete was nearby laughing and dancing with some hunk. Karin sat with Benji in one of the VIP booths. They looped arms and did shots. Toasting the next president?

When we'd first arrived at this club, we'd passed a bachelorette party. Karin had glanced at me to see how I was taking it.

A year ago, she'd thrown me one at the Caly; a week later, I'd walked in on Brett.

Tonight, I'd wanted to shake that bride-to-be, telling her, "Never give a man a wedding ring unless you can be certain he won't ever take it off." *Spoiler alert: eventually most will.*

Really, Brett had saved me the heartache of a divorce.

When my mind turned to heartache, I immediately thought of Dmitri Sevastyan. The guy who couldn't be bothered to make a single phone call today.

Maybe he had another date. At the thought, jealousy churned inside me. Was I more jealous of Dmitri with some imaginary woman than I'd been with Brett and the real-live showgirl in my own bed?

The answer to that question made me uneasy, so I danced closer to the Dane. He grinned, thinking I was in the bank.

Why shouldn't I sleep with him? Then again, why *should* I? *He's not my key. . . .*

I ran my hand over my nape. Damn it, again I felt like I was being *watched* watched. I peered around the club—

Lost my breath.

Dmitri Sevastyan stood beside the dance floor, his eyes

riveted to me. He was dressed to perfection in black slacks and a crisp, blue button-down, but he looked agitated.

How had he found me here? What did he want? He raked his gaze over me, seeming dazed by my appearance. Had he expected the angel from last night?

'Cause she's gone, baby, gone.

As my hips swayed, Dmitri's breaths shallowed. Maybe I should show him what he *could* have gotten if he'd deigned to call me.

I turned to face him, making my moves sensual, as if I danced only for him. Dane took the hint and skulked off with a curse.

In my nearly indecent dress, I raised my hands to play with my hair, then I glided my palms down my front as I worked my hips. My boots had been made for moves like this.

Dmitri's fists were clenched, his eyes glazed with lust. His cock was hard, and he made no attempt to disguise that fact. He looked like he might grab me and rail me against a speaker.

My nipples stiffened. Wondering if my eyes were begging for it, I moistened my lips.

He must've reached his limit. He strode onto the dance floor and grasped my forearm. *"Come with me."* He had to yell over the music. "We're leaving." As he ushered me through the crowd, people stopped and stared at him, but he seemed oblivious to their attention.

"I came here with friends." I couldn't see my crew! "I don't want to leave!"

He faced me, lips drawn back from his teeth. "Were you going to fuck that man?"

"Are you a jealous kind of guy, baby?" The absolute best type of mark for a milk-cow con. Of course, he'd never admit it.

"With you? Yes! I wanted to kill him!"

Oh boy. Had Dmitri meant that . . . literally? "Yet you didn't contact me today?" Could I revive this con?

His eyes darted. "I need to talk to you."

We couldn't continue this conversation over the music, but I wasn't prepared to leave with him yet. "I know a place. Head toward the back." Taking my hand, he walked in that direction, stopping at what looked like a solid black wall.

"Here." I ducked behind a dark drape into the club's secret area.

He followed, drawing up short. "What is this place?"

"The Carousel. It used to be a speakeasy." Carnival decorations from bygone fairs lined the walls. Strings of lights cascaded over ceramic horses from one of the first steam-powered carousels. Drums that still smelled of greasepaint were stacked in the corner. Bright banners and an acrobat's net hung from the ceiling. "Now only locals know about it."

The management opened it for friends' parties, so I'd been here several times. I found the place magical. On slow nights, people hooked up back here since there were no cameras.

"And it's simply . . . here." He surveyed the area, murmuring, "I need help with things like this."

"Like what?"

His gaze held mine. "I need curtains drawn back. I need to be shown things I never would see on my own."

His strange words—plus my cocktails—equaled zero comprehension for me. "How did you find me?"

"This club is popular with Calydon staff."

I scooted into a booth. "What did you want to talk to me about?"

He slid around the table to sit beside me. "I am struggling

to . . ." He closed his mouth. Another try: "I want to . . ." His eyes were fierce with some pent-up emotion, but he also looked frustrated, like he was trying to read my mood and *knew* he was failing. "Are you angered with me?"

I traced the gathered edge of one of my boots. "After what we did, I thought you'd get in touch with me." Like a grifter, he'd given me a taste, then he'd become elusive.

"I went downstairs tonight, thinking you would be at the casino, or that Peter would be."

I *had* told Dmitri I might be working. "But no call?"

"The day slipped by me. I was very . . . distracted. I did call three hours ago."

We'd probably just gotten here. My phone was in my purse. "Do you want a drink?"

He eased even closer, as if he couldn't help himself. "No. I have to keep control."

"Why?"

"Last night I considered doing things to you . . . things that would've unnerved you even more. Had I been drinking, I would have."

"Like what?" I asked, intrigued.

"I wanted to get my mouth on you and prove that you would love oral sex. I wanted to whip you even harder, to make you feel me for longer. I wanted to sink inside the flesh I stroked and fuck you till you screamed."

My breaths shallowed.

"I was nearly overpowered. I hadn't been with anyone for some time, and all of a sudden I was with you." His penetrating eyes said so much, but my buzz blurred the message.

"How long had it been?"

"A very long time. I could argue that I had been waiting on you."

Guh. "What do you want from me, Dmitri?" I met his gaze as I closed the last little distance to him. "Just tell me, and we'll see if we want the same things."

He stared into my eyes, his pupils dilating. "You make it sound so simple."

"Then don't make it complicated. Just bottom-line it for me."

"I must have more of what happened last night," he said, his words laden with raw need.

I leaned in and drunkenly whispered, "You want to drench my tits again?"

He hissed, *"Mercy,"* then yanked me across his lap, settling me over his hard cock.

The heat of his erection reached me through our clothes, and my lids went heavy. "I'll take that as a yes." I wriggled on him.

He inhaled sharply. "I want more of you. More access to you."

His words reminded me of my earlier loneliness and turmoil. "But you didn't call me?" I murmured, sounding drunk and sad. "If you'd called, we could've talked. We could've gotten to know each other better."

"I was not . . . feeling like myself. Do you think I didn't want to talk to you? I feared I would spook you. I'm told I can be overly . . . intense."

"Is that what all the girls say?"

"It's what anyone says."

Though he was dressed as immaculately as ever and clean-shaven, he'd nicked his face in a few places. On a scale between pissed and worried, I tipped toward on the latter.

"Why weren't you feeling like yourself?" Had something happened? My protectiveness toward him lingered.

"I fought with my brother Maksim."

"I'm sorry. You seem close to him."

"I am. After our parents died, he basically raised me."

Why wouldn't the oldest brother have done that? "Do you want to talk about what happened?"

"Maksim stuck his nose into my business." Pure menace burned in his eyes as he said, "And then he told me I will likely lose something I want very, very dearly."

This conversation had strange depths. Once again on this con, I was drunk and at a disadvantage.

"I asked my family to leave," he said.

"Yet you stayed? For the opportunity you're investigating?"

He nodded, his gaze softening. *"Da."* He surveyed the area, exhaling a gust of breath. "I didn't plan for this."

"Do you always plan everything?"

"When something is important to me, yes." He grasped my nape, bringing our foreheads together. I loved when he did that. He seemed to carefully choose his words as he said, "Confusion is not . . . good for me. I handle it . . . badly." His voice was halting, and he looked a little crazy. "I need things solidified. How do I solidify things with you?"

His idea of solidifying couldn't possibly match mine—unless the billionaire was talking about a commitment after knowing me for a day. "You're bringing up confusion, Dmitri? You're sending my brain spinning here."

"Come back to my room with me."

Wow, right when I thought he was interested in more than sex.

Which meant I shouldn't be interested in more than money.

The con was *back* on. Time to plant some more good-girl seeds. "That's not going to happen. I gave you the wrong impression last night. I don't know why I behaved like that." *Truth.* "But there won't be a repeat." *Lie.*

He gave me his thrall look. "Indulge me, and I will indulge you." Did he mean financially? Or sexually?

Because I was drunk, I answered by burying my face against his neck and inhaling him. "Your scent drives me absolutely wild. If you ever got me in your bed, I'd probably just roll around in your sheets and masturbate."

He groaned. "I *never* want to stop seeing that in my head."

When I dragged my head back to face him, his hooded expression made me shiver. I rubbed his chest, loving how his muscles twitched in response. "You must work out."

"Religiously for the last year."

"Lemme guess," I said drily, "you just aren't hot enough?"

"I work out to focus my mind, not to affect my looks. You are obviously attracted to me," he said, as if my attraction was all that mattered.

"Cocky much? What if I was faking?"

"You were too aroused to have feigned that. And I would wager you thought about me when you got off today."

"Yep. I did, a few times. In the shower, I fingered myself and came so hard my knees buckled."

"Mercy, woman!" he said again, his cock jerking beneath me. "You don't know what you do to me."

Oh, but I do. "If you hadn't noticed, I'm a smidge hammered. Will you take care of me?"

Curt nod. "Without fail."

I grinned at him. "I like that. You won't take advantage of me? I don't want to have sex with you."

"So you have said." His tone held a hint of disbelief.

"I'm not looking for an affair—even if you wanted a longer arrangement."

"What are you looking for?" He seemed very curious about my answer.

"A man to prove himself to me." I could say those words believably. Even though I knew my hurdles were simply too high.

"Then I won't fuck you. But that doesn't mean I can't touch you. I need to give you pleasure so much I ache." He reached for me.

"Here?" In the Carousel? We were alone in this darkened area, but for how long?

"Here."

CHAPTER 11

$\mathcal{D}$mitri grazed the backs of his fingers over my jawline, then down my neck. "You could not be lovelier."

I trembled as he traced my collarbone. His hand continued lower. He unzipped my dress until my breasts threatened to spill out—exactly the way I'd imagined when I'd designed it.

His hot hand slipped inside, cupping me. I arched to his touch, and he bit out something in Russian. I could have sworn I'd heard his name at the end.

Was he talking to himself? My question and concern dissipated when he rubbed his thumb over one nipple. Jolts of pleasure shot through me as he rolled the peak, lightly pinching. Then harder.

With a last tug, he moved to my other breast and kneaded it. "Spread your legs wide for me."

I let one knee fall open.

He ran his other hand up my inner thigh. *Higher.* He brushed his knuckles along my sensitive skin. *Higher.* He reached my wet pussy. "You're not wearing panties?" he snapped. I thought he'd be delighted—not infuriated. "Which man was to enjoy this surprise? The one you were dancing with earlier?"

"Maybe next time you'll call me."

"Maybe I will teach you to want only me." His half-crazy expression was back. "I am the only one who knows what you need."

Hadn't I already suspected he was my key? Apparently, he suspected the same. "Tell me what I need, Dmitri."

"I'm about to *show* you."

"But I want to touch you." I dipped my hand down.

"Ah-ah." He seized my wrist, placing my hand on his chest. "This is for you alone."

"Maybe you think I'll get so turned on I won't care if you fuck me."

"I want to see you that abandoned." His voice was low, his eyes hypnotic. "But tonight I'm only touching you, Vika. Submit to my wishes."

Vika. The endearment of my name. Strike *sexy*. He was *molten*. At that moment, I yearned to submit to this man. But a show of resistance was in order. "Why am I always the one feeling vulnerable? I've shared more of myself than you have."

"Share? What if I tell you a secret? Would that suffice?"

"Try me and see."

In a husky tone, he said, "I jerked off in the limo on the way back from your apartment. I wanted your taste on my tongue when I came again. Two strokes later, I ejaculated into my cupped palm, licking my lips for you."

A breath shuddered out of my lungs. I repeated his words: "I never want to stop seeing that in my head."

He might've given me a micro-smile, but it faded when he teased my entrance with a fingertip. "Do you want it inside?" Somehow he grew even harder beneath me.

"Yes," I panted. "Yes. . . ."

He adjusted my body so we faced the same way, my spread legs over his knees, his hands resting on my thighs. "Then raise your arms and clasp your hands behind my neck. Keep them there no matter what I do."

I had no choice; I obeyed.

"Good girl." In reward, he sank his middle finger between my soaked lips.

I cried out as my pussy contracted around it.

He gave a rumbly groan. "Ah, God, you are *tight*. And so slick for me. You love to come, don't you?" He rotated his finger inside, stirring me. Then he began to wedge in a second one. "There you go," he rasped. "Take them for me into your sweet little pussy. Do you want me to finger-fuck you? Then take them both deep."

That dirty talk in his sexy accent made me melt!

With his other hand, he pressed down on my pubic bone and above, which made the fingers inside me feel even bigger. He withdrew them, then thrust. Again. And again. "I would give anything to replace these with my cock."

My body ached for that hot, swollen rod. Though he hadn't touched my clit, I already neared the brink. "Dmitri, I need to come!"

He ignored my plea, never increasing his maddening pace. He twisted his fingers as they plunged, then twisted them again as he withdrew.

I marveled at his skill. Even as he gave me more pleasure than I'd ever felt, in the back of my mind, I wondered how I was going to live without this.

As if he'd read my thoughts, he said, "You're going to have to keep me around just for this. You fingered your pussy in the shower, but you can't do this to yourself. You can't twist and get deep, hitting all these sensitive spots."

"Make me come, please!" *Or fuck me.* I imagined him impaling me on his big, pierced dick.

"I will. Eventually." He made a beckoning gesture deep inside me.

I shot upright. "Oh! *Ohhh.* I can't take much more of this!" I could bring myself off in a nanosecond, was tempted to. Yet I kept my arms back. "I know what I said about sex, but I didn't mean it! Do you have condoms? I'm on birth control, but we should probably double-up."

Between breaths, he said, "I've never had sex without one, so I can with you." He wasn't lying.

"Does that mean we're going to?" My tone couldn't have been more eager.

He groaned again. "I would do murder to fuck you. Think of what I'd do to possess you completely."

I gasped—because I didn't think he was lying about that either.

"Which means I must keep my word."

I panted with frustration. He'd kept me hovering right at the brink for what must be years! "I'm going to come apart!"

"That's the idea. *This* is BDSM," he said at my ear. "Dominance, edging, play. I won't always whip you." He withdrew his fingers.

"Nooo! Need those. Put them *back in.*"

He used two fingers to make a V around my clit, trapping it, pressing the sensitive nub outward.

I undulated over his lap, his cock. "Touch it," I whispered, "touch it. Baby, please, please touch my throbbing clit."

With a growling sound, he used his other forefinger to slowly rub the exposed flesh.

My head lolled back against him.

"You would do anything for me right now, wouldn't you, beautiful?"

I made unintelligible sounds. He owned me. He controlled me.

This man had broken through all my barriers until I was nothing more than raw, dripping need.

My approaching orgasm felt bigger than ever before. Deeper.

Frightening.

Right when I was about to crash over the edge, I spied a man enter through the curtain. "S-stop, Dmitri. We're not alone." I dropped my arms.

The guy—a blond surfer type—told someone unseen, "Back here."

A pretty redhead and a handsome dark-haired male followed. They looked as buzzed as I felt. The trio sat across the room from us in another booth. The two men put the redhead between them.

They would be able to see me from the waist up! My tits were nearly spilling out, lit by the glowing collar I wore. "You can't do this!" I hissed to Dmitri, even as I rolled my hips.

"They can't see underneath our table. Do you really want me to stop?" He kept rubbing. "Say, 'Dmitri, stop touching my pussy.'"

I couldn't say the words, couldn't do more than whimper.

The three glanced over. Dmitri's arm was moving. They had to know what he was doing.

The guys cast me wolfish looks, and their hands caressed

down Red's body. She met gazes with me, then her eyes shot wide. We were both getting fingered in this room—and we both knew it.

Red's lids soon grew heavy. She didn't seem to mind an audience.

Did I look as turned on as she did? Was Dmitri aroused by the girl? I glanced at him. His eyes were locked on me.

I murmured, "I can't let you do this."

"Of course you can." He was a devil in my ear, mesmerizing me with his thrall.

Of course I can. No! *Vice, get hold of yourself.*

"We won't be doing anything they're not," he continued. "This situation heats your blood, doesn't it? Then surrender to it, Vika. To *me*. Put your hands behind my head again."

Such a vulnerable position in front of others.

"Do it, or I won't let you come."

Nooo! Shaking, I reached up and locked my hands again. In reward, he pinched my nipples through my dress, giving me a shock of sensation. I had to stifle a cry.

Red put her arms back too, but the dark-haired guy upped the ante, tugging down her sheath dress to bare her perky breasts.

The girl liked being exposed. She arched her back, and I could tell she was rocking her hips on her partners' fingers.

As I stared, her hands descended—as did the zipper of my dress. Dmitri was going to bare me too? This couldn't be happening.

I wanted to die of humiliation. Or come. Again everything got confused in my mind, and the embarrassment fueled my arousal.

I tensed to stop him, but then I realized both of Red's

hands were moving under the table. She was jacking off both guys.

While all three stared at me.

"This is . . . wicked," I whispered. *Forbidden.*

"Submit to me," Dmitri grated. "I am giving you what you need—because you *are* a wicked girl."

Dmitri was *making* me into one. Suddenly, *I* was arching my back. "Yes, yes . . ."

He peeled the dress wide, uncovering my tits.

The others' reactions—hooded lids and parted lips—made my nipples even harder. Dmitri himself was virtually a stranger to me, and now three others were getting a show.

"Feel how wet you're getting!" he murmured, doing those heavenly/sinful things with his fingers. "You crave their eyes on you."

I did! This primal need to be controlled by him—and watched by others—pulsed through me.

Sensing my surrender, he nuzzled my ear. "Doesn't it feel good when you do as I say?"

My moans grew constant. I was going to dissolve in front of these strangers. I shook so hard my breasts quivered for my audience.

Dmitri pulled my head back to his chest with a decisive tug on my hair, which made me—and Red—cry out. "You want them to know how wet you are, don't you?" He delved those two fingers deep inside me as his thumb worked my clit.

"Ahhh!" So close, so close . . . Oh, dear God, four people were going to watch me come.

"Shall I show them my fingers glistening from your pussy?"

"No, *nooo.*" My face heated just to think of it. Showing my tits was one thing—I'd been known to flash them myself—but not something so intimate!

Yet Dmitri brought his soaked fingers up, revealing them by the light of my neon collar. Red gave a cry at the sight and writhed. The dark-haired guy groaned, and his body jerked. The blond bit out a curse, gritting his teeth, struggling not to come.

I went wild. Couldn't catch my breath. About to lose my mind. "Gonna . . . scream. Don't let me . . . scream."

"I won't. Just take a taste. Then I'll bring you off." His other hand took over, frigging my clit as he brought his wet fingers to my mouth. With his hot breaths against my neck, he commanded, *"Suck."*

So fucking forbidden. Would I really do this in front of others? I couldn't form sentences. "How . . . you . . ." I trailed off, whispering, *"What's happening to me?"*

"Obey, Vika."

With a cry, I leaned toward his fingers. I sucked them, tasting myself. My eyes rolled back in my head, my hips grinding against his other hand.

In an agonized tone, Dmitri bit out, "They're watching you. Staring. Show them how much my wicked girl loves to come."

I mindlessly licked his fingers as he withdrew them.

He clamped that palm over my mouth. With his other hand, he shoved his fingers into me and vibrated his grip—

Edge. Over. *RELEASE.*

I exploded, screaming against his palm as my body spasmed. His mouth was at my ear, his voice ramping up the strength of this already blinding orgasm. He told me how beautiful I was. How he'd never forget this sight or the feel of me unraveling in his arms.

He told me I was perfect.

Floating. Bliss. This *man*.

In time, I came down from the strongest climax I'd ever had. That I'd ever *dreamed* of having.

He uncovered my mouth. Still murmuring praises, he lovingly petted me until I had to move his other hand away.

All I could hear was our breaths. I buried my face against his neck and inhaled his scent. I licked his skin as gratitude and affection bloomed inside me.

The music of the club grew louder and louder.

The club.

Reality returned. I'd orgasmed that violently. Here. In front of strangers.

I gathered the courage to raise my face. Red was out of breath, her breasts heaving. She'd collapsed against the brown-haired guy, and he had his head tilted back. The blond was gasping, had obviously just come.

They'd all gotten off while watching me.

Mortification overwhelmed me. I couldn't face them.

And Dmitri? I turned to him. His pupils were blown, his jaw clenched. He looked crazed to come. Our interlude *wasn't even over.*

I guessed he planned to fuck me right on the table. The thought made me whimper with need—and that alarmed the hell out of me. He could have done anything to my body just now.

Anything.

Even though I'd trusted him to protect me, had asked him to. *Another man betraying me.*

I hadn't wanted *him* to betray me.

I yanked on the zipper of my dress, putting it back to rights as best as I could. "Let go of me." *Escape.*

"Vika?" He sounded baffled.

I struggled against his hold. Between gritted teeth, I said, "Let. Go."

He finally released me, and I scrambled up.

"What's wrong?" He adjusted his stiff cock with a wince.

"You were supposed to look out for me. Not talk me into putting on a show for strangers!" Unable to meet the others' eyes, I rushed from the room.

Dmitri was right behind me. "Just wait, Vika!"

"Leave me alone!" I zigzagged through the crowd to get to our table. Karin and Benji peered up at the huge Russian behind me.

"I'm going home!" I told them. I grabbed my purse and headed toward the exit.

Before I could hail a cab, Dmitri caught up with me outside and snared my wrist. "Come back to the hotel with me!" His expression said he was about to lose it. That lifeline look now scared me. "We will talk—"

"I trusted you, and you took advantage of me! I don't ever want to see you again!"

"You do not mean that." His eyes darted, as if he had no idea how to handle this rapidly deteriorating situation.

Pete, Benji, and Karin rushed out of the club, gazes bouncing from me to Dmitri.

In a low tone, he said, "Come with me, Victoria. Now."

I yanked my arm from his grip. "Just leave me alone!"

My family would ask questions later. For now, they were in protective mode, flanking me.

Pete stepped in front of me. "Mr. Sevastyan, this would be a good time for you to go."

His eyes locked on Pete, and his face turned deadly, as if he was about to tear out my cousin's throat with his teeth. "Do not ever get between me and her." His fists clenched and unclenched. "You do not want to do that, Peter."

Anyone would've been terrified, but Pete didn't back down. "We can all pick this up tomorrow when tempers cool, huh?"

Dmitri turned to me, losing his murderous look. His brows drew together, but I shook my head. "I told you—I never want to see you again."

His eyes dimmed, and that wrecked me. Even though I hated him at this moment.

"As you wish." He turned and left.

I watched his towering form striding away, scarcely noticing when tears began to fall.

CHAPTER 12

*P*ausing at the door to my parents' modest ranch house, I adjusted the basket of dirty laundry on my hip and listened.

Pete said, "You'd have to see the way Sevastyan looks at her."

"He looked that way *before* she told him to piss off forever," Benji pointed out. "Sevastyan did something in the back of the club that she was not down with, and he got the message loud and clear."

I'd refused to tell them what had happened. This morning, as the events from the night flooded into my hungover consciousness, I'd thrown an arm over my face. I'd gotten sexually Svengali-ed by Dmitri.

I was in Benji's camp. I didn't think the Russian would call. I replayed the light dimming in his eyes and felt a pang. How could I have become so attached to the man in two nights? Especially after what he'd done to me?

I'd cried over that asshole. I hadn't cried even when I'd ended things with Brett!

"I'll lay ten large he calls," Pete said.

Benji answered, "I'll take that action."

I yanked open the door, striding into the living room to glare at everyone.

Pete sat in a careworn recliner, practicing cards on a TV tray. Benji was on the lumpy family-size couch with camera parts spread over the coffee table. Mom and Dad sat next to each other on their love seat. She sewed a dress; he worked on his laptop.

Karin had just deposited Cash into his playpen by the couch; he gurgled in welcome. Gram and Russian Al sat at a fold-up bridge table, drinking sherry out of little crystal glasses and playing chess.

Through the sliding glass door, I could see my aunts and uncles out by the pool with all their kids. Though my younger cousins were mini grifters who already cheated at Marco Polo, I would still dominate the water.

After laundry. I cocked the basket higher on my hip. "You guys are betting on me? Like I'm a doped horse?"

Mom set aside her sewing to give me a hug. "Technically, the boys are betting on Dmitri. He's the doped horse in this scenario." She'd covered the circles under her stunning chocolate-brown eyes with an expert application of makeup, but I recognized the scent of the brand. Of course she wasn't sleeping, was too worried about Dad.

"Let's don't say Dmitri's name again, okay?" I muttered, my head hurting me worse than a busted flush.

Benji snorted. "You want us *not* to talk about the elephant in the room?"

Al piped up. "Very beeg elephant." He stroked his long gray beard. Maybe he grew it so long to make up for his bald head.

"Victoria, dear," my grandmother said, "why don't you explain to us exactly what happened in the club with your rich Russian gentleman?"

Squick. "Uh, another time, Gram."

Her dark eyes were merry. Sherry always made her merry, and Al was quick on the refills.

After Al's wife had passed away, my parents had worried he might be lonely, so they'd invited him over for Sunday dinner. Twenty years ago. He'd kept showing up every single Sunday, so eventually we'd adopted him too.

The evidence that Gram and Al were friends with benefits was getting more difficult to ignore.

Mom put her hand on my shoulder and took a deep breath. "Honey, did you truly tell an infatuated billionaire you never wanted to see him again?" She asked this the same way another mother might ask, *Honey, do you do* the drugs?

"I . . . did." What was it about him that made me behave so unexpectedly? "But I'm going to rope a Canadian whale tonight. I'm turning this all around."

Dad closed his laptop, about to weigh in. He would never get mad at me, but I hated disappointing him. Mom rejoined him on the love seat. They were always tied at the hip, best friends as well as partners. Their fake art canvases leaned against every available wall. "Did Sevastyan hurt you, sweet pea?" He narrowed his fierce blue gaze. "I'll kill him if he so much as—"

"No! He didn't. He's not the type."

"I'll back her on that," Pete said. "He might've been about to wipe the street with my face, but that guy would never hurt a woman."

Our two opinions appeased Dad on the matter.

Karin tilted her head at me. "It seemed like Sevastyan scared you."

Yes! "A little. But it wasn't him." I frowned. "It was kind of him." They were still waiting for an explanation, so I said, "I just don't like who I am when I'm around him, okay?"

"He'll call," Karin said. "Trust me."

Trust me? Everyone had to chuckle.

With a contemplative expression, Al said, "So now ve vait for call to come."

"Don't hold your breath, folks, or you'll suffocate." I tossed my messenger bag on the couch, then hauled my basket to the laundry room. Every Sunday I washed clothes here. Every Sunday Mom made sure to leave the washer and dryer stuffed full for me to process.

Once I'd finally gotten *my* clothes going, I rejoined the group. I leaned over the playpen to give my little guy a *mwah!* kiss on his head. Cash blinked his big leaf-green eyes and reached for me with chubby hands, which meant I was putty. I lifted him into my arms, then sank onto my favorite spot on the couch.

The love I had in my heart for this little human staggered me. "You're getting huge! Just between us, you might wanna lay off the beer and hot wings, kiddo."

Blink, blink, gurgle.

As much as I adored this kid, you'd think I'd want some of my own. I'd been prepared to spawn for Brett, but I hadn't looked forward to the prospect.

Cash gurgled again, showing off his first tooth. With those eyes and his dark-brown hair, he would grow up to look just like his father.

Fifteen months ago, Karin had accidentally gotten pregnant

by a mega-rich CEO. When she'd broken the news, he'd accused her of a paternity play, and walked away. The catch: she'd truly loved him. The one time she hadn't been conning.

The guy's last name was Walker.

Fitting.

After her baby was born, Walker had started sending monthly checks without a word. So she'd named the guy's son Cash. We all thought that was hilarious.

And if a gal couldn't make a joke when she'd been knocked up and deserted, when could she?

We'd considered sending Walker monthly checks for the sperm. Once we settled the debt and got back on our feet. Speaking of which . . .

I asked Benji, "Is the congressman's package away?"

"Yep. Right now he's watching a surprisingly well-shot video and shitting himself." *You have to play to pay.*

In our blackmail packages, we demanded total compliance or else we would send the evidence to every major paper in the country (truth). We also warned that if we got any pushback from the blackmailee, Anonymous would add them to their list of high-profile dirt bags to financially destroy (lie).

Though Benji excelled at his job, his artistic talent was wasted on badgers. As a teen he'd wanted to be a wildlife photographer, had continued exploring it in his free time. Before we ran out of free time—

A message chime sounded from my bag; everyone grew quiet. Benji leaned over and took Cash from me. "Check your messages, Vice."

As I dug my phone out, I grew jittery, didn't know what I was hoping for. I glanced at the screen. "It's an e-mail from Brett."

Groans sounded. "Steady Brettie," Pete muttered.

Benji added, "By-the-Book Brett."

I rolled my eyes. "You guys don't even get how ironic it is to call Brett steady and by-the-book. He really wasn't either, was he?" They'd disliked him because he was a law-abiding Muggle who would never understand our secret way of life. The few occasions I'd brought him to family gatherings, they'd been paranoid and miserable with the gull around.

For the longest time, I'd suspected them of running a badger game on Brett to get rid of him.

The woman I'd caught him with had been off-the-charts hot, a legit showgirl. Brett hadn't even known her last name. So what had she been doing at the party we'd thrown?

My grift sense had screamed something was off about the entire situation.

None of my scoundrels had copped to it, so I'd let it go. Maybe my ego had been trying to protect itself by drumming up a conspiracy theory.

"You have to give the guy credit," Dad said. "It's been a year, and he's still not giving up."

"I never understood that relationship." Mom fished for something out of her sewing basket. "I will say this till I'm blue in the face: We're a breed apart. Which means the only mate for a grifter—"

"Is another grifter," I finished for her. Mom and Dad were the perfect example. He'd been the married mark in one of Diamond Jill's temptation scenarios, but he'd been wed in name only—for a scam of his own.

A grifter for a grifter.

I used to balk at Mom's wisdom; now I accepted how right she was. Always watching what I said and did around Brett had gotten exhausting. "If I had a dollar for every time you've told us that, we wouldn't be in so much freaking trouble."

"Hear! Hear!" Gram took another swig of sherry. "But I disagree with the grifter mate theory. You just have to find a fellow who loves you more than life. For a man like that, anyone who thinks to ruin his relationship—such as another woman—might as well be trying to murder him."

Dad grinned at me. "Plus, in my case, I'd have to assume your mother hired a honey trap. She already trapped me once that way."

Mom play-slapped his stomach.

Sooner or later, I'd be forced to check my mailbox, might as well do it now. I opened Brett's weekly message and read:

Tailgate, Fourth of July. You got a lightning bug to land on your palm, and it reflected in your eyes as you laughed. I'd never wanted a kiss more.

I'll always love you, B

I recalled that night. He had kissed me, his earnest hazel eyes glinting as he'd told me how much he loved me. . . .

Then I frowned. Was this ache in my chest even for Brett?

Oh, shit. I was feeling emptiness—because of Dmitri.

"Speaking of gulls who are interested in Vice . . ." Pete turned to me. "How about you text Sevastyan?"

"That'd be an unconventional play," Benji said, his voice lowered because Cash had conked out against his chest. "But then, he's an unconventional mark. Dude owns two of the top fifty highest-grossing tech patents."

Gram sighed. "I don't know what that means, but it sounds just divine. What could he have done in a club that was so bad?" She was still angling to find out.

"I wasn't thinking clearly last night. I was hammered."

"Victoria Valentine!" Gram tsked. "Never drink on a con!"

"Not fair. It was my night off." I set my phone aside and pulled my deck out of my bag.

"When Karin goes to the casino tonight, I think she should scout things out with Sevastyan," Mom said. "If he's attracted to Vice, he'll be attracted to a woman who looks so similar to her."

Marcia! I cut cards and shuffled. I wasn't going to point out that Karin had already had her shot.

Dad said, "Your mom's right, sweet pea. We should switch primaries—just this once—since you're still getting into the swing of these new cons and he's a unique target."

Mom was more direct. "You tossed away the biggest mark this family has ever had a line on."

Al made a move on the chessboard. "Only in America, with the catching and releasing."

Karin sank onto the couch beside me. "I struck out with Sevastyan, but if you help me find an in, maybe I'd have better luck. Since you're not interested in this guy, you shouldn't mind, right?"

The idea of Dmitri touching my sister . . . his deep voice rumbling in her ear . . .

Bile rose in my throat. Jealousy clawed at me.

"No go," Pete said, saving me from having to answer. "This guy wants Vice. Only her. *Trust* me." Again a round of laughs. "He seems obsessed. When I stepped between him and Vice, for a second, I thought he was going to kill me."

Recalling his sinister stare gave me chills. "Yeah, something's way off with him. He's pinging my radar left and right." Because he was crazy! Admittedly! He talked to himself and handled confusion "badly." His likes included spanking strange women and humiliating them in nightclubs.

"Has he lied to you?" Dad asked.

"Not a single time. Still, something is wrong with him." I was about to add, "Trust me," but stopped myself.

"We're not asking you to marry him," Mom said. "We simply need you to fleece him for as much as humanly possible in the next couple of weeks."

Al said, "Type on phone to man. Tell heem you had change of heart."

Dad cast me an encouraging smile. "We wouldn't ask this of you if the alternative wasn't so daunting."

"Daunting?" Pete crossed his arms over his chest. "Is that what we're calling murder?" He faced me. "'Cause that's what Uncle Joe is looking at if we miss the payoff."

Frustration welled. "Then we need to run!"

Cash woke in Benji's arms and yawned, taking in the scene.

"This is our home." Dad's tone was firm. "These are our people. That's our absolute last play."

I shuffled. "Even if I reestablish contact with Dmitri, how do we monetize it? And every second I waste with him, I could be targeting another guy. Pete's got those whales coming in—"

Another chime sounded. Again everyone tensed. Holding my breath, I put down my cards and checked my phone. "It's him."

Gram exclaimed, "Oh, thank Lady Luck!"

"What did he write?" Karin scooched closer to me.

"'I will pick you up for dinner at seven.'" Excitement surged inside me, and I feared our desperate situation was only partly to blame.

Pete said, "I like it. Direct. No explanation. No rehashing."

"What do we write back?" Mom rose, beginning to pace.

"We need more engagement. Lots of question marks, Vice. Flirty, but not *too* flirty."

If I was going back in on this con, I'd do it my way. I typed two letters.

Karin said, "What the hell?"

"What did she do?" Mom cried. "What did she *do*???"

"Vice told him . . . no."

I glanced up, shrinking from their horrified expressions. "I'm playing a hunch."

Dad said, "Ballsy, sweet pea. Let's hope he likes the chase."

Al took one of Gram's rooks. "Vee Russian men do like chase."

Another chime. **DSevastyan: Other plans?**

Mom clasped her hands. "Please, just be . . . nice."

Again, I was typing.

Karin translated for everyone: "She wrote that she and her friends might go clubbing. She punctuated her text with emoticons of a martini glass, a prescription pill, and a dripping syringe."

Al glowered. "Vee raised you better than thees."

Mom looked like she was about to faint, so I said, "Elusiveness. If I'm going to milk-cow him, I should be elusive, right?"

Gram said, "Elusive, yes. Impulsive, no. Long cons are long because we spend time *plotting*, my dear."

I caught my parents sharing a glance. They were . . . scared. As if I'd just taken a dive and shanked our game-winning shot.

Come on, Sevastyan, please text back.

No one spoke. Gram's sherry bottle clinked against her little glass as Al refilled her.

Please, Dmitri, please, please, please.

Another chime. Relief made me sag.

DSevastyan: Are you busy now?

Karin read the text aloud while I answered. Vice: Not really.

I jumped when my phone rang a second later. "It's him."

Karin snapped her fingers. "Paper! Pen!"

Mom scrambled past canvases and sewing materials to toss Karin a notepad and pen. "Put it on speakerphone, Vice."

What if he mentioned what we'd done? But he was a mark, and we worked these cons by committee. As Mom always said, "It takes a village to play a mark."

Karin said, "Sound like you're smiling when you pick up."

I scowled at her, was scowling as I pushed the speaker button and answered, "Yo." All around me, my family went mum, not a peep to give them away. Even Cash seemed to be holding his breath.

"What did you think of the gift I sent you?" Dmitri asked.

The sound of his deep, rich voice filled the room, sending an unwelcome thrill through me. "I'm not at home." I made my tone bored as I said, "What'd you get me?"

"A car. The deliveryman took a picture of it. Would you like to see?"

A freaking car?? I sighed, "I s'pose."

A photo popped up in my text-message queue—a cherry-red Porsche convertible parked in front of my dusty apartment building, standing out like a diamond in coal.

I texted the pic to the conference line Benji had set up for our consultations and confabs.

Phones all around vibrated. Silent checking of screens; soaring eyebrows. Karin wrote a dollar sign with a question mark and flashed her note to Al. He held up five fingers.

The car was worth five hundred thousand dollars? Then my

face fell. "Dmitri, what made you decide to *lease* a car for me?"

"No lease. The title is in the glove compartment. It is yours regardless of whether you ever see me again."

I mouthed, *Holy shit!*

"Though I do hope you will have dinner with me."

"I don't think that's a good idea. I'm not looking for an affair. And you obviously are."

Another bout of silence from his end of the line, which anyone on earth would be tempted to fill with babble. I used the move often. I patiently cut and flipped cards. *I can sit here all day, Russki.*

He finally asked, "Am I, then?"

"I'm not having sex with anyone outside of a committed relationship."

Karin scribbled: *Too soon!*

"Understood. I still want to see you."

"I'll have to check my plans. And I might be called in to work."

"Then I will tell Peter not to call you in."

Sevastyan was assisting in his own grift! "If not an affair, what do you want from me?"

"More, Vika. I will always want more from you."

Jaws dropped. Gram fanned herself. I saw Mom squeeze Dad's hand, as if she was too scared to hope.

Dmitri was either the best player we'd ever heard or he was really, actually taken with me.

"Okay. Pick me up at seven."

"Where would you like to go?"

The prospect of free food awakened any grifter's appetite. "I like Italian."

"Then we should go to Italy."

Mom and Karin shared an *awww* look, until I said, "I want to stay local—in case I need to bail."

At that, Gram swayed like she might fall off her chair. Mom glanced heavenward.

"Then I will be on my best behavior, *moy ángel.* Until then. . . ." He ended the call.

I exhaled a long breath.

Pete ran his hand over his face. "So that just happened." Then he turned to Benji. "You owe me ten large, partner."

Al leaned back in his chair, his hands over his belly. "Russian man ees smeeten to our girl. Called you *my angel.*"

Reminded of something else Dmitri had said, I asked, "What does *prosto rai* mean?" He'd repeatedly rasped that when we'd gotten off together.

Al chuckled. "*Prosto rai* means . . . *sheer heaven.*"

CHAPTER 13

"*Should I stay or should I go now?!*" Karin and I belted out the song along with the stereo. Top down in our new convertible. The Clash playing. Hair blowing. Sun shining. Singing at the top of our lungs.

"*So you gotta let me know . . . SHOULD I COOL IT OR SHOULD I BLOW?!*"

I was happy, truly happy, for the first time in forever. We'd just cruised the Red Rock Canyon loop, the Porsche dazzling against the sandstone and red washes.

When Karin and I had driven it by the folks', everyone had looked at me with new respect. The car wasn't a seven-figure score, but I had another date with a billionaire, another iron in the fire.

When the song wound down, Karin turned off the stereo. "Now that we're alone, you want to tell me what he did in the club? Must've been pretty bad for him to send you this ride as an olive branch."

I'd known this question was coming. "It's one for the sister vault, okay? He . . . he got me off. In front of other people."

She blinked at me. "And then?"

"And then? That's not enough? I wasn't prepared for it!"

Karin looked confused. "Was it good with him?"

"That was part of what freaked me out so bad. I got off harder than I ever have. Harder than I knew was possible." So help me, if a crazy Russian was my key . . .

Karin waved that away. "So you have a fetish. It's perfectly normal."

I did a double take. "I don't have a fetish. Are you high?"

"You're an exhibitionist. You always have been, you know."

"What are you talking about?"

"When you were little, I'd dress you up really cute to use as my shill, and the second I turned around, you'd be stripping. I was lucky if I could keep you in a diaper." She chuckled. "You've never noticed all of your baby pics are of you running around parties naked?"

"Yeah, but by all accounts I was a hard-partying, rule-breaking kid. And what does that have to do with me as an adult?"

"Not the same thing, of course, but you've always been a little nudie."

"This isn't funny."

"Vice, for God's sake, I do badger games. Talk about exhibitionism. Benji watches me do stripteases and dance around in lingerie. I'd be lying if I said it didn't get us worked up."

"So you know about his crush?"

She nodded. "He thinks it'll be weird."

"Weirder than a congressman acting like his wife died in a fiery car crash so he can get a piece of ass?" When I downshifted for a stop sign, the engine purred. Giving up this car would've been impossible for anything or anyone outside of my pack.

"Benji also thinks I'm still in love with you-know-who."

"Are you?" I asked, though I knew the answer. Karin was lost for Walker.

She gazed away. "That would be idiotic, wouldn't it? He made his feelings clear."

The man had a ready-made family but was too stupid to see it. And if Karin and Benji ever did get together, it'd be too late for the asshole. "Are you holding back with Benji because of his history?"

He'd been sexually abused out on the streets. When I was young and didn't know better, I had asked him distressing questions like, "Why are you scared to go outside at night?" and "Why do you cry when it's bath time?" I often wished I could go back and spare him that extra pain.

"He's worked through a lot of it," Karin said. "But, yeah, getting with his adoptive sister might spin some things off axis."

He'd always called me sis, but never Karin. I don't think he'd ever bonded with her that way.

She frowned at me. "Enough about that. There's more you're not telling me."

I could never fool her. "Say I do have a . . . fetish." Which I would be looking up online as soon as I was by myself. "It was Dmitri who got me so worked up. Maybe having other peoples' eyes on me was the seasoning, but the main course was all him. He's really dominant. I did those things because *he told me to.*"

"He sounds like a thrall."

I slapped the gear shift. "Bingo. Everything about him—his voice, face, body, scent, intensity—makes me lose my ever-loving mind. In the same situation with another guy, I wouldn't have reacted as I did. I felt completely out of control."

"I understand why that would be so scary. Especially for your first time."

I exhaled. "I trusted him to take care of me when I was drunk, and instead he pushed me to do things I wouldn't ordinarily do."

"Maybe he sensed your fetish. What if he was trying to please you?"

He'd told me, *I need to give you pleasure so much I ache.* I cleared my throat. "Then I would say I might have possibly overreacted and blamed him unfairly." The look in his eyes . . . I'd hurt him. That damn sense of protectiveness rose up yet again.

"What if you ended up with him outside of a con?"

Of all the women he could have, Sevastyan was pursuing *me.* At least for now. "He lives on a different continent. And we have nothing in common." I refused to believe I could fall for Sevastyan, with his sinful voice and talented fingers. With his lifeline glances, the ones that both lured me closer and scared the hell out of me. "Plus, I could never trust him. I don't think another man will ever convince me I'd be enough for him. It's like in the movies, when the lead guy makes a grand gesture, sacrificing everything to prove his love. Stupid, huh?"

"Not stupid at all," Karin said.

"Catching Brett made me doubt myself in a way I never did before." Wasn't I desirable enough for him? Wasn't I enough woman? "Besides, if I were ever going to settle down, it'd be with another grifter. Which means a tech billionaire is out of the running."

"You must've considered a Peggy Sue by this point." A wedding con. "I'm sure we all did after that call."

The thought had tickled at the back of my mind, but I'd mentally scratched it away. "Dmitri's way too clever. He'd lawyer up with a prenup so ironclad it'd clang when it hit a desk. Plus he's got those two bodyguards."

"*Hate* bodyguards. Still, it's Vegas, baby. Make him crazy for an hour, and you could seal the deal."

"Crazy, huh?" *He's got that covered all on his own.*

"I could run a badger on him." That multi-purpose con could be used for more than just blackmail. "I'd mick him, and you'd find us 'together.' You'd scream and cry, telling him there's only one way you could ever trust him again: the bonds of holy matrimony. Give him the ultimatum, and he'd be toast."

I could cry on cue, but the idea of Karin even "fake" getting together with him made my fingers clench the steering wheel. "I'll stick with the milk-cow."

"Then wear the man-eater."

I'd cut that sleeveless gown from scarlet body-hugging silk. The overall look was simple yet sultry. Illusion straps and a plunging neckline bared plenty of skin in the front, while the back cutout dipped almost to my ass. The hourglass silhouette gave way to a thigh-high slit.

When a woman wore a dress like that, it told men: *I'm getting laid tonight. And when I do, some lucky bastard's balls will scream for mercy.* "You don't think it's too soon?"

"No, but he's going to be all over you."

At the idea, my body purred like the Porsche's engine.

Whatever she saw in my expression made her lips thin. "You cannot sleep with him, Vice."

"Listen to me." I met her gaze as we made the Strip. "There's no way in hell I'm going to sleep with the Russian."

CHAPTER 14

Okay, I might *sleep with the Russian.*

When I opened the door for him, lyrics from the incomparable Madonna sprang into my thoughts:

I'm in trouble deep.

He was just so . . . so unimaginably beautiful. His tailored dark gray suit emphasized his height, the wide set of his shoulders, the narrowness of his hips. His understated tie had a thread of amber through it, highlighting his eyes. My fingers itched to touch his clean-shaven jaw and chin.

He stared at me as if he'd forgotten how to blink. I guessed he liked the man-eater.

Pete had already called to tell me when Dmitri left the casino and what my date was wearing (my cuz had warned me Dmitri looked "excruciatingly hot"). Thanks to intel from Giovanni, the concierge, I also knew our destination: Murano's, a romantic—and extravagant—Italian restaurant.

"Am I dressed appropriately?" I asked as I turned in a circle. "You didn't say where you were taking me."

Dmitri's gaze drifted down, then slowly ascended, as if he

were committing every inch of me to memory. His answer was a curt nod.

Not a word about my appearance? I'd painstakingly braided my hair into three plaits, then pinned them into a crown atop my head. My makeup was expertly applied—kohled eyes, curled lashes, glossy lips, vamp nails. My only jewelry was a pair of onyx earrings. I carried a matching clutch for my keys, phone, and gloss.

When I'd donned the man-eater and the clinging material had glided over me, my nipples had stiffened; the dress had done nothing to disguise them. Now his inspection was making them peak again. By the time his gaze reached my face, my cheeks were on fire. I waved in his direction. "Uh, you look great."

Another nod.

Wow, cocky much?

"Come." He placed his big palm on the bared small of my back. His nostrils flared and his fingertips dug in a little as he led me toward his limo.

I got a hit of Dmitri's aftershave and caught my customary buzz, my lids growing heavy.

When we passed my new car, I said, "Thank you for the gift." Al already had a buyer interested.

Dmitri scarcely acknowledged it. "I have another one for you."

Oh, do you?

One of his bodyguards, the brown-haired one, opened the door for us. A blond was behind the wheel. I dubbed them Starsky and Hutch (not quite eighties, but close enough). Starsky shut the door behind us and got in with Hutch up front. With a low hum, the privacy divider closed.

Dmitri didn't sit close to me. Weird. As we started off, he didn't reach for me and drag me into his lap.

I'd thought my bared thigh would merit a glance, but he seemed determined not to look down. Puzzled, I fidgeted with my clutch and stared out the window. . . .

I frowned when we passed a white Yukon like the one Brett drove. I only got a glimpse of the driver but suspected it was my ex. No matter how many times I'd told him our relationship was over, he continued to cruise my neighborhood. How could I get him to stop with the e-mails and drive-bys and move on?

I didn't need to be thinking about Brett; I needed to be working. I sank back in the seat, watching Sevastyan out of the corner of my eye.

His shoulders were rigid. When he subtly blew out a breath, as if trying to get a handle on himself, I relaxed a fraction. Had I thrown him for a loop?

With more confidence, I asked, "So what do your bodyguards do when you're on dates?"

"Dates? I have no idea what they do when I'm not around."

"Any particular reason you travel with a pair of them?"

He shrugged. "They buffer me from irritations."

"With their holstered weapons?" I'd spied a flash of one.

No denial. "Better safe than sorry."

"An enigmatic answer from an enigmatic guy." I turned to face him more fully. "Before we get to the restaurant, I want to talk about last night. I had a chat with my sister, and it helped me realize some things."

"Like what?"

Two tears in a bucket . . . "Apparently, I have a . . . fetish. This is going to be hard to believe, but I didn't know I'm not, um, vanilla. I got spooked by the intensity and the situation, and I overreacted, blaming everything on you."

"I do believe you. You were shocked afterward. I should have taken things more slowly." He rubbed his palm along his pant leg. "I am learning my way. With you. I see now I should not have pushed when you'd been drinking."

"Well, yeah, maybe. I wasn't just shocked, I was also nervous. A woman could get hurt doing things like that."

He tensed even more. "I would *never* let anyone hurt you. You think I couldn't have defended you against a mere two men?"

"How do I know that, Dmitri? I don't even know you. This is our first real date."

He exhaled. "Point taken. Thank you for explaining these things to me. Please continue to do so in the future."

"I feel better with that off my chest."

"After speaking to your sister, did you investigate your newfound fetish?"

"I did a little digging online." I'd discovered a porn subgenre called CMNF—clothed male, nude female—and watched a video of a naked girl on her knees sucking off a fully dressed guy.

My greedy gaze roamed over Dmitri's impeccable suit. "It was . . . enlightening."

Two nights ago, Dmitri had stripped me while remaining dressed, had even remarked I might like that. Already sensing my leanings?

Thinking of that first night reminded me—had he really jerked off on this very seat?

I would run a con just to see that.

"I suggest we establish a safe word," Dmitri said.

"Isn't that for whips and chains?" Though I might like to recreate what I'd watched today, I wasn't down with bondage.

"If we'd had a safe word, you could have alerted me I was pushing you too far."

Would I have forfeited that explosive orgasm at the time? For now, I'd humor him. Searching for a word, I scanned the luxe limo interior. My attention settled on the fancy bar. "I'll say cognac."

"Very good. I will stop immediately."

I was accustomed to code words. *Blue skies* for cops. As in, "Nothing but blue skies around here." *Juke* for change location. *Cougar* for currently on a grift. *Rep* for lookout.

Teotwawki—the end of the world as we know it—was my family's code for an emergency meeting. Three months ago, my dad had texted that to our group line. Karin, Benji, and I had been at a photography exhibit, our phones chiming all at once. Without a word, Benji had sprinted ahead to get the car as Karin and I ditched our heels to run. We'd hauled ass to Mom and Dad's.

The cartel had just lowered the boom on us.

"What are you thinking about?" Dmitri asked.

What I am. What's at stake. I met his gaze. Time to flirt. "Last night. I haven't been able to think of much else."

"Nor I."

"Those things you did with your fingers were mind blowing. How'd you learn stuff like that?"

"Videos and books," he said. "I studied the subject of sex as if it were my field. I made it my job."

"Why?" I asked, imagining him watching porn and masturbating. Five minutes into this date and my thong was damp.

"So I could impress a woman such as yourself." His words could've been teasing, but he was serious. "And make her addicted to me."

"Consider me impressed." Understatement of the year. "When did you figure out you like to show off your dates that way?"

"You think *I* . . ." His eyes narrowed. "I do *not* like to show you off." In an accusing tone, he snapped, "I want to take you back to my room right now! I want no one else to see you like this. I both love and *hate* that dress." He didn't seem to realize he'd gripped the hem, was letting the scarlet silk flow through his fingers.

My lips curled. *Crazy man.* "Is that your way of telling me I look nice?"

"Nice?? You took my breath away. I haven't regained it yet." He muttered something in Russian, but I recognized the tone: *Fuck me.* He blinked down at his hand and released the dress. "Last night, your appearance strained the bounds of my control. But this . . ."

My breaths shallowed, my boobs rising and falling under his brows-drawn gaze.

"I told you I am a jealous man. I'd prefer no one to see you but me."

"Then why'd you show me off at the club?"

He met my eyes. "*My* fetish is making you wanton and mindless."

Then last night *had* been for me. "How did you know about my fetish before I did?"

Voice gone husky, he said, "Your reactions the first night."

I blushed to recall grinding his hand.

He clenched his fists. Recalling that as well?

I noticed jagged cuts across his right knuckles. Before I could ask what happened, he said, "All I can think about is seeing you come again, and you wear this? You must enjoy tormenting me. I asked you for mercy, but you've given me none."

"I wore the dress because I like the way it makes me feel."

He rasped, "Irresistible?"

God, this man got me hot. Maybe I liked playing with fire. "And yet . . . you're *resisting*."

He lowered his face while gazing up, his spine-tingling expression giving me goosebumps. He looked as if he was barely stopping himself from snatching me close. "You told me on the phone you didn't want to have sex with me."

But . . . but that was before *I saw you in a suit.* Inner shake. "You're right. If I do, you're going to get the wrong impression of me. I'll feel pressure, and I hate pressure." This was true.

"Then I will make you a promise right now. I vow I will never seduce you to have sex until we have both agreed to take that step."

I shook my head. "Not enough. I'll get too caught up with you, begging in the heat of the moment. When you showed up at my door tonight, my very first thought was that I wanted you to fuck me."

"Victoria . . ." His roughened voice made heat cascade through me. Seeming to steel himself, he said, "I vow I will never sleep with you until we've both agreed to take that step—agreed *outside* of a sexual situation."

"What does that mean exactly?"

"It means we will sit down and discuss taking this"—he motioned between us—"further. It means you can enjoy time with me without feeling pressure."

He'd just given me all the tools I needed to milk-cow him.

I nibbled my lip, as if I were undecided. Of course I was going to play his games. Because I was working. What *I* wanted didn't necessarily factor.

Keep telling yourself that, Vice. "Okay. We've got a deal."

"One that will likely be the death of me." With a pained groan, he adjusted his cock in his pants.

I inhaled sharply, wishing he would keep touching himself ... like he had two nights ago in this limo. I imagined him rubbing his big pierced dick, filling his palm with cum—

The limo glided to a stop in front of the restaurant.

Dmitri said, "Are you ready, *moy ángel?*"

As if waking from a spell, I nodded dumbly.

Starsky hurried around to open the door. When Dmitri helped me from the car, my nipples were straining against the thin silk.

The valet stared at my tits; the doorman stared. Each time someone noticed my swollen breasts and the lewdly jutting peaks, a forbidden thrill shivered through me.

Dmitri kept his warm hand on my lower back, his stance proprietary. I glanced up at him. His gaze was locked on me, as if he was making an effort to block out the others' attention.

He'd been telling the truth. Dmitri Sevastyan was a jealous man—who was unfortunately fascinated by his date's reaction to exhibitionism.

Later, I would let him know *he* was the one making me wet. His cock adjustment—and my brief fantasy about him—had primed me just as much as showing off my breasts.

He leaned down to murmur at my ear, "I'm going to feed your body, Vika, then later you're going to be my dessert."

A breath shuddered out of my lungs.

Trouble, Vice. Deep.

CHAPTER 15

I could get used to this.

A warm breeze blew into our cabana, flickering the table's candle. The flame reflected in Dmitri's eyes, his irises looking like backlit amber.

I dragged my gaze from his heart-stopping face to survey the picturesque scene. The outdoor seating surrounded an elegant pool, and each table had a private cabana.

I'd always wanted to eat here, but the prices were exorbitant. Murano's sourced seafood from all over Italy and flew it in daily.

When the tuxedoed waiter, a ginger-haired fortysomething, had taken our orders a few minutes ago, I'd marveled at the menu, choosing the Mediterranean blue rock lobster. Dmitri had selected Venetian crab ravioli with artichokes.

I turned back to him. "You're staring."

"You're stunning."

Each time I caught him checking me out, my cheeks heated. To relax, I'd been drinking again, sip after sip of the delectable wine he'd picked out. Plus I was nervous about his promise to make me his dessert. Did he plan to go down on me?

When he lifted his own wineglass for a sparing taste, my gaze fell on his banged-up knuckles. "What happened there?"

He put his glass back. "It's nothing."

I reached across the table, taking his hand in both of mine. When I stroked the skin beside a cut, his muscles tensed and he exhaled a long breath.

Did even an innocent touch of mine affect him so much? How . . . *heady*.

I wondered what he'd do if I blew him. Visions of taking him between my lips filled my mind. Sucking and teasing his dick. Tonguing his silver piercing as his powerful body quaked. Making him desperate to come . . . until he was helplessly fucking my mouth. . . .

"There," he suddenly said. "Your cheeks grew flushed. What were you just thinking?"

I released his hand. "This and that." My panties were going to be soaked.

"I would kill to know what you're musing about when you blush. Will you not tell me?"

"Hmm. Maybe I'll show you later."

"Tease."

Only always. I lifted my glass again. "You really don't drink a lot, huh?"

He shook his head. "I don't relish feeling out of control. Except for during sexual play with you. Then I want to keep control—right up until the time you steal it from me."

I almost fanned myself at his hungry look, a sight I'd never forget. In the candlelight, he was spellbinding.

I wasn't the only one who thought so. Two babes sashayed past our cabana—for the *third* time—audibly sighing over him.

"You get that everywhere, huh?"

"Get what?" He was oblivious.

"Attention from women." I swirled my finger around the rim of my glass. "What was your last relationship?"

"I've never had one."

I waited for that nails-over-chalkboard sensation, but he was telling the truth. "So you *are* a player."

"No. I am not."

"You can't have it both ways." I could do the math. If he took a new lover anytime he wanted sex, the notches on his belt would start adding up.

"What was *your* last relationship?" he asked.

I let him get away with not answering me. "About a year ago, I broke up with a guy I'd been with for nearly two years. We were engaged." Brett had been so normal, his life an open book. Back then, I'd equated normal and open with honest. "The wedding was weeks away." I'd just gotten a passport for our honeymoon to the Caribbean, and I'd been finishing up a wedding gown that had given me fits for months. Creating it had felt like drudgery, which should've been a clue.

"He allowed you to break up with him?"

Allowed? "What should he have done?"

Dmitri held my gaze. "If I'd been him, I would have fought for you."

His words sent a tingle through me. "Who said Brett hasn't been doing just that?" Each Sunday, I pictured him struggling to come up with another e-mail, to tap into my memories of better times and reach some part of me not hardened by his infidelity.

"Yet you haven't taken him back."

I raised my chin. "He cheated on me."

"I am very sorry, Vika," he said in a sincere tone. "That must have been painful."

"It was." I'd considered my wedding gown so tainted with bad luck I'd scissored it to shreds instead of selling it. "You know, everyone had bet against us, but I was determined." Being with Brett had made me ask questions I'd never asked before.

What if I didn't have to grift? What if I gave people my real name—all the time? What if I made clothes for a living? "I really thought we had a shot."

"Are you tempted to return to him?"

Life had been pretty good. I'd moved in with him, and he'd paid for my car. I'd limited my grift work, and enrolled in fashion design classes. He'd cooked, and I'd cleaned. We'd lived modestly.

Yes, hiding my cons had been stressful, but nothing like I struggled with now. Even if my family settled our debt, I was still getting evicted and driving an unreliable truck. Of course, now I owned a Porsche. But not for long. God, this was all so confusing. I absently murmured, "I don't know."

A muscle in Sevastyan's jaw pulsed. "And this is why you're so cautious."

Partly. "Let's not talk about him anymore."

After a hesitation, he said, "Agreed. Tell me more about you."

"Where should I begin?" I'd been intimate with Dmitri—twice—yet we knew so little about each other.

"What makes Victoria Valentine tick?" A wayward breeze tousled his black hair.

Right now golden-eyed Russians make my pulse race. "Compared to the women you usually meet, I'm sure I live a boring life."

He didn't address that. "Where did you go to school?"

"I was homeschooled. My parents wanted me to go into the family business. They could teach me better than anyone."

"Tell me about your family."

"My folks are still mad for each other after thirty years of marriage. My big sister, Karin, is my best friend. My brother is my hero. I have an extended family I love. In their own way, they're all overprotective of me. But I think . . ." I trailed off.

"You think what?"

They underestimate me. "Nothing. What about your family? You said Maksim basically raised you." Some of Maksim's charm must've rubbed off on his little brother. Maybe that was why I detected such a mix of polish and uncertainty in Dmitri.

"My mother died when I was five, my father when I was seven."

"I'm sorry." I was about to ask him how, but his changeable expression gave me pause. Instead of sadness, I perceived . . . anger.

Dmitri's busted knuckles whitened on his glass. Then he inhaled, as if for calm.

I grasped for a change of subject. "You seem to get along really well with Lucía."

"Yes. I like her very much." He frowned, then said, "At first, I didn't. I didn't like the *idea* of her. I didn't like how my brother was acting. I was not shy in letting him know." His tone implied an understatement.

"What do you mean?"

"He was a sworn bachelor who saw only escorts. His longest 'relationship' was an hour. Then I heard rumors he was obsessed with one woman—after a single date—and living with her after their second. For him to veer so drastically from all the years before, I wondered if he was having some kind of early midlife crisis."

"What changed your mind?"

"It's not a pretty story."

I waved him on. "Please."

"A man targeted her for her money, learning everything about her, then courting her." Oh. Shit. He sounded like a con artist, maybe a serial groom. But a true grifter would never target a good person.

Aren't I right now? No sins, still in?

Dmitri continued, "He tricked her into marrying him, planning to murder her once she'd signed over everything."

"My God." *Not* a con artist. He was a killer who'd stolen some of our methods to do evil. Step nine in the progression of the long con was not *murder your mark.* "The man sounds like a psychopath."

"He was. She ran from him for years, but he found her and stabbed her in the chest before my brother could reach her."

My eyes went wide. I couldn't imagine anyone taking a knife to the lovely girl I'd laughed with. "Then what happened?"

"The man pulled a gun on Maksim, had a bead on his head, but my brother charged him anyway." Dmitri couldn't sound prouder. "Maksim would have died if Lucía hadn't found the strength to hit that fuck's arm at the last second. Maksim took a bullet in the shoulder."

"I had no idea."

He shrugged. "It's not something we lead with."

I put my elbow on the table and rested my chin on my hand. "Your brother charged a loaded gun for her?"

"*Da.*" Now Dmitri couldn't *look* prouder. "He was ready to give his life for her. How could I deny what that meant?"

So Maksim *was* part of the three percent. Had his younger brother been cut from the same cloth? "What about Aleks? You're not as close to him?"

"Before one year ago, I did not speak to him." The mended fence. Yet another of Dmitri's changes that had taken place around that time. "I had not even been in the same room with him in decades, not since we were young."

"Why?" I couldn't imagine being estranged like that from a loved one. Sure, my family could frustrate me, but they would lay down their lives for me in a heartbeat. Just as I'd do for any of them.

"He was not there for me when I very badly needed him to be." Dmitri gazed away, the wheels of his complicated mind turning.

Oh, yes, this man had been hurt. And he'd longed for his oldest brother to have helped him in some way. Dmitri's history was a puzzle, but I could be patient, easing information from him here and there.

Yet then I frowned. I only had eighteen days with him, at best. Surely, he'd be called back to Russia soon. "I'm sorry, Dmitri. But you've since worked things out with Aleks, right?"

"Yes, we've reconciled," he said, his thoughts still clearly mired in the past.

I wanted to jolt him back to the present. With me. "Hey, big guy, did you have a near-death experience about a year ago?"

His gaze snapped to my face. "Why would you say that?"

"You started talking to Aleks, you began working out, and

you got the idea to try BDSM. You also got pierced." So that things would be *different*. "Did you make any other changes?"

"Yes. Many. It was time for me to." Making his tone lighter, he said, "Come, let's speak of happier things. If you didn't work at the Calydon, what would you do?"

He hadn't answered my near-death question, but I let it go. "I would design and create clothing. I made this dress you both love and hate. I make all my clothes."

He raised his brows. "You must want to pursue your talent."

Another instance of gazing at the stars. I was past that.

Even if my pack wasn't in crisis mode, I needed health insurance, for fuck's sake. At the very least, my own personal credit-card cloning machine wouldn't go amiss. *Please, Santa, please.*

Everyone in my family was sacrificing. We all had dreams we'd put on hold. Karin wanted to save up and be a full-time mom. Al and Gram had been planning to go on a world cruise to fleece obnoxious tourists and teach them never to travel again. Mom and Dad dreamed of owning a real art collection to replace the scam props littering the house. Benji, with his artistic soul, wanted to pick up a camera and document wildlife, instead of degenerates. And Pete . . .

Actually, Pete was delighted with his plum new position at the Caly.

I told Dmitri, "We all have dreams, huh?"

He canted his head. "I am starting to believe that."

The server came back to refill our wine. Had I downed a glass? I struggled to resist Dmitri in the best of circumstances. If I had a couple of drinks, he could make me plead for it. Again.

The idea of begging turned me on so swiftly, my face grew heated once more.

"Tell me about your hobbies," he said. "Do you ride horses?"

Eyes on the prize, Vice. "Um, not in a while." Not since we'd worked a real estate con near a ranch in neighboring California. My family had hated being away from Vegas; not me. "Do you ride?"

"I once did, avidly. I'm thinking about picking it up again." *Must be nice.* "Do you like the seaside?"

"Dunno. I've never been to one."

"How can that be? Would you like to travel more?"

"Sure. We have so many replicas of other places here. I'd love to see the Giza pyramids or a real castle or the Eiffel Tower. Just getting a first stamp in my passport would be huge for me." Hell, I'd be happy to drive back to Cali. I always said if I won the lottery I'd get a vacation place there. "But I could never stay away long. My family's here. Sunday dinner is mandatory. You only get to miss a few a year."

"You must be very close to them."

"They're everything to me."

"You are loyal to those you love," he said quietly.

"I will be till I die." I had a catalog of faults, but I possessed loyalty in spades. Once I identified someone as part of my pack, I always would. "'To the grave' is our family motto." That also described how long we Valentines kept secrets.

Dmitri's lips almost curved again, the closest that man came to smiling, and he raised his glass to me. "A toast to loyalty."

I clinked glasses with him.

The intensity of his stare made me feel awkward, so I cast about for something to say. "I couldn't find much about you online."

"I work to keep it that way."

As I suspected. So what was he hiding? More than his eccentricity? "Are you a 'have more than thou showest, say less than thou knowest' kind of guy?" Grifters lived by those words.

"Ah, Shakespeare's *King Lear*."

I grinned. I shouldn't be surprised Dmitri recognized the quote. My mark was scarily brilliant. "So what do you do now? Since you've already finished a lifetime of work?"

"Now I'm a steward for my own holdings."

"I think that's a non-braggy way to say you oversee a financial empire 'cause you're so rich."

He inclined his head. "I've got it down to a science, actually. I can work an hour a day from anywhere. I've decided it's time to enjoy myself more."

"Doing what? What are you looking for out of life?"

"The same as most men. A wife and a couple of children."

I couldn't believe he'd admitted to wanting a wife. And he'd also revealed yet another way we didn't fit: kids. "A family of your own, huh?"

"Wealth is meaningless without loved ones to spend it on."

"I'll have to take your word about the wealth. Though I am surprised you haven't settled down then."

"I hadn't met the right woman."

Hadn't met? As in, he had *now*.

He'd told me he wanted to get something *solidified*, but that was a far cry from *settled down* and having kids. Lucía, Natalie, and Jess had gone on about Sevastyans falling at first sight. Could Dmitri truly think I was the one for him?

No, no. Russian was his first language; he'd probably mistaken the tense of the verb. Or I'd misheard him.

So why was he looking at me so keenly. . . ?

CHAPTER 16

As Dmitri and I talked over more wine and shared a decadent tiramisu, I discovered we did have a *few* things in common.

We liked some of the same art and books and even some of the same music. He didn't laugh or smile, but he did have a sense of humor. "Perhaps you'll be the one to make me appreciate eighties hits," he'd said, his eyes crinkling at the sides. "My tutors failed at every turn." Whenever he *almost* smiled, my body grew tingly.

Now that I was more in tune with his moods and expressions, we'd found a comfortable ebb and flow. But sometimes I would sense that social discomfort, as if he was out of practice conversing.

What a confusing, complicated man. Polished at times, but unpracticed at others. Gorgeous, yet oblivious to the babes sighing as they passed our cabana. Brilliant, but he couldn't read people. . . .

When my phone started vibrating in my purse, I figured it was growing late and everyone wanted an update. "I should be getting home."

He signaled for the check. "Tomorrow I am taking you on a trip. We will spend the week anywhere you want to go."

After last night's detour, I was back to step five: gradually making my desires known. "I have to work. As much as I'd like to, I can't live in the Porsche you bought me."

He grew very still as he said, "I want to take care of you." In a way, he was pitching me too.

I playfully asked, "Dmitri, are you offering to be my sugar daddy?" In Sin City, the going rate was a bauble an orgasm.

He gazed at me as if he sensed a verbal trap. "I want . . . not to send you running from me again."

"I'm not going anywhere. Talk to me."

He sighed. "I have more money than I could possibly ever spend, but it brings me no enjoyment. Being with you does, and so I crave time with you. I resent your work for keeping me from what I want. Will you accept more from me?"

Holy shit! I'd never dreamed of a mark like this. The richest, hottest man I'd ever met was teed up for the kill. But my doubts flared again. The nicer he was to me, the harder this job felt. "Why don't we slow things down a little?" said the con artist to the unbalanced billionaire.

He looked frustrated. "I'm spooking you."

"You must be leaving Vegas soon."

He seemed to be weighing his words. Finally he said, "Not without you."

My jaw slackened.

"That was one of those things I shouldn't have said aloud, isn't it?"

Red flags waved all over the place. "This is going too fast." I struggled for equilibrium.

"Compared to most other couples? Yes. But you and I are both aware of what's happening."

I sputtered, "Spell it out for me, big guy."

"You are going to be mine," he said. "Exclusively. You're as good as already."

I blew out a breath. "Exclusively." *I* was supposed to manipulate him over the finish line. This was supposed to take all of my cunning and skill, and assistance from all kinds of rogues across the underbelly of Sin City.

Dmitri was offering himself up for the taking!

It must be a ploy of some kind. My eyes narrowed. Of course! "This is very convenient." I glared at him.

He looked perplexed. "Now I definitely can't read you."

"You promise no sex, hinting about a relationship first. Then, coincidentally, you tell me you happen to want a relationship. Right now! Even though you've *never* had one before. Why, we could sleep with each other this very night!"

"You beautiful stubborn girl," he said. "I'm not in this merely for sex. I swear to you I won't fuck you until you are mine alone." His eyes flashed. "Tonight, you will beg for me inside you, and somehow I will deny myself yet again."

I studied his face. *I could get this guy to marry me.* But without a prenup?

It'd be the ultimate con on a billionaire mark. . . .

✦

*B*ack in the limo, he dragged me into his lap.

I wanted to curl into him and soak up his heat, but I needed to tantalize. "Why do you keep putting me in your lap?"

"Tell me you don't fit me perfectly, and I will stop." He started to harden beneath me.

"You said I'd beg for you tonight. You just assume we'll be intimate?"

"With the way you eye-fucked me all through dinner?" I realized he was playing with me when a glint of humor shone in his eyes. "We're not only going to be intimate. I'm going to show you how much you'll enjoy bondage."

Was I curious? Of course. But I didn't think I was ready to give up all control. "I'm not sure."

"You have a safe word," he said, but his tone held a challenge, as if he dared me not to use it. "You'll either say it, or you'll surrender to me."

I tore my gaze from his face and glanced out the window. "Why are we headed toward my apartment?"

"I want to see where you live."

Just in case, I'd stowed anything grift-y, and I'd told my family it was off limits. "My place is lame."

He brought our foreheads together in that way I loved. It made me feel connected to him. *Too* connected. "You won't be there much longer, Vika." Because he wanted to do something about my living situation!

"If you're so determined to tie me up, you should know I'm fresh out of bondage gear."

"You'd be surprised what I could improvise with. All I need is a scarf, maybe a couple of belts. I'm sure someone with your interest in clothes will have the items I require."

"If not for sex, then why would you want to tie me up?"

"To get to the dessert I truly crave." His cock pulsated beneath me.

I just stopped myself from rubbing my ass against it. "What exactly does that mean?"

He held my gaze as he rasped, "That means I am going to kiss your wet little pussy until your thighs tremble and you drench my tongue. I won't stop until you scream for me."

I swallowed. Despite my misgivings, I was so torn.

Because part of me desperately needed a screaming orgasm from this man.

Then reality returned. "I told you I wasn't interested."

"Denying me again? Why?"

My cheeks heated as I admitted, "I can't come from oral sex."

"Not all of your blushes are the same. I'm going to learn every one." He reached up and began to pull pins from my hair.

"I'm serious, Dmitri." I jutted my chin. "Statistically, I'm not alone."

"You say you can't simply because you never have before?" As he unbraided my hair, his watchful gaze followed the movements of his hands. I got the impression he'd never freed a woman's hair before, and wanted to get it right.

"After the last two nights, do I believe you could make oral sex feel amazing? Absolutely. But I'm just not built to orgasm from it. The average woman takes twenty minutes to come like that, and I'm not average."

"You are in no way average, *moy ángel.*" Another braid loosened.

"Which means I would be stressed out because you would be down there wearing out your tongue and inwardly cursing my name. So when would you call it a defeat? We could set a timer."

Once he'd unbound my hair, he ran his fingers through it. "I see what the problem is."

"What's that?"

He leaned in to murmur at my ear, "You believe I would be eating you out for your pleasure instead of for mine."

CHAPTER 17

I hadn't said my safe word when he'd pressed me back naked in my bed. I'd remained silent as he'd used a scarf to tie my wrists to the headboard.

But now, when he snapped one of my leather belts, I was tempted to scream, "Cognac!"

"I don't know about this." So why was my voice so throaty?

"You know your choices." Still dressed, he stalked around the bed, his eyes dark and fierce, like an animal surveying a meal it was about to devour.

I had called him a beast just two nights ago. Felt like ages had passed.

When he licked his lips, I shivered and my nipples puckered tighter.

His predator's gaze locked on them, noting my response. "Your body wants more. Safe word or surrender. One or the other."

Fucking Russki. In the club, I hadn't known what I was getting into, but now I did. Refusing to flinch, I followed his gaze from my aching breasts to my hair fanning out, then to my eyes, to my lips. Back to my breasts, before dipping lower . . .

"Bend your knees and bring your heels up against your ass."

"We can do other things, Dmitri," I said, though I'd brought my heels up.

He wrapped my braided belt around the middle of my thigh and my shin, securing one leg in a bent position. *"Nyet.* You said I'd inwardly curse your name? You'll outwardly curse mine. Understand me, Vika, I will kiss you for as long as I like." Then he secured my other leg with a second belt. "If you come without permission, I will keep tonguing you with no care for how sensitive you'll be."

Though this sounded titillating, I wasn't sold. My head fell to the side, and I sighed. I should just fake it.

Brett had gone down on me one night early in our relationship, and I'd known it wasn't in the cards, but he'd kept trying, so I'd faked it.

And he'd still massaged his jaw and waggled it with an adorable grin that had made me feel awful. Sex shouldn't hurt.

Dmitri Sevastyan was a mark; why should I care how he felt? "You can still back out."

"I've made sure you cannot." He'd bound me tight as hell.

I couldn't believe I was doing this. Or, rather, that *he* was doing this to me.

"Unless you use your safe word," he added. "Otherwise I won't relent until you've come so many times I pity your tender pussy."

"You expect *multiple* times?"

"The only thing I expect of you this night is your submission." He sat beside my waist, facing my feet, stretching a possessive arm over my torso.

His fingers brushed over my mound. "Never remove this light hair of yours. It drives me wild." He ogled me so close I could feel his breaths. "Let your legs fall wide. Show me where you're wet."

Face heating, I . . . did. I had to bite back a moan when my damp labia parted for him.

He bit out, "You are *exquisite*. I'm going to learn every inch of you."

The idea of his eyes on me, roaming over my most secret place, made my spread pussy quiver.

He must have seen it because he gave a rumbling groan. "You need to do as I say, don't you?"

Yes. My nipples were so hard, my areolas were raised. My breaths had shallowed. I felt myself getting even wetter, my folds swelling. "I'm trusting you with this."

"Your trust humbles me, Vika." He sat up on the bed and removed his jacket, tossing it onto my cheap office chair.

Would I finally see him naked?

He bent to remove his shoes; I heard the creak of costly leather. When he stood, I watched his every movement in fascination.

His clothes were like art to me. *He* was art to me.

As he shrugged out of his shirt, I was treated to the sound and scent of its starchy crispness. The long lean muscles of his arms flexed as his broad chest was revealed.

My gaze drank him in. His pecs were rigid planes of muscle, his torso defined perfection. Just following the black trail of hair leading down from his navel had me rocking my hips.

He undid his belt and unzipped with fingers that looked masculine and rugged—especially with his busted knuckles—

yet they'd played me like an instrument the night before.

His slacks whispered down his muscular legs, his buckle pinging as it hit the floor. His cock bulged in his gray boxer briefs, and sexy precum wetted the material. I could make out the shape of his piercing.

He pulled off those briefs, and his dick bobbed. *Oh, my God.* He stood before me naked, shoulders squared, letting me look. His body was a bonanza. His shaft jutted ramrod straight, the crown taut. His balls were large and looked in need of cupping. Would he like it if I gently tugged on them?

Or even, *not* so gently? My fingers clenched and unclenched.

He stalked beside the bed, looming over me. As I gazed up at him, his veined length pulsed so hard it jerked.

Oh my.

My, my, mine.

Seeing him like this made me a thousand times more aware of my bonds. I couldn't simply walk over and explore him, couldn't heft the weight of his big dusky balls or fondle his pecs. Couldn't follow that trail of hair below his navel—with my mouth.

I couldn't tongue his piercing. I found myself licking my lips as I stared at it.

He caught me. "Again, you show me no mercy." He gripped his shaft. "Is this what you want?"

"*Yes.* I wish you'd just let me suck you."

He rested a knee on the side of the bed. "Perhaps afterward."

"How long will you do this before we call it?"

"Look at my cock. I'm this hard from mere anticipation. Watch my reactions if you want to know how long I'll do it."

He leaned down and used the pierced head to rub one of my nipples.

I gasped, arching upward.

"Do you know how difficult it was to clean my cum off you the other night? I wanted my seed slathered on your tits, wanted you to wear my mark."

I whimpered.

He caressed my nipples, giving them light pinches. "I had to control myself. But not for much longer." And then what would happen? "We talked last night of getting things solidified. Tonight we will."

"What does that mean?"

He laid his faultless body beside me, one possessive hand covering a breast.

I couldn't touch him back. Could only lie back and . . . receive.

"It means you belong to me. You are mine."

Did he think I needed to be romanced? With lines? "Is that right? For how long?"

His gaze bored into mine.

I swallowed. "You're not saying what I think you're saying."

"I am saying for always."

To be with this mesmerizing god of a man forever? Then pesky reality caught up with me again. This guy wasn't a player; he was insane!

And he'd tied me up. It was dangerous to lead him on, to keep seeing him. When I broke things off with this obsessed Russian, would he be as bad as the cartel kingpin?

No. Dmitri might be obsessed, but I knew he would never hurt me.

I would hurt him, though.

He nuzzled a breast. "When you told me you never wanted to see me again, I barely stood it. Vika, I could not do it a second time."

Guilt twisted my chest.

He trailed kisses down my body. I tried to hold on to my remorse, but his warm, firm lips were melting it away. On his way down, he rubbed his cheek over my hip bone. When he moved his head between my bound legs, he stretched his big body perpendicular to mine so I could see that magnificent cock.

"You wanted to know how I hurt my hand?" As his palms glided up my thighs, he pressed a kiss above the binding on one of my legs. "Last night, you left me seething. I wasn't to see you again? To touch you? I repeatedly punched a fucking wall. Trying to feel *anything* but that emptiness."

"That's not right, Dmitri! Crazy . . ."

His hot breaths whispered across my upper thigh. "Never said I was sane." He nuzzled my outer lips.

"*Oh!*"

"No matter what I do to you tonight, remember one thing: this pussy belongs to me." He licked my labia, giving a groan of pleasure.

My thoughts scattered. "Oh, my God—"

I jerked against my restraints when he sucked on a lip. "Dmitri!" Then he *nibbled* that damp flesh! I could only whimper. He never neared my clit, just played with my lips, yet the mix of sensations already had me tripping closer to the edge . . . and he seemed to be just warming up.

"*Prosto rai, ángel.*" Sheer heaven. He was in love with this! As he feasted, his cock strained. With each visible throb, more precum beaded the slit.

I yearned for that length inside me. Needed to milk it with my body. I'd grown so wet my slickness had seeped down between my cheeks. My bound thighs trembled around his head. "What're you doing to me?" My voice sounded awed.

How could bondage feel so . . . freeing? I didn't have to do all the work. All I had to do was surrender.

"Trying to go slow." Lick. "To *not* devour you." Suck. "My luscious woman." He clenched my thighs with shaking hands, yet he kept a leisurely pace.

He planned to tease me like last night! If I ached any more for his cock, I'd go as crazy as he was. "You said I'd beg you for sex—I am! Please, Dmitri, *please*."

He groaned again. "And break my promise to you? You, who mean so much to me?"

Before I could register his words, he began flicking his tongue over my lips. "Ahhh!" I could almost feel those vibrations where I needed them most. "Then please lick me harder. Higher!"

"No, you're not to come yet. Not without my permission."

"Dmitri!" I was so close, couldn't stop undulating to his tongue. How quickly I'd gone from *no oral sex* to *pretty please eat me raw!*

He drew back to say, "Look at your hips rocking. You had better not disobey me."

I wanted to snatch the back of his head and grind my wetness against his mouth. "I can't take much more of this."

He leaned down until his breaths heated my clit. "Should I make you come? Bring off your needy . . . soaked . . . pussy?"

"Yes, yes, yes!" Just those words in his sinful, accented voice . . . My head thrashed. "Going to come! Oh, oh, I'm close!"

"Nyet."

I cried, "Why?"

"I could be moved to mercy. But I don't think you're mindless enough yet. You'd have to convince me."

Again he controlled me. He'd taken ownership of my body, my mind. The thrall had me in its grip. "Mindless?" I raised my upper body so I could meet his eyes. I barely recognized my voice as I begged, "Please tongue my clit. It throbs so bad, I can't stand it! *Lick it. Taste it.*"

His fingers bit into my thighs. "Would you prefer my tongue on your clit? Or *in* you?" With a husky groan, he licked right at my entrance—then he fucked it with his stiffened tongue.

Once my mind caught up with what my body was experiencing, I screamed. Shattered. *"Oh, my God! YES!"* My back arched like a bow, thighs closing around his ears as he licked me deep. . . .

But once I'd peaked, he kept going, ravenous. He spread me wide with both hands to lap up my cum.

I twisted beneath his mouth. "Too much! Too much, Dmitri!"

He ignored me! I tried to break his kiss, but he wasn't budging, too busy making a meal out of me.

I couldn't fight him, couldn't push him away, was helpless to do anything other than take the pleasure he forced on me. He'd warned me of this!

Finally, I surrendered to it.

To him.

Only then did he give me a reprieve. He nuzzled me again, his harsh breaths tickling my hypersensitive flesh.

My head fell back. "Oh, my God." I'd just come harder than ever before—from oral sex. And he hadn't even touched my clit.

There'd never been anything wrong with me. I was floating. *I love you, Dmitri Sevastyan. Not really. Maybe. I couldn't.*

My pussy is in love with your mouth and wants to get married.

He didn't sound as enamored of me when he said, "You neither asked for, nor received my permission to come."

Weirdly, I wasn't satisfied. I needed *more*. I leaned up. "You wanted me mindless—I am!" I didn't care about the mixed signals I was giving. I didn't care about anything but sex with this man. "Please fuck me." I'd had a sampling of his fingers and tongue. What could he do with his entire body?

"You'd hate me afterward." He pressed a loving kiss to one of my thighs.

His emotions were only heightening this already mind-blowing experience. My hips decided to roll for him.

"Look at you offering up your pussy to me. How could I not want to possess you for my own?" He tilted his own hips, showing off his mouthwatering shaft. "I'm about to spill without a single touch. Watch my cock when I make you come next."

"Next?"

"Uh-huh. At least two more times like this." His tongue returned to my slit.

"Ahhh!" I jolted as much from sensation as from realization. He really was going to do it. . . .

My world diminished until all I knew was his tongue. The flat of his tongue, the sides of it, the *tip*.

The frenzy in me built once more. "Don't torture me again!"

"Do you want me to kiss your clit now?"

"PLEASE!" I twisted frantically.

"Though you don't deserve it . . ." He engulfed my bud with his mouth.

Suction? He was sucking on my—

"*YES!*" I screamed my release. "*Fuck, fuck, YES, YES, YES!*" My thighs shook, body writhing through another bone-melting climax.

But he kept nursing my bud, his groans vibrating it.

The staggering sensations only ramped up. The intensity mounted until I feared what would happen when I came. Would I black out?

Right when I was on the verge, he stopped sucking. "Your sweet little clit couldn't be more swollen. Woman, it *does* throb."

"No more teasing, Dmitri!"

He sank his finger inside me, curling it as he'd done last night. "Tell me you belong to me."

Instinct whispered not to. He would take my words to heart, considering this some sort of real promise to him. "Let me come!"

"You will be mine, Vika." He worked in another finger. "Tell me you belong to me. Say the words."

Desperate, I told him, "I really, really, really think you should fuck me now."

"*Nyet.*" He gave a hungry suck on my clit.

The more I lost control, the more I talked. "Then l-let me give you head. I need my mouth on your cock. Dmitri, untie me, and I'll suck it so good for you."

His voice sounded crazed as he bit out, "Would you swallow my cum?"

"Yes!" I craved to take him down. Needed to be as wicked as he was. Comprehension: *I crave his cum.*

"Say the words!" His brows drew together in pain. "And I'll give it to you."

My fists clenched again. "Okay, okay! I belong to you."

"If you want to come again, say them like you mean them." Another brief suck.

My head thrashed. "I belong to you!"

"Again!" He licked and fingered me at the same time.

"I belong to you!"

"Tell me I own your body. No one else is ever to touch it but me."

I babbled something to that effect. The body he wanted to own was levitating.

"Who owns you?" A graze of teeth . . .

"You do! *YOU DO!*"

"Beg me for your orgasm." He sucked me hard—

Too late. "Oh, oh, *GOD!*" Just that command had set me off. I bulleted into yet another climax, screaming his name.

Sensation racked me, spasm after spasm . . . until I couldn't take it anymore. Still he licked, consuming me. "Please, no, PLEASE!" *Need safe word!* What was my—

"Cognac!"

With a growl of displeasure, Dmitri relented, drawing back. If he'd looked crazy before, now he appeared in agony and crazy, his amber eyes wild with lust. His dick was so engorged, the head was plumped up around that piercing.

As I leveled off, I wanted only one thing: my mouth on him. Between breaths, I said, "Untie me. Dmitri, I need to suck you off."

He straddled my waist, all rippling muscles and whipcord sinews. Voice a harsh grate, he said, "Too late, *ángel.*" He fisted his shaft, bringing the head an inch from my mouth. "Open for me. Take my cum like this, and it will be etched into my memory."

When I opened, he aimed for my tongue. "Look at me," he groaned. "Keep—me—here."

Don't know what that means. But I looked up at him. Our gazes locked, and time seemed suspended. The moment was electrifying, made even more so because we were staring at each other, exposed and exposing, both awaiting his pleasure.

A single pump of his big fist wrenched a bellow from his lungs and his hot cream free.

I never looked away as it spurted between my lips, landing on my tongue. His agonized expression transformed into one of ecstasy, his eyes gleaming gold.

Only then did he break his stare, to throw back his head and roar so loud the walls seemed to shake. Fist flying up and down his cock, he jacked it for more.

I eagerly took every drop. *Never get enough of him. . . .*

As he emptied himself, his hand slowed and his yells faded. With his mighty chest heaving, he gazed back down at me.

Only then did I swallow with a moan.

His bewildered groan made my toes curl.

A pearly drop remained on his pierced crown. I couldn't help it; I eased forward as far as my bindings would allow and lapped it up.

"My God, Vika." He shuddered. "My God." He dropped back in the bed, sprawling across the mattress.

CHAPTER 18

"Um, Dmitri?"

Eyes closed, sucking in lungfuls of air, he held up a finger. "Minute."

I wondered what he'd meant when he said, "Keep me here." The second time he'd told me that. Was it some kind of Russian thing?

When he finally faced me again, he didn't bother hiding his amazement. "I had heard a man could spend so hard he saw stars, but I never believed. Vika, that was a detonation."

Instead of waggling a sore jaw, he licked his lips, gaze hooded. "And you'd thought to deny me that?" With effort, he made it back to his knees. His hands were unsteady as he loosened one of the belts.

"I wish I'd had something to do with getting *you* there." I straightened my leg, wincing a little at the pinpricks.

He began massaging them away. "You mean beside your taste, your scent, your moans? Your response wrested that pleasure from me. Speaking of which . . ." A look of pure masculine pride lit his face. "Shame you can't come from oral sex."

That *look*. "You're really hot when you're insufferably proud and cocky."

He unbound and massaged my other leg. "I am proud—to have pleasured you thoroughly." He leaned over to untie my wrists, his semihard dick wagging in front of my face.

Need. He'd told me he wanted to make a woman like me addicted to him. Was I already there?

Once he'd freed me completely, he asked, "So how many times did you get off?"

I play-slapped his hip. "Four, you smug asshat."

He pulled back the cover. "In you go."

I dutifully crawled under. "Have I lost all your respect?"

"There are many things I feel for you right now. Respect is among them."

"How did you keep from fucking me?" The way his cock had strained . . .

"How is trust evaluated? By testing it." He showed me his palms. Ragged cuts and dried blood marked both. He'd dug his nails in! "It was everything I could do to keep control of myself."

Crazy man! "Why is it so important? Any other guy would've just done it."

He squared his shoulders, as if proud of what he was about to say. "I reminded myself that if I broke my promise, I could lose the best thing that's ever happened to me."

I whispered. "Me?"

"You, *ángel*."

But I wasn't an angel. I was so far from it.

"Those bites of pain were well worth my reward." He rose, unfolding his tall frame. My gaze locked on his dick.

How would I make it through another night without sex?

He headed to my bathroom, giving me the view of his powerful back and shoulders, his lean hips. . . .

His ass.

Good thing I'm not standing.

His taut cheeks were sculpted with hollows on the sides. The play of contracting muscles taunted my nails to dig into them. I wanted to grip that flesh as he pounded me. I imagined nipping him there, and a whimper escaped my lips.

He paused, then walked on, saying, "Are you objectifying me, Vika?"

A laugh bubbled up.

When he returned, he pulled on his clothes before my rapt gaze. I kept thinking, *That god of a man just came from* my *bed. . . .*

Dressed, he sat beside me. "I am pleased we have things settled now."

"Settled?" Oh. That.

"You and I are exclusive with one another."

As I stared into his thrall eyes, I figured, *Well, we* could *be exclusive.*

Ah! I dragged my gaze away. "I can't look at you."

He pinched my chin, forcing me to meet his eyes. "Why, *ángel?*" Hurt flashed across his expression.

"Because I feel as if I'm under some kind of spell. You look at me like this, and I can't think. And worse, I can't seem to tell you no."

"Then never tell me no."

"You're crazy." I bit my tongue as soon as the words left it. I hadn't meant to say it earlier either.

"Yes. I am on occasion. But tonight I wasn't."

I needed to get to the bottom of this. There were different levels and types of crazy, right? He was probably just a social oddball, an eccentric—

"I have a gift for you."

Gift???

He reached into a jacket pocket. "Close your eyes, and keep them closed."

I did.

"I hope you like diamonds." Cool metal glided over my collarbones and neck. The strand was *heavy*. "You can look now."

I gasped at the necklace. A dozen large diamonds were spaced randomly down a platinum chain, each one set in a bezel of tiny sapphires. The stones came in all different shapes: oval, pear, marquise, triangular. The necklace had no discernible pattern. I loved it!

Though ridiculously picky about clothes and jewelry, I could wear this piece forever. "Are you dicking with me?"

"No. I am not."

I dragged my gaze from the sparkling rocks. "Ah, you *do* want to be my sugar daddy. A piece of jewelry for an orgasm. It is Vegas after all."

"If I paid you what that orgasm was worth to me, I'd be back in the research lab because I would be penniless."

And here comes the charm. I couldn't stop a grin.

"I gave you that necklace because it's a good start for your collection. I warn you now, I will spoil you to an embarrassing degree."

I tilted my head. "You're not the first man to tell me things like this. To make promises."

"Then I'll be the first man smart enough to keep them. I will pick you up tomorrow at one. Pack for warm weather." I got the sense that leaving me pained him. As soon as the thought occurred, he informed me, "This will be the last night I part from you."

I couldn't allow myself to believe the promise in his eyes— because it was way too soon. Plus, he was a man.

But what if . . . ?

At the door, he said, "Have sweet dreams, *moy ángel*. Mine will be of you."

What if, what if, what if? Once he'd locked me in and I heard the limo leave, I squealed with happiness, drumming my feet on the bed.

CHAPTER 19

At ten till one, a knock sounded. I was still in my underwear! "Just a sec," I called, shimmying past my overnight bag to reach my closet.

I grabbed a simple black linen sheath I'd made. The shortest part of the asymmetrical hem hit just above my knees. I smoothed my hands down the front, proud of my work, then stepped into pointy-toed black pumps.

My gaze lit on my new necklace, laid out on my duvet. Last night, I'd sent a picture of it to the family's conference line along with a message: Got drama from night before worked out with Sevastyan. Had great dinner. Going on trip tomorrow at 1:00. All good. Please, sleep better.

After I'd signed off, I'd danced naked to *A-ha* while I packed. I was dying of curiosity about our "warm" destination.

This morning, Karin had called for a real update.

I'd filled her in, admitting, "He gave me a taste of something I don't think I can live without." So how would I feel if he took my key away?

"Listen to your voice, Vice," she'd said. "You're falling in love with him!"

"No, I'm not." Falling in lust maybe. But those flashes of crazy kept me on edge. "He's got more red flags than Soviet Russia. He *is* obsessed with me. He's jealous and possessive and controlling."

"Yet you're letting him take you on a trip?"

"We're running out of time." With Karin's recent score, Lucía's watch, my car, and the necklace, we had to be getting close. "To the grave, remember?"

"We didn't mean *your* grave."

"He'd never hurt me. My grift sense cleared him. . . ."

Now I pulled on the necklace, brushing my fingers over the stones. Soon Dmitri would be out of my life, his gift converted to cash. All I'd have would be a photo of this to remember.

My eyes threatened to water. Maybe *I* was a softie.

Inner shake. I finished dressing, then quickly assessed my outfit in the mirror. I'd kept my accessories simple—a light silver pashmina and my little silver purse looped over my shoulder—so my necklace would be the focus. I'd lined my eyes, but wore nude lipstick. I'd left my hair free to curl down my back.

Work the con, Vice.

Ha. I kept assuring myself I was acting in the interest of the con. But I feared I *was* already addicted to him.

My stomach felt fluttery as I carried my bag to the front door. With a wide smile, I opened up. "Hey, big—"

Brett.

I froze.

He looked like hell, his face unshaven with dark circles under his eyes. "It's so good to see you, Tori." The nickname dredged up a slew of memories.

Tori, w-will you go to the movies with me? . . . I love you, Tori. . . . Will you marry me, Tori? . . . Please, Tori, she didn't mean anything to me!

He pointed to the green notice on my door. "They're gonna evict you?"

Finding my voice, I said, "That doesn't concern you."

"Of course it does. Come back home. *Please.* I'll do anything."

Home? We'd been broken up for a year. And Dmitri would arrive any minute! "You've got to go. Now."

"Why?"

"I have a date who'll be here shortly. This isn't fair for you to barge in on me like this."

He frowned. "Then why did you tell me to come over at one?"

"What are you talking about?"

He took his phone out of his jeans pocket and showed me an e-mail—sent from my account two hours ago—that did indeed ask him to come over to talk.

Who the hell had sent it? Anyone in my family could have accessed my account—they all knew *!jiepdll!ozqkml14*** was my password—but they also knew Dmitri would be here at one.

They'd never let anything interrupt my budding relationship with a jealous, possessive, controlling billionaire—

My eyes widened. But they'd do anything to accelerate it.

Whoever had e-mailed Brett was using him as an unwitting shill—to create a crisis of jealousy for Dmitri.

Too soon in the timeline! Too freaking *personal.*

Just yesterday, Karin had talked about manufacturing a crisis. Had it been her? "I'm sorry, Brett, but I didn't e-mail you. Someone must be . . . playing a prank. Or something."

"A prank?" The pain in his eyes was stark. He'd gotten his hopes up.

I reminded myself I'd probably shown him the same stark look when I'd caught him with another woman.

Brett's gaze lit on my diamonds, then dropped to my luggage on the floor. "You've got an *overnight* date? Who is this guy?"

"That hasn't been your business since you cheated on me."

He swiped a hand down his face. "I fucked up with you. I know how bad. But this can't be over. We were made for each other."

"I used to think so."

"It's still true. Please forgive me. Please take me back. Every second of the day, I'm trying to come up with something to say to convince you to give me another chance." His eyes glinted.

I once loved those hazel eyes, had thought I'd wake up to them for the rest of my life. "I can't come back from what I saw, Brett. I'm just not capable of it."

"I wish to God I could go back in time and change that night!"

Though I'd spent twelve months shying away from that memory, it welled up in my mind.

Brett and I had thrown a pre-season football party, but my family had called me in for a last-minute assist—drinks with promising investors/marks. I'd closed the tax-evaders early, so I'd hurried home, wending through shit-faced friends to get to the bedroom and change into my jersey. Brett and the tawny-haired bombshell hadn't heard me open the door. . . .

Now I told him, "When I walked in on you two, it took me the longest time to register what I was seeing."

"Tori, please don't."

They'd been naked in the bed I'd shared with him, frantically kissing, and he'd had his fingers inside her. Getting her ready. She'd been stroking him as his hips bucked to her fist. Unlike me, she had enhanced breasts and legs for miles.

As I'd choked back bile, my mind had been a chaos of jarring thoughts:

He's about to screw her. How long has this been going on? He and I had sex there hours ago. We talked about getting a puppy after our honeymoon. I just washed those sheets. I spent the entire day cleaning for our football party. He knows I don't even like football. But I'm supportive. I was supportive. He's about to do it.

Between kisses, he'd said to the woman, "I don't even know your last name."

The words had jolted me out of my stupor. He'd thrown me away for a *quickie*? A one-nighter with a stranger? I'd snapped, "Guess I should've bought motherfucking name tags for our party."

As I'd stormed out, I'd spotted her *Jubilee!* showgirls T-shirt on my freshly vacuumed floor. . . .

What if I hadn't caught him? What if I'd lived my life not knowing what pushed my buttons?

Black-haired, golden-eyed Russians with dominant streaks and wicked games.

I'd been devastated by Brett's actions, yet never been able to *empathize*. I'd never been able to imagine a desire so strong I'd risk everything to ease it.

After Dmitri, I had a clearer picture. In a haunted tone, I said, "I could see how much you wanted her; you were about to explode from it." Queasiness overwhelmed me. "There's no way you would've pulled away from that girl."

"I was about to, Tori!"

I cringed. Nails on a chalkboard.

How could I ever trust another man not to fall prey to his desires? I'd recognized I would need a grand gesture, some kind of overwhelming proof that I was the only one a partner would ever want.

Looking at my ex-fiancé now, I realized *no* action would ever be enough to convince me. "You're here to reconcile, and yet you're lying right now."

He opened his mouth to tell me another one, so I raised my hand to stop him.

"I'm done." Over his shoulder, I saw a long, cool limo roll up. *Shit.*

Dmitri was out the door before the car fully stopped, six and a half feet of furious Russian, crossing to stand beside me. "Victoria?"

I swallowed. "Dmitri, this is Brett Wilson. Brett, Dmitri Sevastyan."

Former linebacker Brett had to gaze up to him. "*He* is your date?"

Even with his murderous expression, Dmitri looked every inch the billionaire. "I'm more than a mere date. Come, Vika, we will be late for the courthouse. For our wedding."

I did a double take. *Wait, what?*

Brett grabbed my arm, his face panicked. "Wedding?"

Dmitri's demeanor turned even more chilling. "Release. Her. Now."

"Or what?" My ex had at least twenty pounds of bulk on Dmitri. "Don't make me hurt you."

"Brett, he's got bodyguards." Starsky and Hutch stood beside the limo on high alert.

Dmitri's voice made the hairs on my nape stand up as he said, "No one touches what's *mine*."

"What's yours, pal?" Brett bowed up, readying for a fight.

"I'm giving you one last chance to let her go. As you already did before."

"Fuck off, man, or I will lay you out. This is between Tori and me—"

In one lightning fast movement, Dmitri yanked Brett's hand from me and launched a punch to his stomach.

Brett's breath left him in a rush.

"No! Stop this!" Before I could get between them, Brett recovered, yelling with fury. He swung for Dmitri's face.

Neatly dodging him, Dmitri stepped back. With his lips curving into a sneer, he raised one hand and motioned for Brett to try again.

Brett yelled and swung, but Dmitri drew his head back with plenty of time—and with utter confidence.

The Russian knew how to fight. "I'll thrash you simply for not appreciating what you had." The menace in his eyes . . .

When a man like Brett fought, he might give somebody a shiner, maybe knock some teeth loose. When a man like Dmitri fought, *someone was going to die.*

The bodyguards made no move to intervene, not that they needed to protect their boss.

"I'm leaving with you now, Dmitri!" I said. "Please, don't hurt him. Let's just go."

Never taking his gaze from his opponent, Dmitri slowly shook his head.

Brett threw another punch. Dmitri dodged and launched a hit of his own. His fist connected with Brett's nose.

A distinct crack sounded. Brett fell to his knees, holding his face. Blood poured through his fingers.

"Jesus!" I dropped beside him, laying a hand on his back. "Are you okay?" I gazed up at Dmitri. "Damn it, don't hit him again!"

Though Dmitri's eyes were wild, he pulled me to my feet so gently. "Then come with me."

To separate them, I let Dmitri usher me into the limo. As we drove away, I looked back through the rear window.

Brett lurched to his feet, blood pouring. "Please don't do this, Tori!" he yelled. "Ah, God, please don't!"

I squeezed my eyes shut and put my hands over my ears, wanting to block everything out. When I felt the limo turn a corner, I dropped my hands and turned to Dmitri. "What the hell was that?"

"The thought of you getting back with him drives me insane." He *looked* it, as if he was barely holding himself together. "I'm eaten alive with jealousy that he had years of your life." Dmitri didn't touch me, kept his clenched fists lowered. "Last night at dinner, you told me you didn't know if you would go back to him. Today, I find him at your door. You're still in love with him!"

"No, I'm not!" I said, frowning as I realized I wasn't—at all.

"You'll prove it, then," Dmitri said. "You'll wed me."

I gaped. I thought he'd mentioned marriage to screw with Brett.

Married to Dmitri Sevastyan? I frowned down at my chest—because my heart pounded as if it'd just heard the best idea ever. "You can't be serious." Dmitri was playing right into my family's hands. The manufactured crisis had worked; step seven of the long con. "Where are you taking me?"

"I told you. To the courthouse."

"You're missing one important detail—I haven't said yes!"

His gaze held mine, enthralling me. "You *will*."

What if I did? Two tears in a bucket, right?

No, no, no! *Stop thralling me!* "This is moving way too fast!"

"From the moment I first saw you, I knew you were going to be mine. You got under my skin, into my fucking blood! After last night, I know you want me too." He stabbed his fingers through his hair. "I've never felt this way about anyone else."

The congressman had said the same to Karin. "I've heard that line before."

"It isn't a goddamned line!"

"We met Friday, and now you're talking marriage!"

"Maksim knew Lucía would be his after one night. Aleksandr decided to marry Natalie after one look. My timing is cautious by comparison."

I thought of the con. What a coup this would be.

But my mark might be mentally unwell, and that made him vulnerable. Yet these were desperate times. I knew I needed to break the code, but I still said, "Give me one reason why you're so intent on this today. Can't we wait a day or two? What would one day hurt?"

"What would one day help? I told you I don't handle confusion well. I despise uncertainty, have had more of that in my life than any man should have to bear. I will not tolerate uncertainty with you."

"What does that mean?" I asked, fearing his answer would be over the top and crazy.

"I must know you are either completely mine—or you're not."

"*You* are giving *me* an ultimatum?" I was supposed to give him one! How had things gone so sideways?

"Say yes, Victoria. Or say good-bye."

Hadn't I just worried what would happen when he took his sexual intensity away from me? "Why are you looking at it in such black-and-white terms?"

He grasped my nape. "I feel as if I'm scalded with acid whenever I think about you. And I think of nothing else! My mind seethes. My body seethes."

"You fucked-up man! That sounds *painful*—not good."

"It *is* painful! It's goddamned misery. The only thing that soothes it is being with you."

His words brought to mind what Gram had said—about finding a guy who would never jeopardize his relationship. Because it equaled his very life.

Why was I thinking about that now? This "relationship" wasn't real! He couldn't feel this way already.

And if he did, his feelings would *fade* just as quickly.

His hand tightened on my nape. "And now another man— one so unworthy of you—threatens what we could have?" Dmitri gave me a brief, hard kiss. "You will marry me, *ángel.* Accept this as inevitable."

CHAPTER 20

"He, uh, wants to get hitched. Today," I told everyone on the conference line. "In fact, he gave me an ultimatum. Marry him, or never see him again. Ironic, huh?" I'd already relayed the fight with Brett and grilled them about that e-mail. Nobody had copped to it.

Pete said, "Where are you now?"

"At the courthouse, in some little room. He asked me to wait here for him to return." I felt like I was getting sweated by Johnny Law. What was taking Dmitri so long? His family had left Vegas, so he couldn't be waiting on them. He hadn't mentioned anything about mine.

"Find him! You're letting him get away!" Mom cried. "Right now his lawyers are telling him all the reasons why he can't marry you. At best, they're cobbling together a prenup. You need to be hauling Sevastyan over the finish line!"

"Mom's right," Benji said. "You're losing the heat of the moment. If he gets out of crisis mode and starts thinking clearly—"

"Vice isn't ready for this." Dad's tone was stern. "A marriage con can play with your mind. I know this."

Gram made a sound of agreement. "It's so true." After losing my grandfather, she'd married a string of wealthy men.

Pete said, "Then what if Vice kept him?"

"How would that work?" I asked, longing for a deck of cards to soothe my frayed nerves. "Hi, Dmitri, I know we've only been married a few days, but I need a blank check for a fortune, and I can never tell you what it's for." I pinched my temples. "Besides, I thought I was going to settle down with a grifter, someone I could take home to meet my family. My *real* family. If I keep Dmitri, what kind of future will I have with you guys?" I'd belong in neither world. "I'm not talking about cutting him loose this minute, but we must be getting close—without a wedding."

Dmitri opened the door. "My apologies."

I said into the phone, "He's back. Gotta run," which was code for *stay on the line, because I'm only acting like I'm hanging up.* I set it facedown on the bench. "What's happening?"

"I've been making arrangements." Pulling together a prenup? He sat beside me. "You've probably dreamed of a certain kind of wedding, not a courthouse ceremony, but we will host a celebration for our families once we've settled in."

"Settled in?" Oh, fuck me. He was planning to take me to the motherland! "In Russia?"

"No, in California. We have an estate on the northern coast."

We have. Wait, California? *Oh, come on!* My dream location. Lady Luck seemed to be smiling down on me.

He tucked a curl behind my ear. "I would never expect you

to live far from your family. The flight there is only a little over an hour by jet."

"Just hold on a second. I need to talk to you about all this—"

"Here." He pulled a ring box from his jacket pocket and handed it to me. "Perhaps this will make up for the abruptness of everything."

The weight sent a tremor through me. "This ring box is heavy," I said, secretly narrating. I opened the lid and sucked in a breath.

Monster rock . . . jackpot . . . don't scream, don't scream!

"Dmitri, it's unreal. This marquise diamond must be . . . fifteen carats." The band was platinum, my favorite! "How did you get a ring like this so quickly?" That was where he'd been!

"I have ways. Do you like it? We can get you another—"

"NO." *Monster rock MINE.*

"I'm pleased you approve. I also sent one of my men to collect your bag and lock up your apartment. The car remains. Perhaps your family would like to use it? I will get you another one." *Another?* He took my hand and stood. "Come, they're ready."

So soon? "Where's the paperwork? Surely a prenup will take some time."

He frowned. "We have no need of that."

"Pardon?"

"I intend to make you happy in our marriage. What's mine will become yours, and you will never make me regret trusting you with all that I have."

My brain exploded. I could make five hundred million dollars in the next ten minutes. If I were an awful person.

But the threat to my family . . .

I wished I could just *nibble* enough to save my parents; why did Dmitri have to force me into this major commitment?

Think, think! What would my sister do? Karin would be on her honeymoon by now. "Your brothers and everyone will think I'm a gold digger." They would make him get this annulled. He'd plead insanity or something.

"My family wants us to be happily married." Dmitri looked so trusting, and I was so . . . rotten.

"Don't you want them to be here?"

"At present, I have some matters to resolve with them. It's not important. What's important is you. What does your instinct tell you?"

No prenup? "That you're too good to be true, big guy." All my life I'd wondered how people could be so stupid as to get grifted. *If something seems too good to be true, it motherfucking is, idiots.*

"I'm not," he said. "There are things . . . issues I need you to face with me. We will prevail; we will be happy."

Issues? How vague. But could they possibly be worse than the cartel's threat of a burning tire?

"And when I make you my wife, you will be looked after no matter what might happen to me."

Happen to him? Freaked out, I cried, "Are you dying?"

His tone was almost amused when he said, "No, *moy ángel.* But I want you to be a Sevastyan. It will make everything easier."

Victoria Sevastyan. Get the hell out! "This move would put us *both* firmly in the crazy camp. I don't know anything about you."

"I was born to make you happy. To protect you. Marry me, and I will free you. I will give you the entire goddamned world."

Free me? "You don't know anything about me either!"

"Do I not? I have identified the most beautiful, intelligent, talented female I will ever meet. Added to that, she is a wanton who makes my body burn." My cheeks flushed; my family was hearing this. "I will *never* find her equal. Why would I not want to secure her for my own?"

He sounded so logical. Where was the knee-jerk angst of before?

Dmitri cupped my face. "You said when you look at me a spell comes over you. *Let it.* Because I feel the same way when I look at you, and I've given myself up to it. Just surrender."

My eyes pricked with tears. Real ones. I blurted out, "I don't love you." I could imagine my family gazing heavenward. *Silly little Vice, gumming up the works.*

Dmitri canted his head, trying to read my expression. "*Could* you?"

As I considered his question, moments and impressions played in my mind. . . .

His teasing tone as I'd ogled his ass. The way I fit on his lap. My protectiveness toward him. The connection I felt when he drew my forehead to his. How he'd beheld my body as if it were a gift he'd treasure forever. His touch. His kiss.

I told him the truth: "Yes. I could."

He offered me his hand. Cuts remained across his palms from his nails. Because he'd fought to hold out last night. To keep his promise to me.

How could I not take that hand?

His eyes lightened to gold. "You're going to be my wife, aren't you?" His lips curled. His first half-smile.

My heart thudded. And. I. Was. Done.

✦

*J*n front of the justice of the peace, I fidgeted.

The ring was like a brand around my finger. The fit was perfect, but I kept banging my cheekbone every time I tucked my hair behind my ear—a nervous tell I'd trained myself out of when little.

Of course, I had no ring for Dmitri, since I hadn't had the time or the money to buy one. But standing here empty-handed still felt weird.

Since I'd met him, my life had been like quicksand; the more I tried to right myself—to *do* right by my family *and* by Dmitri—the deeper I sank with him. As if fate wouldn't have it any other way.

What were his issues? What would he do when I asked for a divorce?

A traitorous thought arose. *What if I . . . didn't?*

Sounding so proud to be marrying me, Dmitri had already said, "I do," in a deep, resounding voice.

I was really about to get hitched. Not *really* really. But it *seemed* genuine.

My turn. I met his eyes. As Dmitri had asked of me, I let the spell take over. As if from a million miles away, I heard myself murmur, "I do."

When the man said, "I now pronounce you husband and wife," my lips parted on a pent-up breath.

I could see a new emotion in Dmitri's gaze, and it frightened me more than any red flag.

Burning in his eyes was . . . *hope.*

CHAPTER 21

"The property begins here," Dmitri told me as the limo from the private airport turned onto a winding drive.

Gigantic sequoias flanked the way. Their shade was damp and green, so different from Vegas.

At every second on the plane ride here, I'd expected him to regret his rash behavior. Instead I'd detected relief. He'd proudly introduced me—to the pilot, the flight attendant, and his bodyguards—as his wife, Victoria Sevastyan. When he'd taken a brief call from Aleks, Dmitri had said my name a few times in their conversation, his gaze falling on me, satisfaction brimming in his eyes.

When I'd told him his jet was badass, he'd corrected me: "*Our* jet." Then he'd suggested I contact my family and update them while he made a couple of business calls.

To manage his empire? I could be a supportive fake wife. "Of course. Take your time."

I'd furtively snapped a pic of the ring to text, then dialed our conference line, keeping my end of the conversation as bland as possible. Pandemonium had reigned in the immediate family, everyone talking over each other. I kept picturing the Muppets overturning the Muppet Theater.

Dad, Al, and Gram wanted me to keep my new husband and be a happy billionairess girl. As Dad had said, "Sevastyan's mad for you, and we'll work out something on our end. We always do."

Mom, Pete, and Karin wanted me to "lose" the ring, smuggling it to them. After all, Dmitri would have it insured, and the take would be plenty to pay off the cartel for good.

Al had estimated its worth at . . . eight million.

Once the debt was squared, they suggested reconvening on this whole "marriage to a gull" problem. Because grifting wasn't just a job; it was a way of life.

Benji casually mentioned that a nine-figure divorce settlement wouldn't go amiss.

I'd never leave my family to the wolves. Two options remained. . . .

Now I glanced at my *husband*, sitting beside me in the limo.

He held himself very still, staring at me, taking in my reactions. How could he possibly read me when *I* didn't even understand what I was feeling? I knew only one thing for certain: Dmitri Sevastyan's generosity and trust had floored me.

Before I'd hung up earlier, Gram had asked, "Did you tell him the truth when you said you could love him?"

My face had burned to recall some of the other things Dmitri had told me just prior to that question (cough, *wanton*, cough). But again, I'd admitted the truth: "Yes."

What if I lose the ring and gain a husband? Then I wouldn't be such a bad person.

Maybe he needed me to defend him and his ridiculous

wealth—from people like me. I could identify and ward off cons. I could protect him.

But keeping him would mean distancing myself from my past—and my family, to an extent. *Rich people and con artists . . . cats and dogs.*

Barely able to look him in the eye, I turned and surveyed the forest.

"I think you will like our new home," he said, "but if you don't, we will buy more houses until you feel at home."

The second man today to call *his* house *my* home.

Had Dmitri's fight with Brett been only hours ago? My ex would hear that my wedding had taken place; everyone would. I didn't want to hurt Brett needlessly, but this news would force him to finally move on.

"You have been quiet since we left the courthouse," Dmitri said. "And you hardly ate lunch." A four-course affair with silver and china, served at thirty thousand feet. "Again, I struggle to read you. Just don't . . . don't regret this, Vika."

I turned to him, my nerves getting the better of me. "*You* are going to regret it! You're going to wake up and realize what you've done." Again I told him, "You don't know anything about me."

He parted his lips to say something, then clearly rethought it. "I know enough."

"Would you really have told me good-bye today?"

"Never," he said like a promise.

I narrowed my eyes. "Then you lied."

"Did I?"

Say yes or say good-bye. Tricksy Russian!

"Perhaps I manipulated you into this"—*oh, not quite, Dmitri*—"but I will never lie to you."

My family had maneuvered him, plotting in the background, using Brett in the service of our biggest con.

Dmitri reached for his briefcase on the opposite seat. "I had my lawyers draw up a contract for you." He pulled a folder out. "Here. I printed it before we landed." *Our* jet had an office. Natch. "Read this, and sign it."

Ah, the dreaded postnup. With all that talk about trust and spells and potentially love, I'd found myself getting caught up in the fairy-tale-esque nature of our courtship. Now reality reared its head.

Because fairy tales didn't exist.

Though I would probably be divorced soon, I felt a twinge of disappointment in him. I opened the folder, finding only a couple of pages. One was the postnup, the second an identical copy. Both had been signed by Dmitri in a bold, sharp scrawl.

I read it, my bemusement deepening. "This ... this says once the marriage is consummated, I get half of everything in the case of a divorce. Pretty much no questions asked."

"I want you to feel comfortable about the international ramifications of this marriage. That contract will be filed in both the United States and Russia."

Talk about trust. *Or else craziness.* "Are you dicking with me?" I would take a picture of the page and text it at the earliest.

"No. I am not."

Only one thing about the wording pinged my suspicion radar. "Is a consummation clause standard in Russian marriage contracts?" To work my con, I'd have to sleep with him. It fully sank in that Dmitri Sevastyan and I would be having sex. Soon.

"Is that objectionable?"

"No, of course not."

"If you will . . ." He gave me a pen.

I flattened my left hand on the page to sign, but my ring glared at me accusingly. Damn it! I faced Dmitri. "Look, why don't we take care of business stuff tomorrow when you've had a chance to mull everything over?" asked the grifter who was one signature away from five hundred million dollars.

I was having a crisis of identity! All because of this man. His craziness was catching!

"*Nyet.* I need you to sign this now. I told you I dislike uncertainty. Do me this service."

As in, do him a favor? He looked unbending.

Think of Mom and Dad, I repeated to myself. I signed my name to both copies and kept my own. Just because I *could* bilk Dmitri for half a billion didn't mean I *would.* Right? *I only need a nibble.* "Speaking of uncertainty, will you tell me what you meant by issues?"

I got the sense he regretted mentioning that. "We have all the time in the world to discuss such things. For now, let's enjoy our wedding day."

As a grifter, I should let the subject drop right there. Nothing should be allowed to get in the way of our wedding day—and night—enjoyment. Consummation equaled payout.

But as a woman utterly fascinated with this man, I said, "If you'd like to talk, I'm right here."

He wasn't budging. "I will keep that in mind."

I glanced out the window. We were still on the driveway? A brook flowed alongside the drive. Squirrels played on the lichen-covered logs, twitching their tails between rays of afternoon sunlight. *Magical.*

Any minute now I would wake up in my depressing

apartment and realize this had all been a dream. Surreal did not begin to describe my day. And it was far from over. "How long have you lived here?" I asked him.

"I never have. I bought it with the idea that one day I might have a wife and children. The property's size lends it privacy."

"Lemme guess, you bought this place about a year ago?" I asked, angling to find out about his near-death experience.

He didn't bite. "Approximately."

"How big is the property?"

"Thousands of acres. And miles of frontage."

I raised my brows. "Miles of the Cali coast? That must have been expensive."

"I hope you will find it worth the price." He motioned toward the window.

The drive widened, opening up to a breathtaking scene.

Fields of windswept wildflowers. Sun-dappled water. A mansion perched on an oceanfront cliff.

The spectacular structure was modern with glass everywhere. Glass doors, soaring windows, even some transparent walls.

My jaw dropped. "It . . . this place . . . I . . . *seriously*?"

"Vika, your reaction is even better than I had imagined. And I imagined it countless times."

I could barely wait for the car to stop. I scrambled out to see better, Dmitri right behind me.

I followed that stream all the way to the front entrance. To reach the door, we crossed square stepping-stones over the water. "How cool is that!"

We entered, and I about fell over. The stream meandered under the house. I knew this because a winding swath of the *floor* was glass. "Holy shit."

The open layout meant the Pacific was already visible. French doors allowed in a sea breeze and the muted sound of waves. A large pool and a hot tub dominated the terrace out front.

Between breezes, food scents hit me. I followed them to a dazzling modern kitchen.

Two men were finishing up what looked like a banquet for a hundred people. Dmitri explained they were our chef and his assistant.

Our chef. Of course. Why the hell not? The two men spoke to Dmitri in French. He translated: "The refrigerators and larders will be stocked for days."

"Oh. Um, that's great." I thanked them, then resumed my exploration. I started toward the water, but a stairway came into view. The contemporary steps were unconnected, appearing to float in the air.

I headed up, with Dmitri unobtrusively shadowing me. I appreciated that he was letting me take everything in at my own pace.

From the landing, I entered a glass-walled gallery, my heels clicking over the polished hardwood floor. I crossed the threshold of what had to be the master bedroom suite. We passed a dressing room. A middle-aged housekeeper was already unpacking my things.

The smiling woman finished up, speaking to us in Russian.

Dmitri replied in the same, but I heard my new name in there. To me, he said, "This is Galina. She speaks little English. But you'll be picking up Russian soon enough."

Mouth gone dry, I said, "Sure thing." I eked out a smile for the woman as she left. Then I continued inside.

In keeping with the modern design, the master bedroom

had built-ins and sleek cabinets, but minimal furniture. A handwoven rug that screamed of money broke up the stretch of wood flooring. An abstract canvas made a focal point above the fireplace mantel.

And then there was the huge platform bed. We'd have sex there tonight. Whoa.

Opened french doors led to a balcony. As if in a trance, I made my way to the glass rail.

Seagulls hovered on air currents not thirty feet away. Below us, the pool's surface shimmered in the late afternoon sun. A manicured walkway connected the terrace to a cove with a sandy beach.

And beyond: the water.

An endless sapphire expanse.

I murmured, "Dmitri, I've never seen so far." I'd once bought a bolt of cloth in "Pacific blue," but I hadn't comprehended the color.

I'd never understood a sea breeze.

A spray of white caught my eye, then another. Something sliding through the ocean . . . "Look!" I whirled around and grabbed his hand. "Whales! *Real* ones." Not high rollers.

The corner of his lips tilted up. "They migrate past here."

No way! "You can see all of this from your balcony?"

"You can see all of this from *our* bed."

I dragged my gaze from his face and turned back to the water. "Amazing."

"And you haven't even beheld the sunset. I have to warn you, though, it does rain here a lot. Much more than you're used to."

"But that's why it's so green." Unlike my apartment complex, where drifting sand chased me across the parking lot.

He turned me to face him, the warm breeze ruffling his hair. "You want to make our home here?"

I wished he'd simply asked me if I liked it. The odds of me living here for an extended period were slim—not when spending my days with him meant losing days with my family.

I forced myself to hold his gaze. "The property's stunning, Dmitri." *He* was stunning. "I'm pretty sure I've died and gone to heaven."

Never taking his eyes off me, he said, "I am certain I have."

CHAPTER 22

"What do you think?" I asked Dmitri, modeling a bikini I'd designed.

He'd been doing laps in the heated pool while I'd gotten settled and changed, but he treaded water to avidly view my suit. His expression said, *Are you kidding me?*

A cutout in the center of the black bandeau top displayed my cleavage. The red thong bottom had a flirty tie on each side for even easier access. I turned in a circle for him.

Voice rumbling, he said, "I think I am going to enjoy being married very, very much." He swam to the steps. "And this is further evidence you're an exhibitionist. Did you design it?"

"I did." I'd packed the bikini, having no idea it'd be part of my freaking trousseau. "It's made of . . ." I lost track of what I'd been saying when he emerged from the water.

He wore board shorts that hung low on his narrow hips, a dive watch, and nothing else. Drops sluiced over his rugged muscles, his rigid pecs and washboard abs. He was semihard and growing.

The sight of him swindled my breath yet again. I wanted

more of what he'd given me, craved to touch every inch of that body.

"Do you want something to drink or eat?" he asked.

"Hmm? Oh." Gourmet snacks had been arranged on the outdoor dining table in an enticing display, along with a champagne bucket. "Champagne sounds great."

He crossed to the table, shaking out his hair in such a guy way; reminders that he was a mere mortal thrilled me.

He inspected the vintage, then popped open the bottle. After pouring two flutes, he gave me one and took my free hand in exchange. "Watch the sun set with me, *moya zhena*."

"What does that mean?"

He led me to the steaming hot tub. "My wife."

Heart thud. "Sure. Why not?" I sank into the warm water, sitting beside him on the bench. "Your bodyguards aren't going to be coming around, are they? I might be an exhibitionist, but *not* with your employees."

He'd already sent the chef, assistant, and the housekeeper home for a couple of days.

"Understood. *Our* bodyguards have a house on the property, and monitor security through cameras."

"Cameras?" I frowned over my shoulder.

"Only on the other side. No one can approach the house by land without being monitored, but we have privacy on the ocean side. Motion sensors only."

"The place is seriously high-tech." Earlier, he'd introduced me to the house. You could talk to it: "Lights." "I'm cold." "Music."

His expression was amused, eyes crinkling at the sides. "Well, I *am* a tech genius."

I grinned. "I don't even know what you used to do."

"I'll explain my work soon. And you can teach me about clothing design."

Would I be here long enough? *Pang.*

With a sigh, I turned toward the ocean, taking a generous sip from my flute. Right now my family was celebrating with the bubbly too. *Cheers, guys. Go Muppets.*

I wished they could see this sunset. Rays blazed over the water, setting it aflame, and I had a front-row seat.

Because of Dmitri Sevastyan. He'd wanted me to draw back curtains for him? He was drawing them back for me.

"I believe the display is best when there are low storm clouds," he said. "We'll have rain soon."

"It looks too wild to be real." That dreamy sense persisted.

"The night you and I met, I imagined watching a sunset here with you."

I faced him with a smile, thinking he was kidding.

But his sunstruck eyes held my gaze. "With my first sight of you, I was done-in. All this shining blond hair and these shapely curves drew my eyes like a magnet. You looked like an angel to me. One with an edge." An edge? He should see me sharp cards. "My chest tightened, and my pulse raced."

"Really?" No nails-over-chalkboard sensation. He was telling the truth.

He nodded. "When I registered the blue of your eyes, I believed I was having a heart attack. I thought I would die—with you as my last sight."

Intense man! My flute shook on the way to my lips. I'd already drained it?

"Our courtship might have been brief, but it was grueling all the same—because I've never wanted anything so badly, and I knew I would get only one shot at winning you."

"I understand you were attracted to me, but don't you have a history of pursuing something all hot and heavy, then losing interest? It kind of sounded like that happened with your computer work."

He took my empty glass, setting his and mine aside. The muscles in his damp forearm flexed and something caught my attention. I squinted, able to make out the faintest scar running across his wrist, then up his arm.

The first hint of an imperfection on this man's body. From a surgery?

Before I could ask, he said, "I had goals I wanted to accomplish in my career, and once I did, I turned over my work. My goal with you will take a lifetime to achieve."

"What goal?"

"I told you I would always want more from you. Affection. Attachment. There is no limit. I will coax it from you." He pulled me across his lap, then coiled his arms around me.

"You just put a ring on it, Dmitri." God, had he ever. It still branded my finger. "Seems like you got a lot of me today."

"There's a difference between being wed and being married. We were wed today, but I want our lives entangled, until they are seamless. Until the line between us blurs to nothing."

I almost wished I hadn't grown so jaded, so I could believe in fairy tales and love at first sight. Take away my armor, and I would be head over heels for Dmitri already.

He was a dream man who'd brought me to a dream home to watch a dream scene. Lava-orange and yellow and scarlet battled in the sky. "This is all make-believe."

"This can be our life," he rasped at my ear. "I want it to be."

What if you found out something bad about me? I needed to ask him—but that would only make him look harder.

He curled his finger under my chin. "I haven't kissed my wife nearly enough today." He leaned in.

His lips covered mine, and I let myself fall under his spell again. When my lids slid shut, I saw residual images of the sunset—and his eyes.

Lady Luck help me, this felt like . . . a *beginning*. A true one.

Once I was panting against his lips, he drew back, a wicked gleam in his gaze. "I want you to watch that sunset while I touch you. I'm going to play with you till dusk." He untied my bathing suit top, peeling it off my breasts. He cupped one, and his breath gusted over the top of my sensitive ear. "You're not to cover these when we're alone."

I nearly moaned. To walk around topless in a glass house? It was as if he'd bought it with an exhibitionist in mind! Simply being outside and half-dressed was a huge turn-on. Steam kissed my stiff nipples, but then a cool breeze would come tickle them.

He leaned down and nuzzled one peak. He drew it between his lips, flicking it with his tongue.

I whimpered, cradling his head.

He sucked harder, tugging at my nipple just shy of discomfort, but I loved it. As he moved to my other breast, his hands dipped, and he untied the bow at the side of my bottoms, pulling those away as well.

CMNF.

Leaving my breasts aching, he straightened to run his lips up my neck. "I want your body open to my touch." He maneuvered me on his lap until I was leaning with my back to his chest and my feet flat on his knees. Under my ass, his erection strained against his shorts. Then he spread his own legs, forcing me to part my thighs. "That's it." His fingertip grazed my entrance. "Now keep watching. Whenever you see a Pacific sunset, I want you to remember this pleasure." Under the water, he eased his middle finger inside me, lazily thrusting it.

My gasp turned to a moan when he wedged his ring finger into me as well, making a rock-on gesture. "So tight." He thrust his two fingers harder, his palm cupping my clit.

My head lolled, but he said, "Ah-ah, beautiful. Keep your eyes on the sun."

With effort, I did, though he kept up the pumping motion of his hand.

"I need you to be ready for me."

Because we were about to have sex. And his cock was unnervingly large. "How long has it been for you?"

"Longer than you can imagine," he answered. "I *should* know."

What should he know? Maybe his English was off. The thought faded as I edged closer to my orgasm.

"Open yourself to me." Even his voice was hypnotic. "In all ways."

I wanted to. I wished I could.

"Are you watching the sun, Vika?"

Through a haze of pleasure and steam, I watched. On either side of the sinking sun were inky black storm clouds. "It's almost there, Dmitri," I said, talking about the sunset— and my orgasm. "It's so *close*." The winds picked up as the last glowing sliver disappeared. "There. All of it." In the distance, lightning flared over the dark water.

"Are you ready for me, *moya zhena*?" My wife.

I didn't think I'd ever needed sex more than I did at that

moment. Which was saying something after the last three nights. I turned to him, not bothering to hide the need in my expression.

Curt nod. "I'm taking you to our bed." He swooped me from the water, striding across the pool deck with my naked body tucked against him. As he carried me up the stairs, I couldn't keep still. I kneaded the muscles of his chest, rubbing against him.

"Look at you." He gazed down at me as if staggered by what he found in his arms. "I carry my greatest treasure."

Irresistible man.

Inside the bedroom, he told the house, "Fire," and the fireplace near the platform bed flickered to life. He let me slide down his body as he set me on my feet.

"I need you naked, Dmitri." I reached for his bulging shorts, drawing the tie loose, and he helped me work the sodden material over his dick.

The sight of him unclothed before the fire left me thunderstruck. Flames lovingly painting his muscles, his long lean body, his tanned skin. His pierced erection.

I went to my knees on the rug and grasped him with both hands. "You're going to have to pry me away from this." I tenderly ran my cheek against his shaft.

In answer, his Adam's apple bobbed, and he rested his big hands on my head.

Lightly stroking him, I cupped his dusky balls, hefting their warm weight. "These look like they ache."

Slow, solemn nod.

I nuzzled his sac, his scent intoxicating me. He groaned, widening his stance for more. When I tugged on his balls, his cock jerked with excitement, precum beading on the crown.

I leaned in to rub the slippery, plum-colored head against my lips, then I licked them for his taste. *Sublime.* "Swallowing you last night only whetted my appetite."

His brows drew together, as if he was racked with disbelief—and delight. "Vika . . ."

I gave him another lick, then circled the crown. Peering up at him to gauge his reaction, I flicked that ring with my tongue. "I could play with this forever. My new favorite toy."

Flick, flick. Flick, flick.

He shuddered, his torso muscles rippling. "Suck it between your lips."

I gripped the base of his shaft as my mouth closed tight over the swollen tip. *"Ummm,"* I moaned around it, letting him feel the vibrations.

"Fuck! Take it deep for me!"

As I moved farther down his length, I pumped my fist, hand and mouth working together. All the while, I held his gaze.

"Look at your plump lips clinging to my cock! You suck me like you've been waiting your entire life for it."

I felt like I had been! When my other hand drifted down to frig my clit, a ragged groan broke from his chest.

"Are you wet?"

In answer, I raised my damp fingers for him to taste.

His shaft pulsed against my tongue as he quickly leaned down. "Ah, my good wife!" He sucked my slick fingers clean, snarling in bliss, his seed climbing.

He released them with the terse order: "Keep fingering yourself."

When I resumed with another moan, he thrust his hips, then seemed to make an effort to be still.

I wanted to tell him it was okay, but I was too busy devouring him, too busy edging my own orgasm.

"Continue looking up at me! Look at me, and you'll fucking keep me here." What did that *mean*? "I'm close!" His accent had never been so thick. "Can't hold back from you much longer!"

I hollowed my cheeks and sucked him without mercy, until his cock throbbed between my lips and I teetered right on the verge. . . .

Just when I thought he'd treat me to his cum, his body stilled. "Wait. *Wait . . .*" He cradled my face.

I hadn't heard him correctly.

"Wait!" He eased my head back. His cock slipped free of my greedy mouth.

"Dmitri?"

He gazed down at me with such a stark look of hunger, I gasped.

I'd never seen a desperate need like that on a man's face. "Have I done something wrong?"

"*Nyet.*" He looked gutted with want. "I am better off *not* knowing."

Damn it, not knowing *what*? "Tell me what you mean."

He helped me to my feet, then moved to sit on the edge of the bed. He raised his hands to his head, fingers splayed as if he were trying to crush his own skull.

I sat beside him. "Dmitri?" I touched his back.

He flinched.

"What would you rather not know?"

He rose with his fists clenched, the tendons in his arms and neck taut like bowstrings. He jerked his head from side to side, opening his mouth to say something, only to snap it shut. The warring emotions in his eyes reminded me of the feverish colors of that sunset. Just as incomprehensible.

"Dmitri, talk to me, please."

He disappeared into his dressing room, returning in jeans, but his tension had only ratcheted up. Beginning to pace, he broke into an angry spate of Russian, gesturing heatedly. I heard his own name among those words; talking to himself again?

"Please tell me what your issues are."

Seeming overwhelmed with confusion and frustration, he squeezed his head once more. The muscles in his forearms contracted, drawing my gaze to that faint scar. Based on his behavior right now, I worried that mark *hadn't* been surgical.

Without warning, he launched a fist into one of the cabinets, splintering the wood. Another hit and another.

Once I recovered from my shock, I leapt off the bed to reach him. "Stop that!" I grabbed his arm.

He turned heartbreaking eyes to me. "And if I can't?"

I should've been running the other way, but the torment in his expression was killing me. I took his banged-up fist in my hands, and gradually got him to lower it. "Tell me what's wrong, Dmitri."

He shook his head. He was so beautiful outside, and so clearly damaged inside. *Beautiful, fucked-up man.*

"You told me I would need to help you," I reminded him. "I want to, but you have to talk to me."

"If I do this now, and my mind drifts . . . will I come back from it?"

Drifts? "Come back from what?"

His eyes darted. "The more pleasure I feel, the worse it is. And pleasure with you, Vika, is in a different goddamned *realm*. Your lips could turn any man mad."

"What does that mean? What did I do?"

"Maybe I didn't work hard enough, or I wasn't clever enough." Again he squeezed his head, as if he wanted to purge it of thoughts. "I believed I could do this. I misjudged everything." His tone sounded wretched.

"We can figure something out, Dmitri! Just talk to me. *Please.*"

He drew back from me, then strode toward the bedroom door. Over his shoulder, he murmured, "I am . . . sorry."

—————————————

CHAPTER 23

*D*azed, I shrugged into a robe, the terry cloth skimming my sensitive nipples. Dmitri had left me in a state, despite my bewilderment.

I curled up in the bed. What should my next move be? My first impulse was to call my sister, but this situation felt too private—as if I'd be betraying Dmitri to reveal this secret.

Wasn't I betraying him enough already?

Angry Russian words began booming from another room. I really hoped he had made a call and was talking to someone other than himself. Based on the pauses in his tirade, I assumed so.

What had happened to him? What was the source of his damage? I'd never known anyone who'd attempted suicide. Had he?

I gazed down at my ring, and tears welled. There'd been hope in Dmitri's eyes today, somehow connected to having sex with me. He'd worked and planned, but it hadn't been enough.

Dmitri's hopes had been dashed. That wrecked me.

Lightning bolts forked over the Pacific. I got under the duvet and waited for rain. Sure enough, it started to fall. Then pour.

Time ticked by. . . .

I glanced at the nightstand clock. Only nine? The storm still raged outside. Dmitri still raged on the phone.

I reviewed what I knew. Physically, he'd been ready, but not mentally. He'd known difficulties might loom, so this must have happened before. His mind *drifted* when he felt pleasure.

Benji had once told Karin and me he used to dissociate during sex. I'd looked it up and read cases about sexual abuse survivors who would go into a fugue state of detachment during a sexual encounter, having little to no memory of it.

Benji's abuse had been on the streets. Once an orphan in India, he'd fallen into the clutches of a ruthless adoption racket. Shortly after he'd arrived in Nevada, the company had shut down, its victims cast to the winds. He'd been defenseless.

When we'd first taken him in, I'd overheard my mom and dad talking about me.

"I've never seen Vice so protective of anyone," Mom had said.

Dad had grated, "Because no one's ever needed her—or our—protection more."

But I hadn't been able to *do* anything to help my new brother.

Could I help Dmitri?

When he said his mind drifted, did he mean *dissociated*? Had *he* been abused?

His parents had died when he was young. Maybe he and his brothers had been shipped off to somewhere dangerous in the remote north of Russia. Who the hell knew what could have happened twenty-five years ago?

This would explain his driving need to be in control. And

Dmitri had said his trust had been burned "early along the line."

I glanced in his direction. My father was right. Marriage cons could feel real, and right now I wanted to murder anyone who harmed my "husband."

When Dmitri fell silent, I sat up. Would he come back to me or should I go find him?

He returned not long after, much calmer, but he still simmered with . . . *something*. His hair had dried into tousles—far from his perfect look—but I found him even more compelling this way. He was certainly a mortal tonight.

What should I say? I settled on: "Hi."

He nodded. In a halting tone, he said, "You must be confused about my behavior. You must be anxious." He sounded as if he quoted someone. Had Maksim told him that? Whoever he'd called was reasonable at least.

I brought my knees to my chest. "I am."

"I didn't mean to frighten you. We're going to start over now." He drew the duvet away from me. "Take off your robe."

Huh? He wanted to have sex without any explanation? I was about to tell him we needed to talk, but then he unzipped his jeans and pulled them off. A breath escaped me.

Dmitri clearly needed to do something other than talk.

He sat on the edge of the bed and reached for me, stroking the backs of his fingers over my jawline. "When I'm inside you, I want you to look at me."

I met his fierce gaze. *As if I can take my eyes away.*

He joined me in the bed and drew the cover over us. As he guided me down with him, his hands shook.

There we lay, our heads on the same pillow. He moved even closer, and the head of his dick skimmed my belly.

I shivered to feel moisture daub my skin. I was allowing him to begin seducing me. I *wanted* him to seduce me. My mind might be in turmoil, but my body wanted his.

He brought our foreheads together. "I would risk anything to have you." He cupped my face and leaned in, his lips brushing mine. His thumbs rubbed over my cheeks, as if he couldn't caress me enough, couldn't *feel* me enough.

I threaded my fingers through his thick hair. When he dipped his tongue to mine, the contact was as charged as the lightning outside.

He stroked my tongue with his, until we were twining them. Deeply. Sharing breaths.

Oh, dear God, that kiss. I'd known he needed me; he translated that need. He'd given me lifeline looks. Now he was giving me a lifeline kiss.

And it turned—me—inside—out.

I wanted to take him in my arms and give and give and give.

One of his hands descended to cup between my legs. He found me aching for him and groaned against my lips.

His broad crown nudged my entrance. This was happening? I could feel his piercing; the metal was sizzling.

He broke our kiss to catch my eyes. "Are you ready, *moya zhena?*" He rubbed the head up and down my pussy, spreading my wetness. Again and again, he did this—as if he readied to cross a line but still debated it.

Every time the tip met my entrance, I tilted my hips to catch him. I was shaking for it, clutching his shoulders. My wedding ring caught my attention, and a sense of déjà vu hit me, as if it had always adorned my finger—and always would. I faced him. "I'm ready."

His jaw was set, those dark amber eyes claiming me as much as his body was about to. He held my gaze as he worked the head in. His rigid shaft forced my flesh to yield.

He gave a shallow pump of his hips, making me cry out.

So much pleasure. . . .

A groan rumbled from his chest, and sweat misted his skin. He continued deeper, filling me, claiming me.

Changing me.

I was never going to be the same after this. Even in the midst of my chaotic emotions, I recognized that.

Once he was seated deep within me, we lay frozen like that. He rasped, *"Rai."* Heaven.

I panted. "Yes, it is."

"Who would ever want to leave heaven?"

As in drifting?

"Just keep looking at me, Vika. My God, the way your body feels . . . we'll know soon enough." He moved me to my back, resting between my thighs. His powerful frame loomed over me.

I tested his command with his first full thrust—because my eyes rolled back in my head. "Oh, my God." I melted around him, gripping his arms.

"I need to look into your beautiful eyes."

I met his gaze, struggling to catch my breath. *"Dmitri."* His name was my plea for more.

He pulled his hips back, then slowly rocked inside me. "You belong to me now." His voice was hoarse. "Irrevocably."

My back arched, my nipples grazing his dampened chest.

With his next thrust, he bit out words in Russian.

My nails dug into his skin. "English, baby. I want to know. . . ."

"I knew it was you," he said, his expression half-crazed. He gripped one of my hips, stretching his thumb to rub my clit.

I whimpered from the added sensation.

"I knew you'd be my wife. I am obsessed with you, Victoria. Always will be."

Right now I understood. He was a dream lover, using his flawless body to deliver pleasure. Maybe I was already obsessed with him too. My hands dipped to grip his ass.

Still working my clit, he gave a harder thrust. And another. "I would've done anything to possess you! Remember that."

Every time I thought he couldn't go deeper, he'd plunge with more force, making me cry out in surprise. I was captivated by the wild look in his eyes and the feel of his ass working under my fingers.

He clamped the backs of my knees and bucked hard between my spread thighs. Sweat dripped from his forehead onto my bouncing breasts. "Your body drives me *mad*." He shoved inside me, stealing my breath.

My head thrashed. "Ah, God!" I locked my legs around his waist, couldn't get close enough to him.

"Give yourself to me." He clasped my nape and drew me up. "Give me everything you are!" He'd told me he would always want more, that he'd coax it from me. Now he was *demanding* I surrender to him.

To this life.

He was demanding it with his enthralling eyes. With his unyielding grip on my body.

"Dmitri!" I fought the pleasure, wanting this never to end. "I'm so close . . . so close!"

"You wear my ring." *Thrust.* "You always will. You're my wife. Say it." *Thrust.*

Falling deeper under his spell, I said, "I'm your wife."

He gnashed his teeth. "Again!"

"I'm your *wife*!" He made me say it over and over, till I was murmuring it on my own, mesmerizing myself.

At my ear, he confessed: "It was always going to be you. Or it never would have been."

A sudden scream burst from my lungs. I orgasmed, not just from sensation—but from *emotion*. My fingers clutched at him, nails digging in.

"I *feel* you . . . feel you coming for me!"

I writhed beneath him, pleasure coursing through every inch of me. In those shattering moments, I *was* his.

Connected to him as I'd never been to another.

I'd barely drifted back to reality when he commanded, "Cross your arms over your chest."

I didn't ask, only obeyed.

He grabbed my wrists and trapped me with my own arms. I couldn't move if I wanted to. This was bondage—without leather or chains. Just a man taking his pleasure.

Once I was positioned as he desired, Dmitri Sevastyan started . . . to *fuck*.

He rammed his massive body between my thighs, using his grip on me for leverage. Pistoning his cock inside me from hilt to tip, he pounded my pussy.

I'd never felt anything so deep, as if he were taking my virginity. "What're you *doing* to me?"

He seemed to cling to the last of his control. "Fucking—my—wife."

"*Ahhh!*" I came with a scream. He slammed me harder. I came again.

He was railing my mind blank, long-dicking me into

oblivion. Only one thought remained: *I'm his.*

Over the sounds of his skin slapping mine, he bit out, *"Uhn! About to give you my cum! Fucking worth it—"*

His body froze. A guttural yell broke from his chest.

Our gazes locked. His was anguished. I don't think he breathed.

Then he began to ejaculate.

With his first searing jet, he heaved in air. Hips jerking uncontrollably, cock pulsating, he gave a frenzied roar: *"VICTORIA!"*

He plunged furiously, his yells matching each new flood of semen. His release pumped on and on . . . until my body had drained his.

A last groan passed his lips. A shudder down to his bones.

Lost, he rasped, *"Mine."* Then he collapsed atop me.

We lay for some time, catching our breath. My heart raced; his pounded in answer.

"Hurting you?" he asked.

"Uh-uh." Hurt? I floated. "That was more than just sex." My tone was awed.

He rose on straightened arms. Lids heavy, he looked as drugged as I felt. "Still here."

My chest squeezed when a tear tracked from one of his eyes. "Baby?"

"You." His throat was working, as if he was getting control of his emotions. "You don't know what you've done."

I felt alarm. "What?"

"Everything."

I was trying to sort out my confusion when his lips curved fully, showing off even white teeth against tanned skin. His first real smile with me.

I sucked in a breath. His eyes turned molten gold, and he looked ... jubilant. As if we'd pulled off the greatest coup ever.

Deeper under his spell. "Better?"

"Best. A world away from the past." His cock pulsed inside me, already beginning to harden. His jubilant look changed, darkening. "Which means I have *a lot* to make up for, wife. . . ."

CHAPTER 24

*R*ain pattering against the windows woke me. Disoriented, I gradually remembered where I was.

"Dmitri?" No sign of him. The bedside clock read quarter to four in the morning.

He'd taken me numerous times, until I'd passed out with him spooning me, still inside me.

Feeling a tendril of unease, I rose and donned a robe. When I didn't find him anywhere on the second floor, I hurried downstairs.

From the kitchen, I spied a shadowy figure across the windswept field. Lightning flashed, illuminating the scene.

Dmitri?

He was half-dressed, standing at the cliffside. What the hell was he doing out in a storm? I rushed toward a pair of french doors.

I'd never asked him about the scar on his arm. Had he been suicidal? Was he *still?*

Heart in my throat, I tore open a door and raced headlong into the rain, shielding my eyes.

The idea of losing him . . .

The winds howled and waves crashed. The ground vibrated beneath my feet with each impact. Thunder boomed.

He stood too close to the edge; sea spray flung by the waves lashed his ankles. He wore only jeans, his chest bare. He tilted his head back, letting the rain beat against his face, and opened his arms wide.

I blinked against the pelting drops, disbelieving my eyes.

He was . . . smiling.

"Dmitri!"

He lowered his head and turned to me, offering his hand.

Though I was nervous about the drop-off, I took it. Over the wind, I cried, "You don't need to be out here."

"It is a good storm, love."

I put my palm on his warm chest. "You're not cold, but you're shaking. Why are you shaking?"

"I don't know how to describe . . ." His accent was thick. "I feel . . . I feel . . . *so much*. And it is all new to me." Were tears tracking down his face, or were those drops of rain? "I keep thinking about the word *disintegrate*. To cause to fall apart. I was integrated for more than thirty-two years, and now I am something else."

"I don't know what you mean."

He clutched me close, then tilted his head back again, basking in the storm. "I feel skinned alive. Raw and exposed."

"That sounds awful."

He lowered his face, meeting my eyes. His lashes were spiked with moisture, his black hair whipping across his cheeks. "It is *pure*. I live anew now."

Were these mad ramblings? Or was he baring his heart?

Why couldn't I make sense of what he was saying? "I want to understand you. Help me!"

"I planned for this night; I prepared for it. Yet in the back of my mind, I feared my past would win—as it always had before. But I had a wife, a responsibility. Sex was no longer about me; it is about *us*. And I cared more about your pleasure than I cared about registering my own. If I drifted for a time, you probably wouldn't know. If I stayed gone, you would be taken care of."

Stayed gone? As in, losing touch with reality permanently?

"I stopped fighting it." He covered my shoulders with his big hands. "For the first time in my life, I—let—go. My struggles ended. Because of you, I had courage. I stopped trying to bandage my mind and said, 'Let it fucking bleed.'" His hold on me tightened. "But it *didn't*, Victoria. My wounds were seared and closed."

When a towering wave broke before us, he looped an arm around my waist and moved us back from the edge. "You trusted *me*, and I trusted *us*." He traced his thumb over my bottom lip. "*Moya zhena*, my beautiful wife. We can *begin*."

At that, this man, my husband, kissed me.

And I could taste the last of his tears.

CHAPTER 25

*D*awn neared when we began to doze off. After his catharsis in the rain, Dimitri had brought me inside, making love to me again.

Now I lay with my head on his chest, listening to his lulling heartbeat as he stroked my hair. I could have pressed him for answers, but my instinct said to share these hours with him in peace—without dredging up the past.

Reading my mind, he said, "In time, I will tell you everything."

"I know you will." Had he been somewhat crazy tonight? Yep. But I would roll with it for now, letting him set the pace.

"You have an idea though."

I nodded against him. "If you mean *dissociate* when you say *drift*, then yes."

He tensed beside me, then seemed to make an effort to relax again. *"Da."*

So he *had* been abused. My heart ached for him. "Is there anything I shouldn't do? I don't ever want to hurt you or remind you."

"There's nothing you could do. Just . . . just do not leave."
He was such a complicated, intriguing man. Sometimes all
dominant and in command; at other times vulnerable.

I'd known Dmitri Sevastyan for a mere four days. As he'd
said, there was a difference between being wed and being
married. I'd committed to one, but not to the other.

Could I, given time?

Over the day and night, I'd come to five conclusions.

One: I would never be more attracted to, or sexually
satisfied by, another man.

Two: His past only amplified my feelings—because he was
working so hard to achieve a better future. In spite of
everything, he *did* still hope.

Three: Though Dmitri's mental issues had probably
heightened his infatuation/obsession, it was possible he could
grow to truly love me.

Four: He desperately needed someone to look out for him.

Five: Even if I wanted to, I couldn't shed my jadedness
overnight.

At length, I told him, "When you wake up, I'll be here."
After I'd gotten some sleep, I would wrestle with my ever-
growing feelings—tenderness, gratitude, protectiveness, guilt.

"That's enough. For now." He stroked my hair till I was
almost asleep. "Vika?" His breaths were deep and even. He
was about to nod off as well. "Thank you."

"For what?"

"I'm honored to be your husband." He dozed off.

You beautiful, fucked-up man.

In sleep, he clutched the ends of my hair, as if he wanted to
leash me to him.

CHAPTER 26

"*Victoria?*" Dmitri yelled from the bedroom landing. He must've just awakened to find my side of the bed empty.

I quickly called, "Right in the kitchen!" I'd watched him sleep for hours before hunger had driven me downstairs.

Though I was a notoriously bad cook, I decided to make him breakfast in bed. Luckily, each dish in the refrigerators had been labeled with heating instructions and accompaniment suggestions.

As I warmed food, I'd texted Karin an update. Vice: Sister vault. I did a bad bad thing.

She would know what I meant, that I'd gotten too close to my mark, letting down my guard.

KV: How deep?

Vice: I'm attempting to make him breakfast in bed.

KV: WHO ARE YOU???

Vice: Like a sap, I watched him sleeping.

Figuring he needed the rest, I'd let him slumber on. His sigh-worthy face had been relaxed, a world away from the pain he'd shown when he'd balked at sex—or his euphoric expression on the cliff.

KV: I take it "consummation" went well. What's your move now?

Once I'd replayed the events of the night and wrestled with my feelings, I'd made a decision: I still wouldn't reach for the stars.

But maybe I could case their joint and look for an in.

Vice: I want to see where this leads.

KV: Which leaves the ring as your only option. I'll come pick it up, no more than 9 days from now.

Because Al would need time to convert it to cash.

Dmitri hastened into the kitchen wearing gray boxer briefs and nothing else. His eyes were a little wild, and he was out of breath. "Vika?"

"I waited beside you as long as I could, but then I decided to wake you up with food. Look"—I waved at the tray I'd put together—"I even put a flower in a vase, though that orchid I clipped probably cost a bazillion dollars."

"You're . . . topless." He swallowed.

I only wore a lacy black thong. "Why, I am!" I shook my shoulders to give him a jiggle, loving his brows-drawn look.

"Mercy," he said. "Now I *know* I'm still dreaming." Had he awakened only to believe everything had been a dream?

I had.

He stalked closer, all tousled black hair and hooded eyes. "Do you always eat topless?"

"Ah, see, my husband ordered me not to cover these."

He smiled. Fully! "Your husband sounds like a brilliant man."

My breath hitched. "He is. He's a tech genius." I craned my

head up. "I wanted to be there when you woke. I debated an alarm-clock BJ, breakfast, or tickling."

"In the future, I'd prefer two out of those three. And one in particular."

I pouted. "I picked the exact wrong one, didn't I?"

"Depends on what I'm served for breakfast." He swooped me into his arms, and carried me to the kitchen table. "I'm going to eat you up. . . ."

✦

*B*reakfast, take two.

Everything I'd heated would be cold by now. Good thing there was plenty more. "I'm starving," I told him as we began foraging.

"I know, I've never been so hungry." Dmitri rubbed his belly, drawing my attention to his chiseled abs and that black trail of hair leading down. . . .

I dragged my gaze away, needing to concentrate on food. Weren't there some croissants around here? I started the oven again.

"Do you like to cook?" he asked.

"I'm more of a dish-doer." I went to fetch butter and jam. "But I am an ace at heating and eating."

"What do you usually like to . . . ?" His voice faded to nothing.

I'd bent over at the fridge for another stick of butter, hadn't even meant to tempt him. I straightened and whirled around.

"*Vika!*" He crossed the distance in one long stride and grabbed my waist.

"Just a minute, big guy! You gotta feed me—"

His mouth descended over mine.

✦

$\mathcal{B}$reakfast, take three.

"This time I *have* to eat," I said between kisses. He had me pressed up against the counter, trapping me with his body.

"Then why do you keep seducing me?" He continued taking my mouth, so I forced myself to draw back and face him.

"You have two choices, Dmitri. You can control yourself, even when my tits move"—in the throes, he'd told me how wild that sight made him—"or you can go grab me one of your T-shirts."

"And that is the conundrum of my day? I like this life with you."

I grinned. I was liking it too. "I'll strip as soon as we're through."

"Not soon enough." He grumbled in Russian as he strode off. I leaned to keep him in sight. His ass was unreal. I'd left scratches on it over the night.

Inhaling for control, I poured coffee. How would he take his?

When he returned, I traded him a cup for a T-shirt. Had he found the thinnest one he owned? My nipples were visible. Sneaky Russian. "I don't know how you like your coffee—and how weird is that?—so I made it like mine."

He took a sip. "Good. Thank you."

"But it's not how you prefer." I narrowed my eyes. "Do you even drink coffee?"

He shrugged. "Not in a year." He'd had a seriously life-changing year.

"But you accepted the cup anyway?"

Nod.

Awww. "Could you be any sweeter?"

"I am very sweet on you." He set the coffee aside, getting that look in his eyes—half thrall, half dark lust.

I responded like a lit wick. *I did a bad bad thing.* Inner shake. "Whoa, Dmitri. Food."

He sighed. "Very well."

We rummaged, selecting sliced fruit and breakfast ham.

Once I'd satisfied the worst of my hunger, I asked him, "Do you always sleep so long?"

"Never. And never so soundly." He seemed a different man. He'd smiled *several* times—as if his smile had only been awaiting parole. "Maybe it's all part of the process."

I was dying to know more, but I could be patient. So I kept it light. "Did we do good last night?"

He lifted me up on the counter and stood between my thighs. "We did amazing, *zhena.*"

Now that the touch-and-go sexual situation had resolved itself, my usual worry took center stage. My family. I glanced at my ring.

"Something on your mind?"

I gave him my practiced smile. "I thought you couldn't read people."

"I can't," he said, his eyes lively. "But you stopped eating at last, so I figured something else was occupying you."

I play-punched his shoulder. "I've got a comedian on my hands? You should've put a weight clause in your postnup." I slapped my forehead. "Oh, too late . . ."

He almost chuckled. I was beginning to think of his laughter as a muscle that hadn't been worked out. We would ease it into use.

His expression turned serious. "I will always desire you no matter how you look."

I leaned in and nipped his bottom lip. "Lose your rock-hard abs, and I'm outta here." *Excellent, Vice, making jokes about leaving him?* Quick change of topic . . . "How do you foresee our days?"

"I want to take you all over the world. Or as far as we can get between your family's Sunday dinners."

Dinners Dmitri wouldn't be going to. "Don't you have a home in Russia you need to get back to?"

"No. After selling my company, I moved from one property to another." He added to himself, "Fleeing ghosts." Before I could ask about that, he said, "*We* have several properties I think you will enjoy."

"But you'll want to live in Russia eventually." *Say yes. Give me one major stumbling block.*

"No. I like California. I believe my bride does too."

Did I ever. "What would our regular day-to-day be like here?"

"Other than the hour I need to conduct business, I'm at your service. Once we've traveled and enjoyed ourselves, perhaps you'd like to pursue your dream of designing clothes. We should visit Paris and Milan and investigate where your interests lie."

Well, then. "Just hit up the fashion capitals of the world?"

"Why not? Money affords us an enviable entrée. We could attend shows and expos and tour the most famous houses. We could invite your friends or family. Or mine. Or both."

How would my crew get along with the Sevastyans? Didn't matter. I could never risk one of them slipping up and exposing us. I pictured what would happen if Dmitri found out he'd been maneuvered and used. Would he believe anything between us had been real? That I truly cared for him and wanted him to be happy?

"And, of course"—he reached for a breast—"you and I will provide each other vast amounts of sex."

But I leaned back. "Hold up, big guy. We're going to have to ice my pussy if you don't give it a little rest. It's gone from off limits to all access, zero to sixty."

He dropped his hand, squeezing it into a fist. "We're late for an appointment anyway."

"Appointment?"

"Yes, out on the water. So I'll give you a reprieve till tonight. But then I'm going to show you something I think you'll like. . . ."

CHAPTER 27

I sputtered when windblown spray from a whale's blowhole dotted my face.

They were swimming all around our kayak—that close! I cast a shocked look back at Dmitri. "Did that just happen?" I vibrated with so much excitement, I probably rocked the boat.

He flashed me a grin, looking like a god in the afternoon sunlight as he paddled us around. He wore a pair of board shorts. No shirt. The misted skin of his broad chest shimmered. "I'm a witness."

Earlier, he'd told me to hurry into a swimsuit or we'd be late, then rushed me down to the cove to hop in a kayak. When I'd hesitated, admitting I didn't know how, he'd pinched my chin and told me, "I've got you. Just relax, and let me do the work."

Now I breathlessly asked him, "How could you have an appointment for whales? How'd you know when they would show?" Benji would have given anything to be able to take pictures.

"There's an app for that. My phone sounded an alert when this pod started moving down the coast."

"Amazing. You keep boggling my mind. And all I've done today is shake my tits a little."

His grin widened. "I made the better bargain. Tell me, do you like our home?"

"Eh, s'okay, I guess." I shrugged. "Of course I freaking do! There are whales in the backyard!"

Another one surfaced even closer, and it had a baby! I gazed back at Dmitri, wanting him to see how thrilled I was.

"You know, they mate for life," he said, his expression telling me, *As have I.*

Whoa.

Once the pod moved on, Dmitri smoothly steered us farther along the coast. We rounded a headland into the next cove, and I caught sight of several bungalows dotting the hills. Their modern design and expanses of glass called to mind the main house. "What are those?"

"Guest residences." Each one would have a picture-postcard view of the ocean. "For family to visit."

My family consisted of approximately thirty Valentines and company. Hey, maybe we could hide from the cartel here.

Except then Dmitri would definitely figure out what we were. *What I am.*

Worry tempered my happiness. I gazed down at my ring wistfully. How would I smuggle it to Karin? I didn't want anyone to make an official visit, and the security cameras would prevent a drive-by on the sly. Maybe I could hide the ring out in the woods and leave my phone for her to track. I could tell Dmitri it must've slipped off in the ocean, so no one would get blamed for a theft. Yet another lie . . .

The diamond caught a ray of sun, aggressive pinpricks of

light stinging my eyes—as if it knew we coldly planned to fence it.

Yes, I was as superstitious as the next grifter, and I believed wedding rings were symbols.

By sacrificing the ring Dmitri had given me, would I jinx his feelings toward me?

Hell, would that even matter? I'd already stacked the cards against us.

◆

"While we were out, I had some things delivered," Dmitri said over dinner.

We were enjoying apricot-basil chicken salad and heated croissants out on the pool deck. He'd opened a bottle of yummy wine, mainly for my consumption.

The sea breezes were easy and warm, that saltwater scent getting into my blood. "What things?" *He* was getting into my blood. I sighed when the wind ruffled his hair and his unbuttoned white linen shirt. He wore broken-in jeans and was barefooted. I loved this casual side to him.

"Some wedding gifts."

"From you?" I gazed around at the house he wanted to call *ours*. "You haven't done enough?"

"Not until I've given you the entire world, as promised." In a teasing tone, he said, "I warned you I would spoil you to an embarrassing degree, yet you decided to be my bride anyway? Take your medicine, Vika."

I grinned. "Dmitri, I hadn't expected you to be this fun."

He blinked at me. "I hadn't expected anyone to consider me so. I have little experience with it."

Money truly couldn't buy happiness. "Today you had fun, right?"

After kayaking, we'd swum laps—or tried to—but we'd gravitated to each other in the water. I'd given him a slow hand job while he'd done more mind-blowing things with his fingers. Then we'd snacked and lazed naked in the late-afternoon sun.

Once we'd returned inside, we'd christened our large shower. I could swear the bench in the enclosure had been designed just for me to sit and suckle him. Not to be outdone, he'd lifted me to a high marble shelf, one seemingly made for me to relax back and spread for his kiss.

Fresh from coming in my mouth, he'd devoured me—and shown me a trick I could barely believe. . . .

"This has been the best day of my life," he said. "Each day with you easily trumps all others."

They *had* been great, but surely he'd had others make the podium. "No wonderful days from your childhood?"

Looking away, he said, "Not one that stands out."

"What was growing up in Siberia like?"

That muscle in his jaw ticked. "Cold, brutal, miserable."

Okay . . . "The weather? Or growing up?"

"Take your pick," he bit out, his demeanor telling me to back off.

I would. I could give him time, because his wounds were still healing—as part of *the process*. Besides, the less I dug into his past, the less he'd dig into mine. I changed the subject. "What do you usually do in your free time?"

"I haven't had any," he said, his tone softer, as if he appreciated the reprieve. "I've worked diligently on self-improvement."

I cast him a smile. "You and your changes."

"I needed to be ready when my dream woman came into my life."

Smile never faltering, I said, "Can you really call me your dream woman when you hardly know me?"

"I know plenty, Victoria."

I raised my brows. "Like what?"

"I have to pace you during oral sex, or else you come too fast. When you truly open your heart to another, you do so for life, and you're loyal to a fault. You're patient. You're protective. You're secretive. But I know you'll share all your secrets if I share mine. Your zest for life is boundless. And when your blue eyes brighten with happiness, I feel as if I've been drugged. To a man like me, you *are* a drug."

My lips parted.

Then I gazed away, thinking about my past. I could see now I hadn't truly opened myself up to Brett. If I had, I wouldn't be *this* over him. I knew I'd never receive another e-mail from him, and the only emotion I felt was regret that he'd been hurt.

Nothing more.

Maybe I'd tried to force that relationship because I'd been so enamored with *normal*. Maybe I'd held back my heart because deep down I'd known I was meant for a grifter.

So where did that leave me now? I was *married* to a gull, living the most abnormal existence I could imagine. "Wouldn't your dream woman be heavy into BDSM?" I asked. "To match you?"

"Oh, you will be," he assured me, his tone making me shiver. "Already you are an incredibly responsive and giving submissive."

I didn't know if I liked that word. Even if I loved to submit. "Have you been with a lot of submissives?"

"No. None that I know of."

I frowned. "Shouldn't you have tried out some others before you got married? What if you want, or need, to explore this with someone else?" Most men cheated—the nature of the beast, and all that—with far less reason.

"It's taken me my whole life to find you. I will neither want nor need another." God, he sounded confident. Smug, even. Like I might sound if I'd won the World Series of Poker. "Understand me, I will never be unfaithful to you. My wife deserves a devoted husband." He believed what he was saying.

The way he talked reminded me of the shining devotion exhibited by his brothers. If Dmitri *had* been cut from the same cloth, maybe he wouldn't cheat.

He might be the type of guy who went to Vegas with buddies and proudly kept his ring *on*.

But how could I ever trust that? *My hurdles are too high.* And in the end, the point was moot anyway.

With all the lies I'd told him?

"Why didn't you have a lover already?" I asked, only to recall his behavior with babes like Sharon. "Actually, strike that question. Why did you chase women away?"

"Because I was looking for more than a bed partner."

"My sister didn't tempt you?" With her toppled tray?

"I believe your sister must be a lovely person, but she does not compare to you. If you two were side by side, I would not even see her."

No guy had ever chosen me over Karin. "That's difficult for me to accept."

"I wish you could see inside my thoughts." His forehead

furrowed. Then he turned his thrall gaze on me. "Would you like to know how I view the world?"

Would I? I didn't know if I was ready to peek into his tricky, complicated mind. "Okay," I said, the word sounding more like a question.

"Imagine a pitch-black room with a single candle lit in the center," he said, his voice gone low. "The room is the world. You are the candle."

A shaky breath escaped my lips. "How can you be so sure about me?"

He leveled his spellbinding gaze on my face. "When you've been in the dark as long as I have, *moy ángel*, there is no mistaking the light."

Whenever he said things like that, *he* was the dream. *If something's too good* . . . "I worry what you feel for me will burn up like a comet. It's too fast and heated to be sustained." We would hit our two-week anniversary, and he wouldn't be able to stand the sight of me.

"In time, you'll trust my feelings more. After your ex's infidelity, I understand why you find it difficult to relax your guard with me. But I'm not him. I will never lie to you. Everything I do, every action I take, is for your happiness. Remember that."

No nails over chalkboard.

He rose. "Come. I want to see your eyes light up again."

I stood, accepting his offered hand, and he led me inside to my dressing room.

Instead of my few unpacked garments, a store's worth of couture awaited me, plus accessories, purses, shoes, and even more jewelry.

I turned to him with my eyes wide.

He gave me a charming shrug, as if to say, *Can't help it.*

I dove into the closet, stroking materials, inspecting lines, drinking in colors and patterns. This wardrobe made me itch to design, to sketch the ideas that kept bubbling up in my head. "How'd you get all this here so quickly?" Everything was in my size.

"Money expedites delivery."

I held up a divine strand of pearls, running my face against them.

"I told you the diamond necklace was a good beginning," he said, his voice rumbling with satisfaction.

I would explore all his incredible gifts in time; right now I just needed to get closer to this man. I set the pearls away and crossed to him, then stood on my toes to press my lips to his cheek. Gazing up at him from under a curl, I asked sincerely, "How can you be so thoughtful and generous?"

He seemed to stand taller. "I live by one law: what my wife wants, my wife gets. Even if she doesn't yet know what she wants."

For real? *Too good to be true, too good to be . . .*

"And on that note," he said, "are you ready for another surprise?"

CHAPTER 28

$\mathcal{D}$mitri led me back into the bedroom. From his jeans pocket, he pulled a remote control. With the press of a button, all the windows turned to . . . mirrors. "It's a type of smart glass. For full privacy when we have guests."

"You *do* think of everything."

"It gets better." He pushed another button, and the mirrors turned to screens. They displayed the bed from all different angles, even from above.

"There are cameras in the bedroom?" The forbidden thrill made me shiver. "Are we about to make a sex tape?" I asked breathlessly.

"We are. I think my little exhibitionist wife will enjoy replaying our nights over and over again."

The idea left me shaken—in a good way. My tits were already swelling, my thong dampening.

"But first, you get one more surprise this evening." He led me to another walk-in closet, nearly the same size as each of our dressing rooms. Empty earlier, the space was now filled with . . . adult toys.

Wall racks of them. My jaw slackened. Vibrators, dildos, paddles, beads and balls. Implements I didn't even *recognize*. "This is a serious collection, big guy." I couldn't wait to dive into this one as well.

He leaned a broad shoulder against the doorway. "*Da.* I ordered many things."

I would've asked him who set this up, but knew I'd get the same answer about money and expediting. I entered, relishing the scent of leather, my fingers lighting on a clear glass dildo, then a shiny new crop. "What did you have in mind with this stuff?"

"You and I are going to indulge ourselves. Tonight, for every toy or piece of equipment you choose, I'll choose one."

Fun! "Okay." A bar with leather cuffs caught my attention. "How would this thing work?"

"I explain by demonstration only, Vika." With a challenge in his gaze, he asked, "Do you choose it or not?"

I jutted my chin. "Fine. Yes, I do."

That wicked light gleamed in his eyes. He liked my selection? "Then I'll go with this." He chose what looked like a plug. The flat end was a shining blue jewel about the size of a quarter.

When he took a bottle of lube off a shelf, I asked, "Are you going to put that . . . in my ass?" With any other guy, I'd be nervous. But I knew Dmitri would make ass play good.

Because he had with that trick in the shower.

"Considering your reaction earlier, yes."

Once he'd settled me on that high shelf, he'd teased and teased me with his tongue. Then he'd worked two fingers into my pussy. With bath oil on his little finger, he'd penetrated my ass at the same time.

The shocker.

I'd heard about it, but to feel it . . . I'd gone nuts, coming till I'd nearly thrashed off the shelf into his arms. . . .

Dmitri seemed to have unlimited sexual revelations in store for me. Before him, I'd had no interest in anal sex, but if he wanted me that way, I'd try it. I'd try anything he craved at least once.

As far as sex was concerned, he'd earned my trust. I'd have to think about the ramifications of that later.

He held up the plug. "I'll bet you get wet simply looking at this." Light reflected in the luminous metal.

I stared, rapt. "I can't deny it." The jewel on that plug was so eye-catching. If my ass would be adorned, he should have a sensual adornment too. Well, besides his piercing. I turned back to the shelves, selecting a black contraption of two interconnected leather rings. A cock ring?

"Good idea, Vika." He took it from me. "When I wear that, I won't come every time you do."

I swallowed. "Every time, huh?"

He turned toward the bedroom and laid our toys at the foot of the bed.

I followed him. "Tell me what to do."

"Strip."

Undressing didn't take long since I hadn't bothered to put on more than a thong and my beach cover-up.

"Now on the bed."

I crawled onto the mattress and rested on my knees, already thrumming with excitement. This was unreal! I glanced around at all the screens, seeing myself from half a dozen different angles. After today's nude sunbathing, my bikini tan lines weren't as pronounced. The trim patch of hair on my mons looked golden.

He moved to stand at the end of the bed. "Go to your hands and knees, your ass to me."

My face went hot, but after a moment of hesitation, I turned and leaned forward onto my hands.

He groaned, "Woman . . ."

Because of the cameras, I could see what he stared at—my upturned ass and my glistening pussy. Another screen showed me from the side, my breasts shaking from my anticipation. The color of my stiff nipples darkened to a deep pink.

He positioned that black bar near my feet. "This is a spreader." With nimble fingers, he cuffed my ankles on opposite ends of it, forcing my legs wide. "Lower your head and rest on one side of your face. Then place your hands beside your ankles."

Make myself even more vulnerable?

"Safe word or surrender," he reminded me.

I lowered my head, which jutted my ass up even more. "If you've never had a submissive, how do you know so much about this stuff?"

He bound my wrists beside my ankles. "I told you, I studied sex as if it were my field." Once I was immobilized, he stepped back to survey me. "My God, *zhena*."

I could share the same view. My plump labia had parted to reveal my shaded entrance. My cheeks were spread, my ass exposed. I had to stifle a moan.

Never taking his fierce gaze off me, he undressed.

My heart tripped at his ominous expression. "You, uh, you look like you're about to fuck the hell out of me."

He nodded slowly. "Oh, I am. You should know what I'll expect of my wife. What our sex life will be like."

When his jeans dropped to reveal his straining erection,

realization dawned. He could do anything he wanted to me.

Anything.

The idea made my clit *throb*.

He retrieved that cock ring. "You'll give me all my fantasies, won't you, wife? And I'll take all of yours."

My eyes went heavy-lidded as he handled his shaft and balls to adjust the leather into place. "Red-hot, Dmitri." I wished I had a picture of that—

Oh, wait, I'd have a video!

He stood behind me, a giant of a man about to use my body for filthy things. "Look at you. I'm probably dreaming this." He speared my pussy with a long forefinger. "So fucking wet for me."

I moaned, my core clamping down on his finger.

Then he wedged another one inside me. He took his time, scissoring his fingers as deep as they would go.

I turned my head from side to side because I couldn't decide which screen angle I wanted to view. "Dmitri, touch my clit."

He removed his fingers. "I will when *I* choose to. No sooner." He slapped my wet lips.

"Ah!" I jolted against the cuffs.

"Don't make me chastise you again, beautiful. You won't like it." He followed that slap with lighter ones until I'd slicked his big palm. He finally sank his thumb inside, reaching his fingers under me to strum my clit like a guitar.

"Yes!" I wantonly bucked as far as my bonds would allow. "N-need to come, Dmitri!"

"Not without your plug." He'd started to sweat, his muscles sheening.

"Then give it to me! Please . . ."

He removed his hand, leaving me aching. I trembled as he lubed the plug. Though not as big as some I'd seen online, the size was a lot larger than his finger!

Still, I knew he'd take care of me. All he'd ever wanted was my pleasure.

"Are you ready?"

"Yes—" I jolted again when the tip touched my ass.

"Relax, *zhena*." He teased my entrance, circling, then lightly pressing. Over and over. Until I needed him to shove it in! "So tight."

"No more teasing, Dmitri, *please*." I craved that fullness inside me as much as I craved his cock.

"In time, once you're accustomed to this, I'm going to fuck your exquisite virgin ass. Would you like me to?"

My pussy quivered. "Oh, God, yes, yes!"

He eased the metal tip deeper each time, lazily thrusting and twisting it. "Enjoy this for now, Vika." He finally penetrated me, wedging the plug in place.

After a brief stretch, sensation radiated throughout my body. I savored it, rocking my hips to get used to the feeling.

He stepped back so I could view my plugged, jeweled ass too. "So goddamned beautiful." His dick pulsed at the sight.

I would watch this tape to eternity! "Will you fuck me now?"

"Something's missing. Ah, yes, *this*." He spanked me with both hands. "My handprints."

The force made my ass tighten on the plug, intensifying those sensations. I moaned for more.

He spanked me repeatedly, muttering, "Your body gets my cock so hard, the tip wet for you."

I could see it. That black leather ring bit into the swollen base of his shaft, and precum beaded the pierced crown. *"Dmitri."*

"You're going to feel very full with me and the plug."

Between panting breaths, I cried, "Do it! I want to know . . . I want you inside me."

He gritted the words: "My wife wants . . ."

Immediately I said, "I want to come!"

"I don't think you really do. You know how much stronger your release will be . . . if we resist your urges." He laid one of his big hands on my lower back, his fingers spanning my waist. With his other hand, he worked his cockhead up and down my drenched folds.

On a screen, I could see the sculpted muscles of his ass flexing with each stroke. I wriggled my hips, trying to catch him, to tempt him. Tension gathered . . .

"Does your hungry little pussy ache for this?" He began feeding his length inside—

"Oh, my God, *YES!*" I screamed, coming before he was halfway in. *"Dmitri!"* The fullness sent me over the brink.

"*Uhn!* Feel you!" He shoved home, ripping another scream from me. And again. "You would've stolen my cum, just like that."

I writhed in my bonds as my orgasm consumed me, numbing my mind. . . .

Once I finally fell limp, he bit out, "More?" His muscles quaked against me. How badly he must need to come!

"Yes!"

"I will always give you more." He drew back his hips and gripped me around the waist. Then he widened his stance. He was *readying.*

I fidgeted in my bindings. He looked like he was about to

ravage me. And there was nothing I could do but take it. "Um, Dmitri—"

He yanked me back along his cock while his body rammed forward. He yelled; I moaned from the impact.

His position, my position . . . I felt like a sexual plaything. Maybe I was a submissive, because the idea put me right back on the brink.

"Your body needs to be fucked by mine. Taken." He eased out to give me another teeth-clattering thrust. And another. Soon he was *pounding* me. His breaths were grunts; my cry scaled higher.

I screamed his name as I came again.

"*Vika!* Your sweet pussy!" He never slowed, his skin lathered with sweat. "You're milking my cock!" He grew even thicker inside me. "Can't take this . . . pressure much longer." Was he loosening his leather ring? His size was unbearable.

So why was I on the verge of a third orgasm?

His damp hips slapped my ass harder and harder. *Slap, slap, SLAP.* "Victoria!" he roared, his fingers biting into flesh. "Need to shoot my cum . . . so deep inside you!"

My next climax forced a strangled moan from my lungs. I was delirious, babbling, sex-drugged.

Face drawn with need, he met my heavy-lidded gaze in one of the screens. *"I will never let you go!"*

He bellowed with pleasure, neck corded and muscles bulging, as his semen flooded my core. Ramping up his pace, he slammed into me to empty the last of his cum. . . .

With a groan, he collapsed atop me, his heaving breaths tickling my damp neck. Even as he recovered, he grazed tender kisses across my nape.

Though I was restrained, with his weight pressing down on me, I'd never felt freer. Hadn't he promised to free me? Boneless with bliss, I murmured, "Dmitri, I like how our sex will be."

CHAPTER 29

"What will we do today?" I asked, watching Dmitri stretch naked in the morning sunlight. I blew out a breath. *That man.* We'd been married for a week, but my attraction kept growing.

Earlier, I'd awakened him in one of the two ways he preferred. He'd cracked open his eyes—the color of yesterday's painted gold sunset. After a moment of confusion, he'd curled his lips. "An alarm-clock BJ? Are you dicking with me?" he'd asked, using my line.

Imitating him, I said, "No. I am not." I couldn't get enough of his taste.

"Ah, Vika, I like this life with you. . . ."

I enjoyed all the luxury he showered on me, but Dmitri was the draw by a mile. Even if he had no money, I would still be infatuated with him. My toes would still curl when his waking confusion transformed to that golden shimmer of satisfaction. I'd still know more pleasure with him than I'd ever dreamed.

I'd still feel protective.

God, I felt protective.

"We should pack for our honeymoon." He pulled on a pair

of broken-in jeans; the staff must be coming in today. "I want to spend our one-week anniversary in Moorea."

"Where's that?"

"An island near Tahiti."

So far away? How would anyone pick up the ring? They needed it in three days! "Um, I thought we'd be honeymooning here."

He shook his head. "The weather's supposed to turn, but it will be nice in French Polynesia. I plan to buy you everything—even sunny days."

"Maybe we could leave in a week or two?" *Work the con*, I told myself.

Oh, who was I kidding? I kept using the con as an excuse to get right where I wanted to be—with Dmitri.

Married. Falling ever deeper under his spell.

He sat on the bed beside me. "Why the delay?"

"I'm having too much fun here." Not a lie.

Yesterday I'd modeled the clothes and jewels that kept arriving (I called my dressing room "the never-ending story"). He'd rated the looks—until I'd emerged stark naked, with nothing but jewelry all over me, just asking for it.

As he'd fucked me, strands of pearls had bounced over my tits, delighting him.

We'd been having *a lot* of sex. Kink and non-kink. In the shower. In the pool. In the hot tub. Down by the ocean.

In the six-car garage, on the hood of a Bentley.

Each night we watched our sex tapes from the day before. Yesterday, he'd played the recording of the first time he used a plug on me—while he'd worked a larger one inside me. "You're going to ride me, facing away, so I can whip your beautiful ass and control the pace."

Reverse cowgirl? Once he'd stretched out on the bed, naked and hard and glorious, I'd mounted him. Between the video and his husky commands and the fullness, I'd gone into a frenzy, gripping his muscular thighs for leverage and flaunting my jeweled ass as he'd slapped my cheeks. . . .

Dragging myself from the memory, I delicately cleared my throat. "I feel like we're just discovering this place." He and I had gone kayaking a few more times—with me paddling like a boss. We'd explored the grounds, hiking the property's many trails through the hills and the vast forest. "We haven't even gone riding yet."

Yesterday he'd taken me to the stables, tucked away on the other side of a hill, to introduce me to our horses that had arrived—so many I couldn't remember all their names. I was lost for one particular mare with mischievous eyes and a glossy black coat. I'd teasingly asked Dmitri, "Can I take her back to the house?"

"Of course." My eccentric husband hadn't been kidding.

"Oh. Um, maybe another time."

On the way back from the stables, Dmitri and I had taken a different route, a winding coastline path. He'd held my hand. Walking with him like that had felt so natural, as if my hand had only been waiting for his. . . .

Now he leaned over to chuck my chin. "Our home isn't going anywhere. Perhaps you don't like the prospect of being so far from your family."

I didn't want him to think I was an overly attached wuss, but I didn't have a better excuse to give him. "Perhaps." In truth, the idea of heading to another part of the world intimidated me. And what if Dmitri found out I was a con artist while we were there? What if I got abandoned in

French-freaking-Polynesia, with no money to get home?

He said, "If you prefer, we could visit them before we leave."

They would be paranoid and quiet around a gull, and he wasn't exactly Mr. Sociable. Though a visit would present an opportunity to hand off the ring, I'd risk his uncovering more about us—and someone might get blamed for theft. "Maybe not so soon." He frowned, so I added, "And I want to see *your* family again first."

Dmitri didn't seem to like that idea. He'd talked about matters that needed resolving with them. Maybe resolution would take some time.

Honestly though, I *did* want to see them. I'd love to get Natalie and Lucía's take on BDSM. And find out more about my husband.

Wait . . . What if *I* was a matter that needed resolving? What if his family thought I wasn't good enough for him? Or worse, a gold-digger?

He relented. "Then we'll remain for now."

"Great!" I managed a believable smile.

He pressed a kiss to my lips. "I'm going to get my work done early." He religiously spent his hour a day on the computer. "Will you join me?"

I had all week. I would stretch out on the study couch, paying more attention to him than to the new laptop he'd given me. The first day, his heart-melting little frown of concentration had been irresistible to me. I'd crawled under his desk.

He'd hissed in a breath when I'd gone for his fly. *"Prosto rai,"* he'd groaned as he'd let his legs fall wide. . . .

I longed for a repeat now, but I was too unsettled. "I think I'll go for a walk."

Once he'd settled into the study, I got dressed, then headed toward the stables. Strolling along the manicured path, I barely saw the surrounding hills, caught up in debating my future.

The more I bonded with Dmitri, the more disloyal I felt to my family and my upbringing. On the other hand, if I assured myself I'd be back among them, returning to my old life, guilt over Dmitri gutted me.

My determination to save my loved ones meant I had to be ready to betray his trust.

I felt like a snare was closing around me.

Grifters loathed snares, unless sprung on a mark.

My trail crested a rise, revealing a plateau of wildflowers and the bright white stable. Most of the horses were out in the four paddocks, whickering at each other and tossing their heads in the sunshine.

I leaned against a fence and watched.

Being with Brett had made me ask questions. Dmitri, too, made me ask: *Can I fall for a guy in so short a time? Can I learn to trust him? Can I make a life with someone who isn't a grifter?*

One bay colt raised his face to the breeze and sneezed, then hopped around. I caught myself grinning.

This would be an amazing place for kids to grow up.

I frowned. Not a typical Vice-like thought. The other night, Dmitri and I had talked a little about children. I'd teasingly said, "You know a lot about parenting, do you? I'm not so sure I'm cut out for it."

He'd raised his chin. "In the few years I had with my mother, I learned from her how to be a parent: provide infinite patience, love unconditionally, and safeguard with your life." He'd held my gaze. "Victoria Sevastyan, you will be an incredible mother."

Just as I'd planted good-girl seeds, he'd sparked the idea of kids—and it'd grown. The prospect of children with Brett had been unappealing. But when I imagined Dmitri and myself raising a family, I could *see* it.

He'd be a little crazy; I'd be a little shady. Hell, it might just work.

I took out my phone and called my sister. "I like him."

"You like his money, hon."

"Don't forget, I could divorce him today and walk away with half of his fortune," I pointed out. "Karin, I imagined him without a dime. I pictured us living a modest existence. I'd still be hooked on him. He's caring, brilliant, supportive, and protective. And creative. He's even funny." He'd started cracking more jokes. "I *wish* my need for him were as easy as money. Money would be simple. But what I feel for him is scary. What if . . ."

"Out with it. Sister vault."

"What if he and I *were* made for each other?" What if fairy tales existed?

A thought occurred. How could Mom say they didn't when she was living one with Dad? They'd fallen in love at first sight and had been inseparable for more than thirty years!

"Hon, you sound really . . . infatuated."

What if I keep him? Damn it, Dmitri needed to be kept by me. "I freaking watch him sleep. I inhale his jackets for hits of his scent. I catch myself sighing at him when he works. He gets this little frown of concentration that is seriously the most adorable thing I've ever seen. His smiles make my heart twist." They were coming so much more frequently. "When he talks about his work, he gets all excited, and it's sooo sexy."

Two days ago, he'd tried to explain his patents and research to me. He'd been shocked when I'd jumped him. "Vika?"

"I can't help it," I'd told him between kisses. "You're utterly irresistible when you talk about tech stuff."

He'd hastily rasped about ratios and refactoring and vertical traceability and other gobbledygook as I'd yanked at his clothes. . . .

Karin asked, "But what about having nothing in common? You told me he wants kids; you don't."

"I might have changed my mind. I'm not saying I'll be knocked up tomorrow or anything." I was on the pill for now, had been taking them straight through to avoid a period. "But yeah, I can imagine it." I exhaled. "This is the longest I've been apart from him since we got here, and I legit *miss* him." He was just as bad; earlier, he'd been reluctant to go to his study without me.

"Vice, you hardly sound like . . . you."

"What does that mean?"

"You told me he was a thrall, and then all the sudden you're thinking babies and happily-ever-afters? While you're honeymooning in a palace, your family's on the razor's edge, not knowing what you're going to do or where your head's at."

Just because I had a deadline didn't mean I should take to the last second to decide. "You're right. I'm sorry." Though the congressman had ponied-up in full and Mom and Dad had scored on their scam, we were still well short, even with Lucía's watch and my car.

"We can't do this without you. You need to settle on your play today. Lose the ring"—adding more deception to the heaping pile of it—"or lose the guy."

Divorce.

"If you walked now, you could tell his lawyers you'll sign away your rights, but only for a speedy settlement. Say ten mil by the weekend? They'd consider their client's enormous exposure, and I bet they'd pay it."

As if Dmitri would ever let me go . . .

Karin added, "Or you can lose the ring and put off the divorce decision."

I worried my lip. "It's a symbol. What if I jinx this marriage by giving it up? What if Lady Luck is actually smiling on me to this extent? How will she feel if I spat in her eye?"

"Jinxed? Your 'relationship' is built on lies," Karin said, getting exasperated. "You don't have a choice. You can't keep the guy *and* the rock."

My sister made me sound greedy, like a gull. "I would never leave the family in a lurch—you know that—but there's another option. I ask him for the money."

In that scenario, I would anonymously return Lucía's watch. What if it had sentimental value? Like I'd attached to my ring?

Oh, and I wouldn't report the Porsche stolen.

All told, I'd need . . . three mil.

She imitated me: "Hi, Dmitri, I know we've only been married a week, but I need a blank check for a fortune, and I can never tell you why. Though this would definitely spur any sane man to investigate me, please don't. 'Kay? Thanks, baby."

I didn't want to frame my dilemma as *how much I love my parents* versus *how much I trust a virtual stranger to give me millions.*

He was unbelievably generous, but could he sign a blank check—with no questions asked?

If he refused, he'd be suspicious once I lost my ring. Even if he said yes about the money, he might still investigate my family more intensively.

I would be risking everyone I loved, rolling the dice on a man I'd known for mere days—a man with a troubled past.

One who didn't seem interested in divulging much more about it.

So far, I'd garnered only tidbits of his background. When I'd asked him about his parents, he'd said, "I loved my mother dearly." His gaze had gone distant, but his eyes had been full of affection. "My brothers were older and often off by themselves, so I spent most of my days with her. She taught me how to play chess and ride horses. She used to sing to me." Yet he'd refused to talk about his father at all.

Though I still had no idea how his parents had died within two years of each other, I hadn't pressed. He believed once he shared his secrets, I would share mine, and I wanted to postpone that as far into the future as possible. Read: *indefinitely.*

Karin said, "If he finds out we played him, he could get that postnup overturned. You would be left with nothing." She sighed into the phone. "Pete knew this would happen. He told me to remind you we're a different breed."

The only thing we can't cheat is fate. . . .

Dmitri had already been betrayed by someone he'd trusted, likely his abuser, a person who'd targeted and deceived him.

I had targeted and deceived him. My family had manipulated him, arranging for him to run afoul of my ex. Despite our motivations, how could he ever get over the similarities?

I recalled his eyes dimming as he'd said, "We always find out in the long run, do we not?"

"Vice, I'm going to tell you something I've never revealed to anyone." Karin paused, then said, "I considered coming clean about all of us to Walker. I would've bet the house that he loved me. He'd told me he did." I pictured the adoring way that man had looked at her. "He and I have a *child* together, and he still deserted me and Cash. I know how easy it is to get blinded."

On the surface, Dmitri and Walker had a lot in common, both so rich and proud. Would Dmitri react like Walker? Would I react like Karin and never get over the heartache?

Did I believe in that Sevastyan devotion? Or the tears she'd shed?

"Text me your plan," she said. "Today."

"Tell me how *you* would play this."

She didn't hesitate. "I'd ignore my starstruck infatuation, shuck his thrall, divorce the guy I barely know before he divorced me, and take him for all he's worth. Then the family would be safe, and we could all be together again. That's all we've dreamed about for months. Don't you want that too?"

"Of course."

"To the grave, hon."

I gazed down at my ring. *To the grave.*

CHAPTER 30

When I entered the study, Dmitri said, "I finished early so I can take you shopping down the coast."

Of course you did, because you're affectionate and thoughtful. "That sounds really nice."

His brows drew together at my pensive expression. "What's wrong?" He stood.

I joined him by the desk. "Not a thing."

"Come now, even I can tell something's amiss." He rested his hands on my shoulders. "*Moya zhena*, you can talk to me about anything."

I gazed up into his eyes. Between this closeness and his touch, my path seemed to gain clarity, Karin's words fading. After all, she didn't know how wonderful Dmitri was. And hadn't she said any *sane* man would need to investigate?

My husband was a little crazy.

The grift sense I'd relied on all my life was telling me to shoot for the guy, the ring, *and* the cartel payoff. If I believed everything he'd told me since we'd met, then he would do this for me.

Trusting another man, Vice? "I . . . what if I asked you for something I knew was unfair?"

He swallowed, his voice going hoarse as he said, "Divorce?"

"No!"

He blew out a breath, staggering back into his seat. "Then I don't give a goddamned fuck what you ask for. Wife wants; wife gets, remember?"

"But it won't make sense unless you drill down on it or dig. And I know how badly you need things to make sense."

His lips curved. "You're already learning me well."

I backed up a step. "I'm sorry; this was a mistake. Temporary insanity." Had I really just said that? *Shit, Vice, get it together!*

He shot to his feet, moving between me and the door. "I refuse to let you leave until you tell me what's making you unhappy. You know I'll keep us here till we starve."

Yep. Just as I knew he would've let that mare prance right into this house. "Dmitri, if I asked you for something large and unusual, could you swear never to investigate why?" I twined my fingers, touching the ring like a talisman. "To let it *not* make sense?"

"I can do anything to make you happy. But you must talk to me."

I couldn't bring myself to say the words.

He cupped my chin to lift my face. "I won't tell you to trust me." If he had, I would've bolted. "That will come in time. But I will ask my Vegas wife to take a chance on me."

I released a breath. "Okay, here goes. Can I please . . . could I have a check today for three million dollars, no questions asked?"

He dropped his hand. "Sit." He indicated the chair across from his desk.

Just great, Vice, fucking great. How stupid could I have been? Now I'd blown everything! I hesitantly sat, preparing myself for whatever he was about to say.

He sat as well. "I am disappointed, Vika. In myself."

"I . . . what?"

He steepled his fingers. "I haven't made it clear enough that we share this fortune. You never need ask for what's already yours. I hope we can consult about larger expenditures, but it's not necessary."

I could only gape at him.

"You don't have to answer, but is this money for your parents?"

When I hesitated, he said, "I will never drill down on this or dig further." Not a lie. "I ask because we could transfer the money. Immediately."

Sell on the sizzle. "It's a debt." Maybe he'd think we had run afoul of the IRS, or needed to ward off a bankruptcy.

"If you have all the account data, we could complete the transfer now, to spare them any unnecessary worry."

In a daze, I pulled up the information on my phone and handed it to him. "It's under Joseph and Jill"—Gentleman Joe and Diamond Jill—"Valentine."

Dmitri typed in numbers at a blinding speed, then said, "There. All taken care of." He returned my phone.

I started to hyperventilate. "That just . . . happened? Did that really . . . just happen?"

"Of course, love."

Even as my brain exploded from his generosity, I felt the

stress of the last few months evaporating. My family would be safe.

He opened a desk drawer, retrieving a leather portfolio similar to the one that had contained the postnup. He stood and offered it to me. "I just got these in."

Inside were checks and credit cards in my new name. Victoria Sevastyan.

If I wanted to, I'd never have to give a name other than this one. I stared up at him in wonder.

"Vika, if you decide to leave our marriage, this money will be yours no matter what occurs. That should not be a consideration if you choose to stay with me." He pinned me with his gaze. "You should stay because we do very well together. You should stay because I make you happy."

Complicated man! He'd shown such vulnerability earlier when he'd barely been able to utter the word *divorce*; now he was all blazing confidence.

I stood, reaching up to lay a hand against his cheek. "You truly just sent my family three million dollars?"

"No. I sent them five, to incentivize them to come to us when they are in need of money. I told you, I have no parents. Yours will become mine. We will be notorious for spoiling family, will we not?"

I burst into tears. Real ones.

"Why are you crying?" He looked nervous.

"Because I'm so relieved. And you're so wonderful." *Two tears in a bucket—I'm keeping him.*

Which meant he could *never* find out my past. Cold-as-Ice Vice was officially buried. I would put away my decks of cards, my costumes, my fake IDs, and wigs forever. I'd hide my past and keep my family separated from him as much as possible—and as long as possible.

I launched myself at him and hugged him hard, my tears wetting his shirt. "If I have my own money, I can buy anything I want?"

His voice was thick as he said, "Name it, *ángel*, and it's yours."

I drew back to face him. "I need to get my husband a wedding ring."

He swallowed, and could only nod.

✦

"I wish you were here to celebrate with us!" Karin cried over the music playing in the background.

The cartel had accepted the payment and cut us loose! Wham, bam, thank you, ma'am.

They were out of our lives forever.

My family had been drunk-texting me for hours.

"I know. I miss you guys." My tone was hushed; once Dmitri had fallen asleep, I'd sneaked into the bathroom and briefly spoken to the less hammered members of my family.

Mom and Dad had sounded like their old selves for the first time in months.

Even over the tunes on the other end of the line, I heard a champagne cork popping.

Karin said, "I still can't believe you got the guy, the ring, and the money—plus some serious gratis on top. Well done, sis. We applaud your grift sense."

I'd told her all about my angst, as well as Dmitri's promises to spoil our family. I'd begged them never to let my husband know what we were.

Which meant instant retirement for the Valentines. "Is everyone good with stepping out of the game? I mean, Dmitri did say I could spend money however I like. I'll set up accounts for you guys."

"Your husband gave us an extra two *million* dollars. That's going to take some time even for us to blow." She laughed. "Gram is shitfaced and threatening to steal 'rich Dmitri' from you, and Al is lecturing everyone on the generosity of Russians in general. I dramatically vowed to send Walker back every dime he's sent me, plus interest. And maybe a little note along the lines of, *Thanks, but we've got it from here.*"

"I think that's a great idea."

"Apparently he needs the money more than I do. Rumor says he's going bankrupt. Ironic, huh?"

"Never would've seen that coming."

"Enough about him. Can you believe this day?"

I glanced over my shoulder in Dmitri's direction. If there was ever an example of me reaching for the stars . . .

"But, Vice?" Karin said, rousing me from my thoughts. "You know we celebrate our wins whenever we get one, and we're delighted to be off the hook. But the general consensus around here . . ."

"Tell me." Though I knew what she was about to say.

"Watch yourself. Dmitri Sevastyan is too good to be true."

CHAPTER 31

I woke from an afternoon nap to find Dmitri sitting up against the headboard, staring out at the mist over the water. He wore only broken-in jeans, his chest bare.

I'd never seen him this still when awake. And his eyes were so vulnerable. What was he thinking about in his mixed-up mind? Reliving the past? Or imagining his future?

With me.

For the last two weeks, a dense fog had blanketed the property, magnifying the unseen splashes out in the ocean and the haunting gull cries. Dmitri and I had been running the fires throughout the house.

Though this magical place had begun to appear eerie, I liked the gothic atmosphere. I was out in the middle of nowhere, alone with my enigmatic husband. Except I was no helpless waif. I skipped into that toy room every night and delighted in choosing things for my wicked man to show me.

These weeks had been wonderful. Three things prevented them from being perfect:

I missed my family.

I missed working—not conning, necessarily, but doing *something* with a purpose. Like bringing my design ideas to life.

And I kept waiting for the other shoe to drop with my too-good-to-be-true husband.

I studied his compelling face. My antsiness grew each day, and my grift sense had started sounding the call.

Last week, he and I had walked through the woods. We'd been relaxed and enjoying our stroll, but then a briar had snagged my sweater. Dmitri had valiantly rescued me—I'd discovered he loved being my gentleman hero—and we'd continued on. Yet then another briar had caught me shortly after.

My grift sense was like that—a thorn snagging me again and again, no matter how many times Dmitri's affection and love-making and generosity rescued me. My anxiety kept me from surrendering to this life. From falling all the way for him.

My gaze dipped to his left hand, to his bare ring finger. Though I'd said I would buy him a wedding band—caught up in that moment, in his bigheartedness—I now worried I'd acted rashly.

Rings *were* symbols; how could I pledge forever to him with all my lies and doubts standing between us?

Dmitri shifted on the bed, interrupting my thoughts. Still staring out the window, he absently traced that faint remnant of a scar. If he'd been suicidal, how much longer could I go without asking him about it?

As if he sensed my internal debate, he turned to me. "You're awake."

I sat up against the headboard. "How long was I out?" I wore one of his T-shirts, but only because the housekeeper was here today.

"Not long. I just had tea brought in." A silver tea service with snacks sat on the end of the huge bed. He poured me a cup with honey, exactly how I liked it.

I took a sip. Delicious.

He sat beside me and reached for my free hand, as if he'd only been waiting for me to wake so he could lace our fingers together.

Life could be so sweet when I forgot myself and lived in the now. He and I rode horses and explored the coast. He'd taken me on two short overnight trips—shopping on Rodeo Drive and sightseeing in San Francisco—easing me into travel.

Whenever we played chess, he won, which made me itch to challenge him at poker. But I'd vowed to turn my back on anything related to my grifter days, even a simple card deck, my beloved rectangle of two and a half by three and a half inches.

After twenty years, my days as a cardsharp were over. *Pang.*

I took another sip of tea, feeling Dmitri's gaze. He studied me like he was trying to crack a code.

I'd come close to slipping up a couple of times.

When a restaurant server had been hanging all over him, he'd noted my jealousy. As the woman had sauntered off, he'd teased me, "Remember, I'm legally yours." Glaring at the woman's back, I'd snapped, "In that case, I might have some use"—I'd bit my tongue to keep the rest from escaping—*for Johnny Law after all.*

And, damn it, gaming a parking meter was second nature!

My family would be just as likely to slip up. Parents loved to relate stories about their kids growing up, right? Mom couldn't exactly tell my gull husband I'd been a "broad tosser" at age four. *"Can you keep your eyeth on the queen, thsir?"*

I sipped my tea, sighing over the cup.

"What does your family usually do for Thanksgiving?" Dmitri asked.

I swallowed thickly. "Pardon?"

"We could invite them all here."

I still hadn't figured out how his visiting with them would work. My dilemma? *How much I long to see my family* versus *how much I fear losing Dmitri.*

"We'll see." Maybe over time I'd grow more confident in him. Sharing was the key to companionship; once we got to know each other better, he could genuinely fall in love with me, replacing his meteoric flash obsession with something more abiding. If he loved me, his feelings might remain true once he found out what I'd done.

But getting to know him was difficult when he still wasn't talking.

"Vika, this can't go on much longer. You've already missed too many Sundays with them."

I set my cup aside. "I'll broach it with them—once you tell me what you fought with Maksim about."

He exhaled. "In time, I'll tell you everything," he said, his go-to answer. "I suppose you'll have to continue sending your family gifts until we can see them."

Last week, at his suggestion, I'd shopped online while he worked, buying Benji a super-fly camera; spa days for Mom, Karin, and Gram; golf clubs for Dad, Pete, and Al; toys for Cash and my younger cousins.

At the end of his hour, Dmitri had looked at my purchases. "I need you to feel comfortable spending more."

"I don't think that's possible." He was no longer a mark I planned to fleece. Had he achieved pack status in my heart yet? No. But he *could*.

He'd pulled up a spreadsheet on his computer, highlighting a sum. "What we make annually on the patents alone."

I'd squinted. The length of that number couldn't be right. I'd rechecked it, but the figure remained *unimaginable*. "Need . . . to sit . . . down."

He'd helped me back to the couch. "I want us to spend our lives trying to kill our fortune—no matter how impossible a prospect that might be. Will you try to do better tomorrow? Endeavor to shock me."

The next day, I'd cracked my knuckles before hitting the computer. I'd purchased cars, wardrobes, jewelry, and thirty cruise tickets. I'd set up a college fund for Cash and bought my parents authentic fine art. Again, I'd shown Dmitri my take (without the mountain bike and gifts I'd secretly ordered for him).

He'd said, "More income came in overnight. You didn't even scratch the surface. Perhaps tomorrow you will be more aggressive. . . ."

Now he canted his head, forever deciphering my expressions. "If you are anxious, I'm not helping by putting pressure on you. I apologize." He pressed a kiss to the palm of my hand. "You must have a reason for remaining away from them. I look forward to when you can share it with me."

Guh. He *was* too good to be true.

I kept hearing Karin's warning, reinforcing my own experience, yet I couldn't prevent my feelings from growing. My mom had said people got greedy. That they knew better, but they *chose* to ignore all the warning signs.

I was greedy for Dmitri.

And yet I knew so little about him. *Dip a toe, Vice.* "When I woke, you were staring out at the water." *And touching your scar.* "What were you thinking about?"

"Myriad things."

"Such as . . ."

"You should have had a period by now," he said, taking me off guard.

"You noticed?" My eyes widened. "Oh, wait, did you think . . . ? Dmitri, I took my pills straight through, so I wouldn't start this month."

His broad chest rose and fell on a deep breath.

"You're relieved?" I frowned. "But you want children."

"Not yet. We have so many things still to do, and I think a pregnancy would distress you greatly."

But he'd said I would make an incredible mom. "Why do you believe that?"

"Because you have no idea what kind of father I'd be. How could you when I've told you little of my family or of myself?" He was providing me an opening!

"We could remedy that."

He squared his shoulders, as if bracing for a hit. "What do you want to know?"

Impulsively, I brushed my fingers over the scar on his wrist.

He stiffened, pulling his hand from mine. "You are very observant, aren't you?" *Details are my job.* Or they used to be. "Even I can barely detect it. I had the scar removed by laser a few months back, for when I eventually married."

"Dmitri, the sight of it doesn't bother me. But . . . did you try to commit suicide?"

Curt nod. "Years ago. Maksim stopped me before I could do my other arm."

When I thought of how close it must have been . . . *Thank you, Maksim!*

Dmitri gazed away. "I'd made sure not to say anything out of the ordinary—in what I'd thought would be our last conversation—but my brother must've detected something in my tone. To this day, I don't know what made him drive over."

"Why did you do it?" How physically and mentally excruciating taking a blade to one's own flesh would be!

He was clearly weighing how much to tell me. "I couldn't imagine a better life because . . . I didn't know that there would be you."

Those lifeline looks? Might really be lifelines! Did he comprehend how much pressure he was putting on me?

He faced me with a frown. "That's one of those things I shouldn't have said out loud, isn't it?"

This was too much responsibility for another human's happiness. What if our marriage didn't work out?

I was just a freaking grifter!

We stared into each other's eyes until I felt calm enough to say, "Will you explain what pushed you to try to take your own life?"

He scrubbed his hand over the back of his neck. "Maksim told me I would have to reveal everything from my past for us to move forward. Do you believe that?" Dmitri was genuinely asking for my advice.

"I think it can be very helpful." I remembered Benji, struggling, in so much pain. "My adopted brother had a traumatic childhood. If he'd kept everything bottled up, I believe it would have destroyed him."

Dmitri rose to pace. "And he is better now?"

"It's taken years. But, yeah." I didn't get the sense Dmitri truly wanted to talk, more like he was checking off something unpleasant in order to solidify our marriage. "Don't talk to me just to tick a box."

"Perhaps if I shared my past, you would tell me more about yours. I want you to. I want us . . ." He eased his pacing to face me. "Are we getting closer?"

"Do you want to know if we're bonding?"

"Precisely."

"I think so. Do you?"

He nodded. "Each minute I spend with you, I crave a thousand more. I wake and see your head on my chest, and I feel as if I live within a fantasy."

Heart thud. "My toes curl whenever you say things like that. But then I wonder how you can feel so strongly when we still don't know a lot about each other."

He opened his mouth to say something, then must've rethought it. "When I suspected you might be pregnant, part of me welcomed the idea, because a child would bond us."

It hadn't with Walker and Karin. "Dmitri, there are other ways for us to get closer."

Gazing away again, he said, "I will . . . I'm ready to talk about my past." He settled onto the bed and drew back against the headboard once more. "What do you think happened to me?"

I wouldn't flinch from this. "After your father died, you were sent to live with someone who sexually abused you."

He blew out a breath. "You are very perceptive. But actually, he was sent to us."

CHAPTER 32

"*I* . . . it was very long ago." Dmitri seemed to be losing his nerve.

"How old were you when it started?"

He cleared his throat. "Seven years old. From seven to nine."

So young, an innocent little boy. My protectiveness for Dmitri burned like an inferno. "Was the man supposed to be a guardian?" Someone in a position of trust.

"Yes. His name was . . . Orloff." Dmitri's fists clenched. "He . . . molested me, and many other children before me. Both boys and girls. He physically abused Maksim, beating him and locking him in a dark cellar for months."

I eased closer to him. "I'm so sorry, Dmitri."

"I don't know if I want to tell you these things yet. I cannot tolerate pity."

"You don't have to talk to me before you're ready, but you should know I could never pity the man you've become."

Placated, he said, "Orloff wasn't the first to abuse us. My father was a violent drunk. My earliest memories are of him beating me and my brothers and my mother. Especially at night. In the winter, night was unending."

My God. No wonder he and his brothers rarely drank.

"When I was almost six, I woke to a horrific argument. My father had taken issue with something trivial Aleks and Maksim had done, was bent on punishing them. He sounded more enraged than I'd ever heard him. Desperate to protect them, my mother fought back. He shoved her down the stairs." Voice gone thick, Dmitri said, "I will never forget the sudden quiet. I sensed she was gone, but terror of my father kept me from going to her. He left my mother for me to find the next morning."

I would give anything to have spared him that! When I thought of Dmitri as a terrified boy, I wanted to hold him, but he looked like he might bolt at any second.

In a lower tone, he said, "I only recently told my brothers she died to protect us."

Dmitri's words: *provide infinite patience, love unconditionally, and safeguard with your life.* His mother had given her life to safeguard her sons. "You must have missed her so much."

His expression turned fierce. "I need you to understand: there was nothing she could do. There were no shelters. If she'd run with us, my powerful father would have found her. Even if she somehow managed to escape him in the winter with three young sons, she had nowhere to go."

He thought I would judge his beloved mother. "Dmitri, it was a different time and place, a world away from what I know. I would *never* question her actions." But I would judge her abuser.

Seeming satisfied with my vehement answer, Dmitri continued, "When Aleks was only thirteen, our father would've done the same to him. Aleks defended himself, accidentally killing the man instead. Fearing he'd go to jail, my brother fled, leaving me and Maksim behind. Orloff arrived shortly after."

So much violence and horror. "That's why you hadn't spoken to Aleks in so long." Because he hadn't been there when Dmitri had *very badly needed him to be*. At seven, Dmitri had needed a protector.

He nodded. "Aleks was like a father to me. And then he was . . . gone. In my young mind, I viewed it as abandonment. He left us behind and got to shed all our painful history, and then was adopted by a very wealthy and decent man, Natalie's biological father, Kovalev."

That was how Natalie and Aleks had met?

"He'd been blessed with a new father, while Maksim and I had been cursed with a monster. I blamed Aleks for all that befell us. Maksim did as well to a lesser extent. Rationally, I knew Aleks wasn't at fault, but the anger wouldn't subside."

"Did he believe you two were okay?"

"*Da*. And much better off without our father. He couldn't have guessed what happened to us. He only learned of it a few years ago."

He must've felt so guilty. "Will you tell me what happened when Orloff arrived?"

Dmitri hesitated. "In the beginning . . . he was kind to me, doing nothing unusual. When he started to touch me, it was so different from the violence I'd known that I mistook his behavior for genuine affection. He told me all boys my age had a guardian to touch and kiss."

My fists clenched under the cover.

"Maksim sensed something was wrong. He asked me if Orloff hurt me, and I could honestly say he didn't because he never did anything that would cause me pain. Orloff would rather have died than to injure his 'perfect little boy.'" Dmitri gave a shudder of revulsion.

I choked back bile and imagined burning Orloff in a ring of tires.

"Yet then he began firing servants and isolating us even more. At the same time, he pushed me to do things I couldn't reconcile. When I refused, he threatened to kill Maksim. Finally, I saw what Orloff truly was. After that, I was so infuriated and disgusted, I grew detached, my mind and thoughts far from him. Sometimes I would dissociate for long periods."

"How did Maksim find out?"

"My brother sneaked into my room on Christmas Eve to set up toys, but I wasn't there. Maksim discovered me in Orloff's bed."

Oh, God. "That's when Orloff beat him? Because your brother tried to protect you?"

Dmitri nodded. "Orloff flayed his back open repeatedly and locked him in the cellar for months."

I would never have suspected Maksim's traumatic past. Today he was so confident and so at peace with himself, with Lucía. "How did you two escape him? Was Orloff arrested?"

"No, he ... died. An elderly woman was put in charge of us, but it was Maksim who looked out for me, and I got better. Or so I thought, until my teens." He rubbed a hand down his face. "Whenever I felt sexual pleasure, I'd start to dissociate. I fought with everything in me, but I couldn't stop it. After sex, I couldn't remember what had happened. It ruined the act for me, and each time I drifted, slipping away grew easier."

Now I understood more about our wedding night. He'd feared dissociating with me. "Did you get help?"

His lips drew back from his teeth. "I tried *everything*. Any kind of therapy you can think of, I tried. For years. I learned what my issues were and how best to cope with them, but the dissociation continued to plague me. Every day I felt robbed; every day I was reminded of wrongs inflicted upon me. I could deal with my past, but my present was providing fresh misery."

I couldn't imagine having a wound that festered—for decades.

"Logically, I knew there would come a day when I would *stay* gone. I was just twenty-five when I concluded I could never sustain a relationship. Which meant Orloff had left his mark on me, was having the last laugh. That filled me with so much rage. For years, rage was the only emotion I felt. In a way, I was unwillingly being true to him, but I knew how to shuck off that monster's hold forever." He rubbed his scar.

Suicide. The culmination of all that terror and violence and pain.

"After Maksim intervened, he pressured me to go to a facility. A doctor suggested a pill to keep me anchored in reality, one with a notorious side effect. It killed my sex drive. I had a choice. Sane and celibate, or insane and sexual. My protocols of pills and no sex enabled me to concentrate on my work. I spent years like that."

"Before me, when was the last time you were with someone?"

"A while."

I could tell he hoped I would leave it at that. "How long is a while?"

"Years."

"How many years?"

He squared his shoulders. "I was completely celibate for eight."

I masked my astonished reaction. This explained so much of his behavior, starting with our first night together—the wonder in his expression as he'd explored my body in the penthouse bathroom. . . .

Not to mention his family's unnerving enthusiasm at his interest in me.

"I had my work for most of that time," he said, a defensive edge to his tone. "And I wasn't alone in my suffering; Maksim battled his own shadows. His back is covered with scars, and because of what he endured in that cellar, he couldn't stand to be touched."

No wonder Maksim's longest relationship lasted for an hour.

"My brother was as scarred on the outside as I was on the inside. I assumed both of us would be damaged forever, wanting nothing to do with Aleks, the two of us sharing our secret burdens."

"Then he met Lucía," I murmured. Dmitri had told me he'd hated the idea of her. "You felt abandoned again."

He sucked in a breath. *"Yes."*

I put my hand over his. "That's normal. I would've too. Anyone would have."

"I was so frustrated with him." Beneath my palm, Dmitri's hand clenched into a fist. "He and I used to believe in reason and logic above all else, but he swore he felt a connection to her that defied any rational explanation. My ruthless, cynical brother started talking about something that sounded a lot like fucking *soul mates*."

Just as Natalie, Lucía, and Jess had said.

"I derided Maksim for that, thinking he'd gone as crazy as I was. But when he risked his life for Lucía, I accepted he did truly believe. I still didn't."

The jaded part of me wanted to scoff as well, but my parents . . .

"For some reason, Maksim loved her touch alone. He could sleep through a night with her beside him. He laughed. He even reconciled with Aleks." Voice gruff, Dmitri admitted, "When Maksim married, I felt more alone than I ever had before."

I pictured Dmitri by himself on that deck, gazing up at the moon. Lucía had said he was a lone-wolf type. Just like the beast from fairy tales, Dmitri didn't *want* to be.

I took his fist in both of my hands and pressed a kiss to the back of it. "No longer."

His brows drew together. "No longer."

"Please go on. I want to know more about you."

Seeming resigned to sharing, he continued, "Before I hit thirty, I'd made a fortune, but I derived no satisfaction from it. The money was like some grotesque entity, growing faster than I could ever spend it. My wealth *mocked* me, because the more I had, the more I became aware of what money couldn't buy: sanity, companionship, a family of my own."

And that explained why he was so adamant about spending it.

"Eventually I comprehended I was the only thing getting in the way of Maksim's happiness, and that I would always be a burden to him. A year ago, I made arrangements to check myself into a permanent facility in California, but on the way there, I decided to permanently check myself out. A life avoiding pleasure isn't worth living. I was done."

He'd been suicidal again just a year ago? "What happened?"

"A weather front forced the plane to touch down in Las Vegas. We were grounded until the next day. I figured, why not stay the weekend and drink myself into oblivion one last time?"

"Did you make another suicide attempt?"

He shook his head. "That night I had an epiphany, as if light touched all the darkened corners of my mind. I couldn't stop thinking: *What if I might have what Maksim did?* It may sound strange, but I *wanted* to have someone I'd face a loaded gun for."

Crazy, beautiful man.

"Maksim had turned his existence around because he had incentive: Lucía. Aleks too had changed his life because of Natalie. What if my woman was alive and well, only waiting for me to find her? I made a commitment to right my life and become a man worthy of a woman such as yourself."

Oh, Dmitri.

"I stopped taking those pills. They were dangerous and had been recalled in most countries. I improved dramatically just from that. I began working out and eating better. I studied sex to compensate for my limited experience."

And his piercing had made him "different" than he'd been—when abused by Orloff. "You had your scar removed."

He nodded. "I would never want to embarrass my woman in public. I organized my business, becoming more efficient, so I would have more time for the enjoyment I hoped would come. I bought this house, all to prepare for a wife and a life I didn't yet have."

He'd prepared himself for me. Well, not for me, necessarily, but for a future wife. "And you offered an olive branch to Aleks."

"*Da.* I began to comprehend the importance of family. Presenting a unified front is a very powerful thing, no? Then, a few months ago, I swallowed my pride to get his assistance with business matters that were *crucial* to me. He gladly used all his power and connections to help me. In the course of our dealings, I learned more about his life on the streets before Kovalev found him. Aleks had endured his own trials. We came to an understanding, and he has been helping me ever since."

"It took you a year before you found me?"

"You and I met a year later. Everything Maksim had told me—everything I'd scorned as idiotic—was true. I'd once asked him how I would recognize my woman. Theoretically. He'd said, 'You'll feel as if you've been struck by lightning.' That was an understatement. From the moment I saw you, I knew."

Dmitri's first word to me: *"You . . ."* This man believed I was his soul mate.

"Vika, I wouldn't have been right for you before. You would hardly have recognized me." He turned to me fully. I imagined him feeling physically and emotionally open after revealing his secrets. "Even after my changes, I would have liked more time to prepare for you; I still feared drifting. I'd never experienced sexual pleasure with another and not dissociated. The more pleasure, the more detachment. But there you were."

"When we hooked up in the bathroom . . ."

"I wanted to believe I would respond to you differently, but I decided not to push my luck by coming. Yet then you were *too* arousing. I had to release. I went mindless in a completely new way"—he held my gaze—"and I remembered *every blistering second with you.*"

I inhaled sharply. "You really never had before?"

He shook his head. "In your apartment, the same thing happened when I came: pure pleasure. But on our wedding night, when you went to your knees and sucked me, I realized there were yet more heights with you."

"That's why you stopped."

"Yes. I called Maksim, railing because he'd assured me things could be different once I found my woman. I told him I couldn't risk dissociating forever and never knowing you." Dmitri gazed past me as he said, "I just like . . . being with you."

I like being with you too.

He faced me again. "But Maksim said, 'Your wife deserves a full life, with everything that entails.' I decided you would have your wedding night if it killed me. For the first time, someone else's pleasure was more important than my own. Nothing was going to stop me from taking you. So after a lifetime of desperately fighting that dissociation, I stopped."

"You risked permanently losing yourself for me?" For a woman he'd known for mere days at that point? He was either the craziest man I'd ever met or the bravest.

Curt nod. "And when my mind was open like that, and I had surrendered to being ruined forever, you seeped into every inch of me. You took over my thoughts. Nothing could pry me away from the present because I was making love to my wife. Each one of your cries, the scent of your hair, the unimaginable softness of your skin—everything anchored me to you. You seared me."

"You're making me sound like the key to your recovery," I said, concerned about that.

"I *did* the work. I learned to cope. But I never had my own incentive to make truly frightening decisions."

Out on the cliff, he'd told me, "I let it fucking bleed."

I grazed his forearm once more.

His expression was grave. "Can you believe me when I tell you I'm a different man now?"

"Never again, Dmitri. Never, never again. Make me the promise."

"Very well. I can make that promise," he said, adding, "as long as you're alive."

"Dmitri!" I released his hand to pinch my temples.

"One of those things I shouldn't have said aloud?"

What was I going to do if he discovered all my lies? Hadn't I—just like Orloff—insinuated myself into Dmitri's life, deceiving him, using him, betraying him? The grifter in me clamored to rabbit out of this situation. But the snare was closing.

Dmitri had told me he'd known enough doubt and uncertainty to last a lifetime. Though I never wanted to cause him more, it seemed inevitable. Any move I made in the future would hurt him.

He cleared his throat again. "Now that you know these secrets, do you view me differently?" My husband was holding his breath.

He'd just laid himself bare for me. Despite such traumatic beginnings—his father's viciousness, his beloved mother's murder, his brothers' suffering, his guardian's appalling abuse—Dmitri Sevastyan had somehow grown to be proud and strong and courageous, amazing in every way. "Understanding your past makes me care even more deeply for you, Dmitri." *Snared.* "Understanding the risks you've taken since we've met shows me how brave you are."

He drew me into his lap—as if he'd been promising himself

he could, as soon as he'd completed his task. "And how crazy?"

Was he? Yeah, at times. And I wouldn't sugarcoat that. "Well, you kind of are, big guy." I put my hand over his heart. "But I'd still rather have an honest madman than a sane liar."

He wrapped his strong arms around me. "I like that you don't shy away from calling me crazy. For so long, everyone did." He rested his chin on my head, tightening his hold on me. "But I want you to understand something. I took those risks not because I'm crazy. I took them because nothing matters beyond having you. I am obsessed with you. What I feel will never burn away."

My heart turned over in my chest, but my jadedness made me ask, "How can you say that if you've never felt these things before?"

He pressed a kiss to my head and inhaled the scent of my hair. "I believe when a man finds the one woman meant to be his, he associates her scent with happiness. In the deepest recesses of his brain, he thinks, *This woman is where all happiness lies. She is my home.* Every time he catches her scent, that link is reinforced." Another kiss. "My happiness lies with you, Victoria. You are my home. It is *because* I've never experienced these feelings that I recognize them."

My eyes pricked with tears, and I was glad he couldn't see.

He'd told me, *When you've been in the dark as long as I have, there is no mistaking the light.*

Maybe he had found his soul mate. Stranger things had happened, right? But the notion didn't comfort me. *After everything he's survived, my betrayal will be all the more devastating. . . .*

CHAPTER 33

"Here we go." Dmitri guided me as I walked blindfolded through the house toward another of his surprises.

I couldn't see anything through the scarf he'd used, but I thought we were in the vicinity of his study.

Today was our one-month wedding anniversary. Sometimes I felt as if we'd been together forever.

Other times, a day.

This morning we'd driven up Highway 1 in his black Ferrari convertible. The sun had been shining, the road clear, and he'd been sliding me sexy grins. We'd shopped in an adorable seaside town—and he'd tried to buy me everything. Though uncomfortable in crowds, he had made an effort to prolong our outing and entertain me. Or perhaps he'd been stalling in order to get this mysterious surprise in place.

At my ear, he said, "We're almost there."

For his gift, I'd gotten him tickets to an eighties movie fest in L.A. and cufflinks made of tiger-eye for luck and protection.

I had a feeling I was about to be upstaged.

I'd thought about finally giving him a ring. All day, he'd

proudly referred to me as his wife. More than one person had glanced at his bare ring finger. And he'd noticed.

After he'd shared his past, I'd ordered a gorgeous gold band, shipping it here. Dmitri hadn't seen the package among all the others that kept arriving. I'd hidden the band with my many jewels.

Though I was falling for him, my anxiety kept me from giving him that ring, a pledge for forever.

Among our other difficulties, my husband and I remained in a stalemate over my family—and his own.

"Are you ready?" he asked.

I could *hear* his smile. "Yes! Though you don't have to keep buying me things."

"I told you that I would give you the entire world." And that he would free me.

Over this month, Dmitri had freed me sexually. He needed to take control, and I'd found so much freedom in surrender. . . .

He sighed, adding, "And someone must spend our money, since you refuse to."

I stutter-stepped, but he caught me. "You really just said that?" During my shopping sessions on the couch, I'd relaxed and dreamed and felt the power of his fortune.

I'd gifted a huge stipend to a veterans' association in my grandmother's name. My grandfather, the great love of her life, had been a pilot whose plane had gone down while she'd been pregnant with Mom.

I'd set up design scholarships, because I'd wished for one myself.

I'd donated liberally to children's shelters, with Benji—and Dmitri—in my thoughts. . . .

"We're here." He began untying the scarf. "First, I will say something I never thought I'd be able to: Happy one-month anniversary, *moya zhena*." He removed my blindfold.

I blinked in disbelief.

I was looking at a large design studio—filled with dress forms, garment racks, and three brand-new sewing machines. Organizational systems for spools, tapes, and scissors lined one wall. Bolts of luxe cloth were arrayed along another. The fourth wall was blank; I could hang drawings there!

I murmured, "Until this moment . . . I don't think I'd ever understood the word *glee*." I crossed to a cutting table, sweeping my fingertips across the surface. Then I marveled at the sewing machines, the most advanced I'd ever seen. I checked out the assortment of cloth, a rainbow of hues and patterns.

I wanted to explore everything, but, as ever, Dmitri drew my gaze. I skipped over to him. "You are the best husband ever!" Oh, I could tell he liked that. "This is the nicest, most thoughtful thing anyone has ever done for me." I went up on my toes to kiss him. "How did you know what to buy?"

"I contacted the head designer at Chanel for advice."

I laughed, then realized he might be serious. "That wasn't a joke?"

"No, love. It wasn't."

"How did you get this set up so quickly?"

"Money expedited delivery." His standard answer. "I'll show you my favorite part." He said, *"Touch screen."* That blank wall lit up, resembling a thirty-foot-wide computer screen, with icons of various design programs!

With a tight wave of his hand, the image changed, becoming an enormous canvas. "Here." He pulled a stylus from his pocket and handed it to me. "You can draw ideas and save them. The lines can be all colors and different widths. There's shading as well."

I tentatively drew a couple of lines and then, getting bolder, the basic shape of a dress model. "Oh, fuck me. Now we are cooking with gas."

"I . . . are we?"

"Just a saying," I said absently, adding more contrast. I quickly figured out how to change colors, and started to outline an idea that had been tickling at my brain.

When I'd gotten the basics down, I stepped back to view my sketch, only then becoming aware how quiet the room was. I turned to Dmitri.

He was sitting on the couch near the door, elbows on his knees, watching me avidly. And he was hard.

He gave me his charming shrug, the one that said, *Can't help it.* "You're utterly irresistible when you design."

I set aside the stylus and sashayed over to him.

"I want to watch you whenever you're in this studio," he told me, his voice husky. "So I take back what I said earlier. This couch is my favorite part of the room."

My gaze drank in his proud face. Somehow over the last month, he'd grown even more handsome. His eyes were glimmering with satisfaction, his body ready to pleasure mine.

And yet a wave of sadness washed over me. Dmitri Sevastyan was *too* thoughtful, too attentive and intelligent and sexy and caring. He was too . . .

Perfect.

His gift overwhelmed me. This life overwhelmed me.

Earlier, I'd called Karin from the restroom of a seaside

souvenir shop, in the middle of what must've been a panic attack. "I can barely breathe."

"Are you going to confess?"

"How can I risk it?" I would never tell her the tragic details of his past, so she couldn't understand how badly my betrayal would wound Dmitri. "What would happen if I lost him?"

Her tone grew distant. "You find ways to go on."

My poor sister.

"Maybe he cares about you enough to forgive you."

"To forgive *all* of us." I still didn't know who'd placed Brett in Dmitri's path, making Dmitri lose his ever-loving mind to jealousy.

"Hon, it's been a month. Something's got to give."

She was right. Talking on the phone to my pack of scoundrels a few times a week was like putting a Band-Aid on a sucking chest wound. Hearing Cash's laughter . . .

As I waited for the answer to my dilemma, the days slipped by.

"Vika?" Dmitri rose and peered down at me, clearly struggling to read me.

I gazed up at him. I didn't *want* to love someone who would end up hurting me—or being hurt by me; yet I was on the brink of falling totally in love with Dmitri.

Again, I couldn't catch my breath. Freaked out and on edge, I could envision every scenario in the world except one: us living happily ever after.

You can't cheat fate.

My survival instinct kicked in—because if he left me, I'd be broken, a shell of myself, forever replaying this dream I'd once had.

I backed up a step—a grifter sensing the biggest snare of

them all—and muttered, "I'll, uh, lemme go make a call."

"You're doing it again. The more I try to please you, the more you distance yourself. Tell—me—why."

I just needed to hit the pause button for a bit. I forced myself to turn and walk away.

Something's got to give.

I'd made it to the hall when he clamped my arm and pulled me around. I craned my head up to take in his fierce expression, his crazed eyes.

"You're not going anywhere."

"I need a minute—"

"I can't goddamned read you! Except for when I'm pleasuring you." He fisted the material of my dress. "Then you let me see *everything.*" With a yell, he ripped my dress clean from my body.

I swallowed, shaken by the sudden ferocity of his emotions—of *my* emotions.

"Then you hold nothing back!"

"Dmitri, wait!"

My bra and thong joined the torn dress on the floor.

I cried out when he swung me up into his arms, cupping my ass in his hot palms. The intensity seething inside him should've frightened me; my legs locked around his waist, my arms around his neck, his shirt abrading my stiff nipples.

When he yanked his fly open and shoved his pants down his thighs, my pussy was already wet for him.

"You are *maddening* me, woman." He planted me on his shaft, shuddering with every inch he forced inside me. "Ah, God, Victoria!"

I moaned as my slickened sheath welcomed him home.

He pressed me against the wall, his lips crashing into mine, his tongue seeking. But he hadn't moved his hips.

Between kisses, he snatched off his shirt. With his bared chest rubbing against my breasts, he kissed me aggressively, tonguing me, as if his mouth fucked mine. But he still hadn't thrust.

How was he fighting that primal need? He'd given me his cock, yet held it back from me, leaving me aching for more.

The point wasn't lost on me.

He broke the kiss to run his lips up my neck. "You're pulling away from me." At my ear, he groaned, *"Don't."*

"I'm not—"

"Don't lie to me!" He leaned down to lick my tits, nipping them with his white teeth, sucking the delicate flesh between his merciless lips.

As he tormented my breasts in a frenzy, I could only clutch his shoulders and beg, *"More."*

He squeezed me, pinching my nipples hard.

I cried out, frantic for him to move inside me. "I need you! *Please.*"

He stood fully. Sweat dotted his skin, beading his upper lip. His hips slicked my inner thighs. "Look at my marks all over your breasts."

I glanced down. Stark love bites covered them, circling my areolas. At the sight, I helplessly rocked on his cock.

"No!" He pulled me from the wall and slapped my ass. "Feel what it's like to need more."

"Ahhh!" The sting nearly brought me off.

He coiled his arms around me, tightening his ruthless embrace. "I am obsessed with you." He said this the way another man might say, *I am in love with you.* "Feel the same way toward me! Want me like you want your next fucking breath!" When I leaned in to kiss his neck and taste his sweat, his head tipped back and he groaned, *"Think of nothing but me. . . ."*

"Please, Dmitri!" I could feel him throbbing inside me! I drummed my heels into his ass.

"You belong to me alone." When he nipped my neck, my pussy quivered around his cock. "I want to belong to you as well!"

In spite of my emotions—or because of them—I was about to come, tension gathering inside me.

"Why haven't you given me a goddamned ring?"

Because this dream had to end.

"Why?"

I threaded my fingers through his hair, tugging him to meet my eyes. It was on the tip of my tongue to cry, "Any move I make is the wrong one—because I'm falling in love with you!" But I couldn't.

He could tell I was holding back. His fingertips bit into my ass, and his eyes went even wilder. "Fucking give me something!"

When I could only whimper, he abruptly pulled out of me, holding me poised over his cock.

I gasped. "Nooo! Come back—please!"

In a menacing tone, he said, "Do you feel empty inside? Cold?" He looked insane. "It doesn't have to be this way, does it? What you need is so close you can feel it."

I mindlessly undulated for him. "Dmitri?" I couldn't think!

"You are so close to me, Vika, but just out of reach. When I would kill for this—" He rammed his cock home, impaling me.

"Ah, God!" My head lolled.

He bucked his hips, pounding upward. Then again. Deeper. And again. *Deeper.* He was punishing me, his muscles rippling as he fucked. "Give me something of yourself!"

My tits rubbed his unyielding chest. My pussy tightened around him, readying to come. Excruciating pleasure/pressure mounted. Between breaths, I cried, "Dmitri! It's too much . . . *too strong.*"

What my body was about to do scared me.

What my heart was about to do scared me.

He shoved into me with all his might. "Give me something! Goddamn it, anything!"

The truth spilled out: "I'm afraid!"

Astonishment. He eased his feverish pace until he was slowly grinding me. He knew I was talking about more than one thing. "*Moya zhena*, just let it happen. I will always take care of you." He was talking about more than one thing too. "Can you do that?"

Panting, I said, "I *want* to. I-I'm trying."

He nodded. Lips thinned, jaw set, he accelerated his rhythm. He swelled inside me to the limit as he plunged harder and harder, relentless. "Let go, love." At my ear, he groaned, "*I've got you. . . .*"

My orgasm hit me with the force of a shockwave. I threw back my head and cried, *"Dmitri!"* That agonizing pressure gave way, wrenching a scream from my lungs.

My mind blanked. I floated; I begged. I dimly heard him telling me I would be his forever. That he would fight for heaven. That I was making him spend so hard I'd feel his cum like a thrust.

I was still climaxing when his shaft pulsated inside me.

His back bowed, his mighty body racked with pleasure. To the sound of his tortured bellows, he shot his hot semen hard and deep—just like his thrusts.

✦

*A*fter washing and putting on a robe, I returned from the bathroom. Outside, a breeze swept the fog from the grounds, rain beginning to fall.

Dressed in jeans, he sat on the edge of the bed, elbows on his knees, head in his hands. He'd done the same on our wedding night, when he'd believed he could never have sex with me. "Did I . . . did I hurt you?" He sounded wretched. "The marks I left . . ."

In the bathroom, I'd run my fingers over them, getting hot all over again. I sat beside him, putting my hand on his back. "Have you seen your shoulders, big guy?" I pressed kisses to the claw marks across one. "I used you for a scratching post."

He gave a strained laugh.

"You're not capable of hurting me," I said without a doubt.

"But I'm not capable of making you content either." He raised his anguished face to me. "I don't have any experience with this. Tell me how to make you happy. If taught, I can learn."

Realization struck, and I knew I'd remember this moment for the rest of my life.

He is *in love with me.*

No longer could I call it obsession. Or craziness. Over the last four weeks, he truly had fallen. "You are perfect, Dmitri. It's me and my baggage that's the problem."

He drew back with a scowl. "Perfect? Even after what I told you?"

"More so. You revealed a traumatic past you've worked hard to overcome. One you're triumphing over. You're so much more than your past."

Sheer adoration shone in his eyes. And Lady Luck help me, I was close to returning it.

"Then why have you grown distant? You tell me little of yourself. You long for your family, but won't visit them. You get antsy after every gift I buy you, though you know how much money we have. Vika, why are you afraid?"

I would give him part of the truth. "I was raised to believe if something seems too good to be true, it *is*. And I'm superstitious as hell. Put those two together, and I'm waiting for the other shoe to drop." Lightning flared outside, as if to punctuate my statement. I warily noted it before returning my gaze to him.

"I don't understand."

"It's *too* good. I went from having no man to having one who amazes me every second. I went from cocktail waitressing and eviction notices to all this." I waved around. "The whole situation feels like reaching for the stars, which is something I never do."

Tension eased from him, moment by moment. "Why?"

"Because that would involve taking my eyes off the road and my hands off the wheel. Great way to crash." The rain intensified, pouring along the coast.

He shifted closer to me, hope growing in his eyes. "How do we get past your superstition?"

"This feels like a dream, and all dreams have to end—"

"Why do they have to end?"

Not a rhetorical question. He wanted me to explain this? "I don't know why. I just know they always have before."

"You say I'm more than my past. Why can't your dreams be more than the ones that ended?"

I didn't have an answer for that. "Dmitri, what if I'm not good enough for you?"

He looked baffled. "I've told you what you are to me. How you've affected me mentally and physically. Emotionally."

"I'm not responsible for that—*you* are. You got therapy for years, and you worked so hard to improve your life; you still do. All the changes you made must have helped you overcome the dissociation." I could tell he didn't agree, but wasn't going to argue his point. "Now that you're able to stay present, maybe you could find someone else. Someone who's more like Lucía and Natalie."

Someone who isn't rotten from all the secrets burrowing inside her.

He blinked. "I don't follow."

"They're both rich and educated. I couldn't pick them apart with a fork."

He squared his shoulders. "You are rich and talented and brilliant and exquisitely beautiful. You're an artist."

Yeah, a *con* artist. A breed apart.

Dmitri insisted, "I'm far from perfect."

I sighed, giving him a sad smile. "Not from where I'm sitting, big guy."

He narrowed his eyes. "I believe I am ready to tell you more about my past. I wasn't entirely forthcoming." His tone was threatening—as if he intended to hit me with a fatal imperfection.

"Did you lie?" No, I would've caught him.

"I've never lied to you. But what I'm about to tell you

involves another. His secret has been safe with me for twenty-three years, never repeated outside of my family. I will share it with you now."

He'd definitely piqued my curiosity. "Okay. I'll keep the secret to the grave."

Nod. "I told you Orloff died. Which is true. But he was murdered." Another bolt of lightning flashed.

I schooled my expression. "Who did it?"

"My brother and I."

CHAPTER 34

My mind raced as I got my bearings with this bombshell. Orloff had died when Dmitri had been about nine. Maksim would've barely been a teenager. *How do I respond to this?* I settled on: "Will you tell me more?"

Dmitri ran his fingers through his hair. "When Orloff beat my brother and locked him in the cellar, the violence sent me deeper into dissociation; my isolation with Orloff kept me under, until I rarely surfaced. Maksim was down there in the dark for months, suffering, blaming himself for not protecting me. The night of a bitter freeze, I finally woke. Maybe the wind battering the window brought me back. Maybe it was that fuck's smug behavior—he *knew* Maksim would die."

Orloff had fully planned to murder an innocent boy. Maksim must've been so terrified.

"I knew I had to save my brother somehow. When I tried to get the key from the man's pocket, he woke, but I was prepared. Earlier, I'd gone outside and brought in a snow shovel. I hit Orloff with all my might. I freed Maks, and we . . .

we strangled the man before he could ever wake," Dmitri said, his gaze clocking my face for clues.

I wanted to shake him: "You felt guilty about this? You carried this weight? Shuck it right now!"

He swallowed. "I have no idea how you're reacting."

I chose my words more carefully. "That psychopath forced you and Maksim to defend yourselves. You two were so incredibly brave."

As if I were missing his point, he said, "I helped *kill* a man. In the same situation, I would do it again."

"Do you think I would've done less if I could've saved Benji from the horrors he suffered? Those men are still out there, Dmitri. And we have to live with that knowledge. You and Maksim prevented a homicidal monster from preying on other children, yet no one will ever know you're heroes." I cupped his face.

As he'd done the first night, he leaned into my touch. "Heroes?"

"If someone had prevented Orloff from ever putting his sights on you, what would you have called that person?"

He drew back. "I never thought of it that way."

"It's crystal clear to me. Thank you for trusting me with this."

His brow furrowed. "That's it?" His shoulder and neck muscles tensed, his frustration welling.

"If you told me this to make me see you in a worse light, then you did just the opposite."

He shot to his feet, exasperated. "I have other secrets. My family has *mafiya* ties."

Come again? "You're saying your family operates outside the law?"

"After Kovalev's death, Aleks took over the man's position as a *vor*, a very powerful man in the *mafiya*."

Dr. Nat's father had been involved in organized crime? Aleks presently was? "What does he run?" Guns, drugs, girls? All of the above?

"Nothing. He is a former enforcer who is paid for protection. Maksim had political connections to the *mafiya* as well."

Unbelievable. "And you?"

"I have drawn on Aleks's power and influence."

"To help you with those crucial business dealings," I said. "What were they?"

Dmitri seemed to be taking my measure. "You'll get no more secrets out of me, not until you start sharing your own."

How could our investigation of the Sevastyans fail to turn up even a whisper of this? "Wouldn't there be something online?"

"I've kept a tight rein on that information. Over the last year, I've used a great deal of money and skill to bury our backgrounds."

I frowned. "Why did you tell me these things now?"

"Because I want you to understand I'm not perfect. And that I trust you, even with my family's secrets. Perhaps now you'll see I can be as accepting as you are, far more so than you seem to think."

Dmitri and his family operated outside the law. Could he really raise a brow at one or two or thirty grifters?

For the first time in weeks, hope filled me. Dmitri had risked his life to save Maksim, just as Maksim had for him. Then they'd done whatever it had taken to survive. If I explained how desperate I'd been to protect my parents, surely Dmitri could forgive me.

If he loved me . . .

He'd told me his history; he deserved mine. I would confess everything, betting the pot with this man, but only after he comprehended my motivation—for targeting *him*. "Dmitri, you know I would do anything for my family."

He sat beside me. "Of course."

"I believe you'll like them very much. Do you want to go to Vegas for a few days and see what they're like? We could fly out on Friday." Giving them a couple of days to prepare.

Please, please Lady Luck, let him forgive me.

The look in his eyes . . . maybe it would be enough. "Yes, Vika." His voice was hoarse. "I would like that very much."

CHAPTER 35

"*I* don't want to let you out of my sight," Dmitri said, his hands covering my shoulders.

I smoothed my palms over his crisp button-down. "I'll be fine for an hour, big guy." I still couldn't believe I was staying in the Caly penthouse for a week. When we'd arrived a short while ago, other employees had bugged at the sight of me wearing a couture slipdress and diamonds, on the arm of a man like Dmitri, with Starsky and Hutch hovering around to "buffer irritations."

"I would skip work"—Dmitri had already set up his computer and things in the study—"but I have a couple of business calls I need to make."

He hadn't gotten in his hour this morning before we'd been due to leave, which was my fault. I'd caught him vacillating over which ties to pack and said, "You never give this much thought to your clothes."

With his brows drawn, he'd held up his options. "Making a good impression on your family is very important to me, love."

Yep, I'd jumped him, ties flying.

Now I said, "I need to call in our catering order for later anyway." I planned to bring my pack to visit in shifts, starting things slow. All of them together would be overwhelming for anyone, but especially for Dmitri. I'd invited just Karin and Benji over tonight, for wine and dinner on the terrace.

I couldn't wait to see my family, had missed them so much. And I needed to talk to my sister face to face and ask for her advice. . . .

Dmitri pressed a kiss to my head, then drew back to gaze down at me. "I'm looking forward to meeting everyone."

"I kinda figured." Ever since I'd broached his meeting them, he'd been keyed up. "Just like I'm looking forward to seeing your family soon."

"They are on my list to call now." His answer didn't sound that promising.

I adjusted the strap of my royal-blue dress. "Am I the source of the rift between you and Maksim?"

He curled his finger under my chin. "Every single person in my family believes you are wonderful for me—and that you are the only one for me. If anything, they're worried *I* will bungle things with you."

Then why wouldn't he tell me what the fight had been about? "They don't see me as a gold-digger?"

"Not at all. They know I insisted on that postnup. You can walk away at any time with half of our fortune, and yet"—he grinned—"you keep wearing my ring and waking me up with blow jobs."

I arched a brow. "Fine, husband. Go forth." I pushed at his chest. "Work. Provide. I'll see you in an hour."

At the study door, he hesitated. "Vika, everything will turn out well. I will make sure of it."

I wished I could believe that.

Because even after Dmitri had bared his soul, my grift sense still needled me. Something was *off*, that thorn nagging my subconscious. Maybe Karin could help me figure it out.

Left to my own devices, I took a few minutes to check out the penthouse with new eyes. I strolled into the guest bathroom, memories making me blush. Dmitri had waited eight years for that night. *I remembered every blistering second with you.*

No, he'd waited his entire adult life: *Because, beautiful girl, this is the most pleasurable thing I have ever done, and I'll give anything for it to continue.*

I wandered outside to the terrace and climbed up to the deck, with its wisteria-covered trellis and bubbling fountain. My beast's lair. *This is foreign territory for me,* he'd said. *But I like my new guide very much.* It'd been new territory for both of us, for different reasons.

Though the sun beat down, such a change from that moonlit night, I twirled my ring on my finger and replayed our first kiss. *I will play games with you. . . .*

I'd had no idea how much my life was about to change. I'd had no idea I'd ever have to confess to him.

But first, introductions.

I headed back down, deciding to order all of Karin and Benji's favorite dishes, even if none of them went together. Steak, risotto, sushi, pizza . . .

I'd just entered the living room when a text chime sounded from my purse on the coffee table. I hurried over and dug out my pink phone.

I blinked in disbelief at Karin's message.

KV: Teotwawki outside.

What the ... ? I read it again, as if the message would change.

When I'd texted her two days ago to invite her over, she'd replied: I will contact you when you reach the Caly.

The abrupt response was puzzling, but I'd shrugged it off, figuring she'd been upset about Walker. When Karin had sent him back all his child support and that note, he'd written:

> *Apparently you've gotten your claws into a new dupe. But if you think I'll let another man raise my son, think again.*

Now I feared something else had already been wrong. I glanced toward the study. I had an impulse to tell Dmitri, but what if the message was a false alarm? I could go downstairs and be back up before he even knew I was gone. I hurried to the penthouse's main entry, my heels clicking down the foyer.

Starsky stood at the entrance.

"Just going to talk to a friend for a few minutes," I told him. "I won't leave the property."

He hesitated, so I said, "Wasn't asking permission, Starsky," and breezed past him. Even when they were on my side, bodyguards were annoying as hell.

Outside the casino, checkout-time traffic clogged the main drive. I finally spotted Karin, Benji, and Pete in my cousin's new sedan. All three looked pensive as I wove through the bumper-to-bumper snarl of cars to reach them.

When I hopped in the backseat beside Benji, he snapped his fingers at me. "Lemme see your phone."

Frowning, I handed it over. "What's going on?"

While he flew through screens at lightning speed, Karin gazed at me from the front seat with something like pity. "You aren't falling for Dmitri, hon. You're already there, aren't you?"

I hesitated, then murmured, "Yes, I am."

Her expression said, *Welcome to the world of heartache.*

"What the hell's happening? He's going to wonder where I went."

Pete glanced back from behind the wheel. "We're rescuing you."

"From what?"

He honked at the cars blocking his way. "We'll explain everything, but for now, we need to get out of here."

"To go *where?*"

Benji glanced up. "Don't say. Not yet. Her phone is hot."

"Hot??" My heart raced. "Who would bug it? Did you guys just wake up this morning and think 'Vice probably has a bug'?"

Pete said, "Your husband did it."

"That's ridiculous." Panic churned. "Why would he?"

Benji powered down my phone, handing it back to me. "Pretty sure we can talk freely now."

"You can't know it was Dmitri." But who else would do something like that to me? Who would have the chance? "Maybe ... maybe the cartel is monitoring us for some reason!"

Benji shook his head. "You're the only one in the family with a tap. Plus, the hack to pirate the microphone is really sophisticated. Something you'd see from a tech genius. Assume he made a clone and accessed all of your data in real time as well."

Data. Every text, picture, e-mail, and web search. My face heated as I thought of everything I'd written about him, all the things I'd *said* about him while in range of that phone. "Since *when?*"

"No way to tell," he said. "If I had to guess, I'd say from the beginning."

From the first night? Then Dmitri had probably heard me telling Karin I'd never come harder than with him. I cast my mind back. He must've heard my family plotting how to shake him down. He'd called with news about my new car right when we'd been wondering how to monetize his interest! "Then he knows what we are. What we've done." And he still wanted me? I stared down at my ring. He might've started spying on me in the beginning for security reasons. Maybe he regretted it—the same way I wished I'd never used him. Maybe he and I could try counseling. "This isn't necessarily teotwawki here."

"There's more," Karin said. "A couple of weeks back, I was talking to Giovanni, the Caly concierge. He said Sevastyan was at the casino about a year ago."

"Dmitri told me about that trip." When he'd made the decision to turn his life around then.

Karin said, "I used some juice to order security footage of his visit. We got it two days ago." She'd waited for me to reach Vegas before she would risk communicating with me on a potentially hot phone.

My anxiety multiplied. *Here comes the other shoe.* "And?"

"Sevastyan sees you. He followed you."

"That doesn't make any sense. If he saw me and was interested, why not approach me? He's a gorgeous billionaire."

"He wasn't so hot back then," Pete said. "He was much thinner and looked strung out. Pretty sure he was a drug addict. And he'd been drinking like he was trying to kill himself."

He kind of had been. But that was before he'd started to work out and eat right. Before he'd kicked those pills. "Still, I would've given him the freaking time of day."

"No, Vice, you wouldn't have," Karin said. "Because you were at your bachelorette party."

"What are you saying?"

Pete laid on the horn. "He got rid of your fiancé that week."

My mind zoomed back to the night I'd caught Brett. Yes, I'd marveled at how off-the-charts hot that woman had been.

The showgirl who'd somehow found her way to our party. To Brett.

Oh, my God. "My grift sense said it was a badger game! I just suspected you guys of pulling it—to get the gull out of my life."

"Not us," Karin said. "Sevastyan must've hooked up with a private investigator in Vegas and put a temptation scenario into motion."

I had no urge to get back together with Brett or anything, but could any man have withstood that kind of lure? Fifteen minutes ago, I would've bet my life on Dmitri. Now I didn't even know him.

He'd set me up for devastation, ensuring I found my fiancé with another woman. The success of his scheme had depended on my pain.

"We've started digging with detective agencies," Pete said. "We'll know more soon enough." He craned his head, looking for a way to reverse.

I'd love one too—a way to reverse the last month of my life. I'd known something was off, had felt it down to my bones! "You guys think Dmitri's been spying on me *for a year*?"

"Yeah, sis." Benji's solemn eyes made mine water. "I'd bet ten large he was."

That manipulative stalker!

Movement near the hotel entry drew my attention. Speak of the devil.

Dmitri's head jerked in all directions as he searched for me. His frantic gaze darted.

Karin mumbled, "Shit. He's already down here."

He caught sight of us and charged forward, his long strides eating up the pavement.

Pete locked the doors.

Dmitri reached the car, pulling the door handle. Masking his panic, he bit out, "Open this for me, love."

I shook my head.

In a roughened voice, he asked, "What's happened?"

"Don't you already know?" I held up my phone.

His eyes widened. "Let me explain, Vika!"

Explain what? He'd played with my life. He'd played with *me*. I understood the irony, could see the parallels. But short of impending murder, I'd never targeted a decent person.

Why had *he* targeted *me*? Tears welled.

"Just *talk* to me." He sounded so agonized, and even now it gutted me. "Please don't cry, *moya zhena*."

Tears spilled down my cheeks.

Each one maddened him more. "Open this door!" He pounded a fist on the roof of the car.

Karin jumped. Pete snapped, "For fuck's sake."

Dmitri was just getting started. "Goddamn it, let me . . . get to you!" His accent was the thickest I'd ever heard it. "Just give me a chance to explain." Another pounding hit to the roof. A month ago, he'd warned Pete, *"Do not ever get between me and her. You do not want to do that."* This car was between Dmitri and his wife.

I could only stare and cry. Karin reached back to take my hand. An infusion of strength.

He stabbed his fingers through his unruly hair. "I can make this right! Vika, love, I *can*." He looked crazed, as if he was barely holding it together. Like how I felt.

I spotted his bodyguards at the entrance, "buffering" against Calydon security.

I murmured, "Did you set Brett up?" But Dmitri must've heard.

He bellowed with frustration and yanked the car handle so hard I thought it would break.

I had my answer. A sob broke free. But I wanted to hear him say it. "Did you set him up?"

Dmitri swallowed, growing still. "Yes."

I battled a wave of nausea. The anxiety I'd grappled with had never been about fate or luck or a too-perfect husband. I'd subconsciously picked up clues from his behavior and sensed my own impending doom. I'd been tied across the railroad tracks, perceiving the vibrations of an oncoming locomotive.

"I can't even look at you!"

That seemed to snap him past the limits of his control. "Guess what, wife? I'd do all of it again!"

"Stay the fuck away from me! I never want to see your face again!"

The sedan lurched ahead a few feet, but was blocked by a taxi.

Eyes wild, Dmitri yelled, *"Nooo!"* Still yanking on the car handle, he pounded his fist against the window. The car rocked.

Benji muttered, "Jesus."

"Just unlock the door, Vika." Another brutal punch against the window. Blood smeared the glass. "You cannot leave!"

Even now I fought the impulse to soothe his anguish.

Pete said, "Finally!" The car sped forward out onto the Strip, leaving Dmitri behind.

I gazed back as he stumbled out into the traffic, yelling, *"Do not leave me!"*

CHAPTER 36

"*Is she hyperventilating?*"

"*She looks like she's about to throw up.*"

"*Not in my new car!*"

"*Shut the fuck up, Pete.*"

"*Vice, say something, hon.*"

I couldn't, could barely think with the roaring in my ears. I had all this noise in my head, yet my body was numb.

Was this what crazy felt like? How had Dmitri stood it for so many years?

Familiar scenery passed by my window, but Dmitri's dried blood on the glass colored every sight. Vegas no longer felt like my home.

I'd made my home alongside a wave-tossed cliff with a man who was a stranger to me.

I glanced down at my ring, and the tears fell and fell. . . .

After what must've been ages, we pulled up to my parents' house. I let Karin walk me inside.

When Mom and Dad leapt up to hug me, I gave a humiliating sob. Cold-as-Ice Vice had broken into frozen shards. Even Cash's welcoming gurgle from his playpen barely registered. I dimly noticed Al and Gram had traded up from sherry to hard liquor—vodka. Because things were seriously fucked.

Mom brushed tears from my face. "Honey, we're going to figure this out."

Dad searched my expression. "Did he ever hurt you, sweet pea?"

I shook my head. Finally found my voice. "He was . . . wonderful. Obviously too good to be true."

I sat on the lumpy couch, Mom and Dad on one side, Karin protectively on the other.

Mom rubbed my back. "Then help us understand this."

How? When I couldn't wrap my mind around it? "I don't know. I don't . . . I can't *think*."

How much of Dmitri's interest was real? How much of his sentiments?

Everything between us was as fake as the Strip.

I muffled another sob.

"We can't figure out *why*." Mom frowned. "Does he like playing games?"

Dmitri had warned me he would do just that.

Benji sat on my parents' love seat. "Maybe he's a typical rich asshole who enjoys manipulating people. He could've made a bet with one of his brothers or something, then ended up falling for Vice."

Karin said, "Maybe he's an unlovable person—and he knows it. He could've spied on Vice, learned everything about her, then changed himself like a chameleon to trick her into loving him."

They debated possibilities, each one getting more far-fetched.

I finally said, "I want to see the surveillance."

Karin nodded. "Benji put a compilation together."

He pushed buttons on a remote. "I'll cue it up." The TV flared to life.

I noticed they had a new flat-screen, courtesy of Dmitri's money. Good. They'd proudly hung the art I'd bought them.

Video footage of the Caly's main lounge began to play, with a date and time stamp at the bottom. August 21 at ten after ten.

I barely recognized Dmitri sitting at the end of the bar. Because he'd been a drug-addicted, addled, suicidal wreck—a shadow of what he was now.

He'd weighed at least twenty pounds less. His skin had been pale and clammy, his face gaunt, his eyes deadened and filled with pain.

Seeing him like that . . . Emotion squeezed my chest till my lungs threatened to collapse.

Then my group of seven women came on-screen—Karin and I, cousins, and grift friends. We'd booked rooms that night at the Caly; right then, we would've been heading out to a club next door.

Karin, dazzling as ever in a slinky red dress, had led the way. She'd been pregnant, but hadn't looked it, except for her glowing skin and lustrous hair. Every man she'd passed had done a double take. Yet as she'd traipsed past Dmitri, he hadn't spared her a second glance.

I was farther behind her, the last of the group. I'd been wearing a black strapless dress, my hair loose. I'd been laughing at something.

When Dmitri spotted me across the bar, his body jolted straighter. He'd stared at my face as I passed, rubbing his chest.

All of a sudden, those deadened eyes glimmered with interest. . . .

He'd once described his first impression of me. He'd been telling the truth—about the *real* first time he'd seen me: "You looked like an angel to me. One with an edge. My chest tightened, and my pulse raced. When I registered the blue of your eyes, I believed I was having a heart attack."

I swiped my forearm over my cheeks. He'd gazed at me as if . . . I were a candle in a world of darkness.

Hurrying to follow, he'd tossed money on the bar, then strode out of the casino.

The video skipped to later that night at the Caly. With Dmitri secretly observing me, I'd picked a pocket. The guy must've negged me.

Dmitri had canted his head, appearing utterly fascinated. *An angel with an edge.*

Gram murmured, "Nice lift, Victoria."

"Not nice enough. He saw me do it." Between that and the spying . . . "He's known all along what we are." All that worry and covering up for nothing.

Pete said, "Oh, yeah."

At the end of the night, Dmitri had trailed my group to the elevator, then gone straight to the front desk, taking aside the manager.

Had Dmitri paid for my information then? My room number? He could've cloned my phone that very weekend.

Pete told me, "I had a hunch about all your burned marks, so we got more recent tapes. Vice, he busted your cons."

My fists clenched. *"What??"*

Another video cued up, this one from just over a month ago. There stood Nigel in the lobby, fidgeting, smoothing a hand over his head, waiting for me to show. And off to one side—Dmitri, looking a thousand times better, phone in hand. He'd texted something; seconds later, Nigel glanced down at his own phone, paling at whatever he'd read. Dmitri had spooked the man somehow.

Right on time, I showed up in my white drape dress—then looked dumbfounded as my mark bailed.

In the video, Dmitri squared his shoulders, clearly intending to talk to me then. How nervous he must have been!

As he started toward me, I exhaled an irritated breath, texting Pete my humiliating defeat. When I pinched my temples, Dmitri slowed his pace, looking wrecked. As if he hated my pain. Even though he'd been the cause of it!

A group of babes approached him, circling him aggressively, blowing his chance to talk to me. He scowled at them, then reluctantly walked away.

The TV screen went black. I stared at it anyway.

What had he said to me that very night on the deck? "Perhaps I drove the others away so you would appear in front of me."

Dear God, when he'd tipped his face up to the moon and exhaled, he had been longing—for *me*.

Then, as if his wish to the universe had come true, I'd shown up moments later. No wonder he'd been shocked.

Fresh from sabotaging my con, never knowing what was at stake for me, he'd kissed me. *Wait*. He'd known everything. He'd known about the cartel. My eyes narrowed. He'd paid them off so easily because *he'd always intended to.*

So why let us suffer? Why not pay sooner? Couldn't he tell how scared we'd been? For months, we'd talked about nothing else, and he'd been listening in.

Dad said, "I watch that video, and I don't see a man out to hurt my daughter. I see obsession and fixation but not malice."

"Obsession?" Benji turned off the TV and set aside the remote. "You could say that. Today he bloodied the car window trying to get to Vice."

"Then how could he keep himself away from her?" Mom asked. "Once Brett was out of the picture . . ."

Pete scratched his head. "He must've used some of that time to clean himself up." He turned to me. "Is Dmitri off whatever he'd been on?"

"Yeah," I murmured. "Completely."

Benji said, "Before you married him, he mentioned issues. Based on the way he acted today, I'm thinking more than drugs." When I nodded, he said, "So mental issues."

My sense of loyalty to Dmitri still had a stranglehold on me. I would never specify exactly what he'd struggled with. "He worked on some things over the past year. Then he and I resolved some more." *I think. Who knows what was real?* "If you'd talked with him over the last month, you'd just think he was a rich eccentric."

Karin put her arm around my shoulders. "You told me he sent up all these red flags, but I pushed anyway."

She had. They *all* had. Mom had cried, "You're letting him get away!" But then, none of us had had a choice.

Benji leaned forward. "I'm sorry you've been hurt, sis, but marrying him was still the right play. You're rich now. You'll never have to work again."

I wanted *Dmitri*. I wanted my husband. Or the man I'd thought he was.

"No prenup with a known con artist?" Karin shook her head. "What was he thinking?"

"The lawyer said that postnup was legit," Pete said. "Dmitri's left himself with a half a billion dollar exposure."

It's actually a ton more than that, Pete.

Mom nodded. "For whatever reason, Sevastyan gambled. And he lost."

They were making Dmitri sound foolish, and even now it got my back up. He might be crazy, but he wasn't stupid. Just the opposite. He was the most brilliant man I'd ever met. Methodical. Quick to learn—

My eyes widened as realization hit me. I shot to my feet, sucking in a breath.

He did learn! "I see now," I whispered. "I see so clearly what he did." Everything began to add up.

"Don't leave us hanging, Vice," Benji said.

I started to pace. "He let *me* catch *him*." The fox had never suspected the henhouse was a trap.

"I don't understand," Dad said. "What'd he want from you?"

"He wanted us to be together. Married." Not just wed. Our lives entangled.

And he'd had only so much time to snare me.

People who dated had sex. If he'd denied me much longer, I would've gotten even more suspicious. On the other side of the coin, if he'd reacted as he had on our wedding night . . .

He must've feared I'd run away screaming.

Plus, his obsession had grown more apparent every hour. He wouldn't have been able to disguise it much longer. He'd told me, *"I've never wanted anything so badly, and I knew I would get only one shot at winning you."* No wonder he'd called our courtship grueling. I couldn't imagine the pressure he'd felt after a year, after all those changes, and all that work.

"Then why not simply romance you?" Mom asked.

My mind raced. "He and I got any issues resolved because I had no choice; I was already in so deep with him. If we'd had a typical courtship, I would've bolted at least three times. He knew that; he couldn't risk that. He thinks I'm his ... soul mate."

Karin frowned. "What're you saying, hon?"

I pinched the bridge of my nose. "He needed me to ignore the warning signs—and my common sense—and pursue *him*. He needed my family's interests to be aligned with his, everyone pushing for marriage. Which meant he needed heat. The cartel threat was a masterstroke."

"You've lost me, my dear," Gram said.

"He either set up the cartel sting—or he let it roll, capitalizing on it. Don't you guys see? He was pulling *a long con*!"

He had learned. From *us*.

Stunned silence reigned.

I replayed all his actions, seeing them afresh in the logical progression of a con. "After identifying me as his mark, he did his foundation work, cloning my phone and getting rid of any impediments—such as my fiancé. Then he assembled his team." I turned to Pete. "How did you get your job at the Calydon? Did you use juice?"

"It pretty much fell into my lap. Ohhh . . ." Comprehension dawned on his face. "I thought I'd gotten lucky. Jesus Christ, the Russian *positioned* me. Me! I was a shill."

I nodded. "Then came the meet. His sister-in-law said she was surprised when Dmitri recommended they all travel to Vegas. They were unwitting shills as well. He positioned them to orchestrate a memorable first impression. I found them so down to earth and fun; he benefitted just by association."

And step four? Integration? Dmitri had used gifts and sex to insinuate himself into my life.

Mom turned to Dad with a shocked laugh. "The Kansas City shuffle."

Dad nodded, looking thunderstruck. "Conning the con artist. I'll be damned."

Gram raised her glass. "He outfoxed the foxes, didn't he?"

Al shot his vodka, then said, "Vee Russian men are vily."

I gazed from one to the other. "You guys sent Brett to my house to pressure our mark into marrying me. Dmitri used the situation to his advantage, maneuvering *me* into the crisis."

"Only one problem," Benji said. "None of us e-mailed Brett."

I sank back down on the couch. "*Dmitri* did it. He could easily have e-mailed from my account." At my apartment, he'd told me, "This will be the last night I part from you," because he'd *known* we would be married the next day. I darted a glance at my ring. He'd had it on ice, just waiting.

"Oh, he's good," Mom said. "That ruthless Russian is *good*."

Karin said, "Turning down a prenup was his gesture of sacrifice."

I nodded. "To deepen my trust. He even gave me the ultimatum: tell him yes or tell him good-bye." He'd conned my entire family. And right now, they looked equally dazed—and admiring.

Dad muttered, "Well played, Sevastyan."

Mom said, "He was a hacker, a backer, and a fixer."

Pete gave a startled laugh. "Don't forget roper and mastermind."

Al petted his beard. "He played us like chess master."

Benji said, "We got freaking Keyser Söze-ed!"

"Vat does that mean?"

"The Usual Suspects?"

No wonder my grift sense kept sounding the alarm. I'd sensed his plot; deep down I'd known I was getting played! "Why are you guys not pissed?" I demanded. "Understanding his motives doesn't erase everything he did! He listened to our private conversations. He hired a woman to tempt my fiancé. He might've faked the cartel threat!"

Benji pointed out, "You can't get angry about half of those things because they were done in the service of a long con. Either they don't count—or else we're really shitty people."

"But we target assholes!"

Dad cleared his throat. "Sweet pea, his con *depended* on us using him for money."

"But only to save us from the cartel—a crisis he might have manufactured." No one seemed to care about that.

"He didn't want to blow his one shot with Vice." Mom sighed. "I'd suspected him of having all these awful, twisted motives."

"Me, too." Karin stood, heading for the playpen. She pulled Cash in her arms. *Gurgle. Blink.* He'd grown. I needed to hold him, but I was shaking too bad.

"We all did," Pete agreed. "Vice, your biggest fear was that he'd get to know the real you and bail. He had the same fear about you—and so he hedged his bets to hell and back."

Benji told me, "He knows you up and down, and he still tried to fight a car to get to you."

"You wanted a man to make a grand gesture?" Karin sat on the couch arm, adjusting Cash. "Like in the movies? How about devoting a year of his life and risking half his fortune to win you?"

Mom smoothed my hair from my face. "As for you . . . I've never seen you more upset than you were earlier—and yet you didn't take off his ring."

I shot to my feet, pacing again. "You guys are all as crazy as he is!" I pictured Dmitri right now, going nuts, wondering whether his wife would come back to him. *Just don't leave. . . . You are my home. . . .* His voice echoed inside my head.

But I couldn't get over the cartel. Was the whole thing a setup? "We were terrified for months. I thought Dad was going to be burned alive! Think of how many extra men Karin had to seduce, or how many hours I'd tried to run game, never knowing I was doomed to failure. Mom, how many nights did you lie awake terrified?"

And if he'd monitored my conversations and texts, he knew how much anxiety I struggled with over the last month; why not put me out of my misery? Why let me agonize over my ring? Had he been testing me?

A car engine sounded outside.

Benji stood to peer out the living room window. "Holy shit, it's him! Maybe he's tracking Vice."

"He wouldn't need to," Karin said. "He knows her. He knows *us.* And this is our sanctuary."

Pete raised his brows. "He's showing up here? On our turf? The balls on that son of a bitch!"

Al intoned, "Russian men *do* have beeg balls."

I darted over to the window. Exhaled a shocked breath. Dmitri was striding to our front door.

Gram chuckled over her vodka. "This is better than my soaps."

CHAPTER 37

I whirled around when I heard the front door open and close. No knock.

My family was agog at the towering billionaire who'd just barged right into our sanctuary without an invite.

He'd done a lot of things without an invite.

Standing across the room from me, he squared his shoulders, but I could tell how difficult walking into this lion's den was for him. A special kind of hell, as Lucía had said.

He loathed attention; all eyes were on him. This morning, all he'd wanted was to make a good first impression on my family. He'd gone back and forth over ties. Now his hair was unruly, his eyes wild, his hand bloody.

I fought the sympathy billowing up inside me. *Stay cold, Vice.*

"I need to speak with you, Vika." His voice was hoarse from yelling at me not to leave him.

My heart hurt, but I had to be strong. Which meant I couldn't let him touch me. "Anything you have to say to me can be said in front of them. From there."

"Very well." His gaze lit on each of my family members—who looked like they were settling in for the show—before returning to me. "I love you."

My lips parted.

Pete muttered, "I like it. Direct. No explanation. No rehashing."

Dmitri continued, "And you love me."

"Do I? I'm not sure I even know you. You may have tailored yourself to become more attractive to me."

"I did. To an extent. But you *do* know me."

"You spied on me for a year and used whatever you learned to trick me." How frustrated he must have gotten every time I'd thrown up roadblocks, claiming he didn't know me.

Or that his obsession would fade.

"Then wouldn't we have had *everything* in common?" he asked. "I also used what I'd learned to please you. You talked about California. I bought you a large part of it. You imagined travel. I have planned dozens of trips for you. You dreamed of designing clothes . . ."

And he'd given me a studio. Because I was an exhibitionist, he'd bought a mansion made of glass. He'd figured out my fetish and investigated it—though he struggled with it personally. He'd even gotten his scar lasered—for me. "What do you want from me now?"

"I want the wedding ring you bought for me that you think is hidden, the one I've tried on daily since its arrival. I want a ceremony in front of our families, with no secrets between us. I want to be married and not just wed."

He tried on the ring? "How could I ever trust you? How could you ever trust me?"

"Each time I put my faith in you I was rewarded, but I was never surprised—because I *know* you."

"Up and down, apparently."

"Everything," he said shamelessly. "And you can trust me because I have never lied to you."

I thought back. My honest madman hadn't lied, but he *had* been slippery. When he'd described the night he'd had his epiphany, he hadn't quite included me: "I made a commitment to right my life and become a man worthy of a woman such as yourself." He'd meant that literally; I *was* the woman.

He'd even told me the truth about how he'd come to Vegas. He had been on his way to a facility. Seeing the video of his appearance back then, I could absolutely believe he'd been on the verge of taking his own life.

He appeared so different now. He *was* so different. He'd turned his entire existence around.

For me.

I was his "incentive." The one he'd face a loaded gun for.

He took a step closer, his eyes thralling me. "The first time I saw you, you were making jokes and laughing, and you were everything bright that was missing from my grim life. I was mesmerized; I had to follow. You went to another bar. There was a limerick contest. You delivered the winning one with an Irish burr."

I blushed to recall it—one too many syllables coupled with questionable taste—but I'd been hammered.

There once was a laddie from Nantucket, and if he saw a hole he would fuck it. A wooden fence down the row . . . had a nice circular hole . . . a splinter later, he'd come by the bucket.

"Vika, for the first time in memory, I laughed. The sound

coming from my chest startled me. And I knew you were the one for me. I just needed your name."

I cast my mind back. "The emcee asked me to tell the crowd about myself."

His expression grew stark. "And you said you were at your fucking bachelorette party. I'd finally found you, and you were engaged."

"So you took it upon yourself to manipulate my life," said the grifter.

"As I investigated your family, I discovered what a long con was. A badger game seemed ideal to begin with. I put one into place immediately."

My anger spiked. "You *knew* you'd be hurting me!" I started pacing again. "Do you have any idea how bad that screwed me up?"

"I hated hurting you!" He scrubbed his busted-up hand over his face, seeming not to feel his injury. "I made a deal with myself: I would try to entrap him just once. I reasoned if he proved weak enough to fold—especially so close to your wedding—then eventually he would stray all on his own. I told myself if he resisted, I would leave you alone forever." Dmitri gave me that lifeline look. "But that was a goddamned lie—because I never could have given you up. I would've thrown a thousand women at him until he succumbed."

A breath left my lungs, and I slowed my pacing. "Emailing him to meet me was needlessly cruel."

"You have to play to pay." He was using our own logic against us! "You assumed one of your family members did it, but you held no lasting resentment against them."

Shit. Good point. "What purpose did fighting him serve?"

"None. I merely wanted to thrash him for being disloyal to

you." Dmitri's fists clenched. "How could he, after he got to have all those memories with you? I envy him every one."

Obviously, Dmitri had read all my private messages, all of Brett's recollections—but I couldn't talk; Pete and I had rued the missed opportunity to clone Dmitri's phone.

"Ultimately, the blame for hurting you goes to your ex-fiancé. He didn't appreciate what he had," Dmitri grated. "So yes, I made him my mark, because you deserve a faithful husband. And unlike him, I *can* keep my eyes on the queen!"

Oh. My. God. Broad-tosser wordplay. This man could not be sexier.

Gram, Mom, and Karin sighed.

In a sly tone, Al murmured, "Checkmate."

Not quite. "Was the cartel threat even real?"

"Yes."

My pacing ramped up. "Did you manipulate the kingpin for your own purposes?" I could *never* get over that. Not if he'd exposed my family to danger.

Yet I couldn't believe Dmitri would do that.

"I *encouraged* him to accept my money instead of harming Joseph." Dmitri waved to indicate my dad.

I froze. "You what?"

Dad appeared stunned; Mom looked at Dmitri as if he were a hero of old.

"The threat was very real." Dmitri took another step closer to me. "I told you I mended fences with my brother. At first, I did it because you obviously revere family, and I wanted to show no rifts in mine." *A united front is a powerful thing, no?* "But Aleks was of great assistance in those cartel negotiations."

Because Aleks was a *mafiya vor*. "The business matters that were *crucial* to you . . ." Dmitri had gone to his brother—hat in hand after decades of anger—to save my dad and my family.

"I paid the kingpin off, promising even more would come, but I asked him not to inform you that your debt was satisfied."

Pete said, "Creating a sense of urgency."

Dmitri nodded to him, then turned back to me. "I confided to Aleks my plan to win you. He alone understood I couldn't *learn* charm and that courting you in a traditional fashion would end in failure. We both knew I could only hide my . . . limitations—and my obsession with you—for so long."

His sexual limitations. Because people who dated had sex.

"You knew I would pull a milk-cow." The first time I'd told him we couldn't sleep together, he'd seized on it.

He inclined his head.

"Did Maksim and the others know about me and my family?"

"No, not until the morning after you met everyone. He and Vasili, his security head, ran a check on you over the night. Your efforts to hide your background would've been effective, but there is nothing those two can't find."

Benji raised his hand. "Wrong time to ask if I could chat with them?"

Dmitri looked receptive, but I glared at my brother, and he shut up.

"Maksim came to me the next day," Dmitri said, "to break the news that you were a con artist, from a family of them. I admitted I was running my own con. He believed you would end any relationship we might have once you found out. To him, my hopes seemed doomed. My family has not visited us or called you because none of them wanted to lie to you—or reveal my plot before I could confess it to you."

"How did Lucía take the news?" She'd been targeted by a man who'd used con tricks.

"She was fearful I would lose you as well. She's been giving me tips this month."

I worried my bottom lip. "Why not wait longer? You told me you weren't ready."

"Your badger games accelerated my plans." He raked his fingers through his hair, even more tension stealing over him. "I didn't want you seducing other men! So I burned your marks. But investigating each one was time-consuming. Texting Nigel as his scorned wife was easy; discovering her private number in St. Barts was not."

He'd investigated them all? I grasped for my sense of indignation. "Why let me agonize over asking you for money? You knew I considered fencing my ring." The one still comfortably parked on my finger.

"And I was silently willing you to turn to me instead. You believe the ring is a symbol. When you decided to trust me, I had hope you were keeping *me* as well as the ring."

I narrowed my eyes. "You were testing me? That's why you reminded me I could walk with the money at any time."

Nod. "I was certain of you from the beginning, but I wanted proof for anyone who might doubt your intentions toward me."

"Like your family."

Slow shake of his head. "Like *you*."

I swallowed. "Would you ever have come clean about everything you did?"

Another step closer. When had he gotten within a few feet of me? "I told you I would reveal all my secrets once you revealed yours. Explaining what I'd done would have been a lot easier—*after* you disclosed what you and your family did for a living."

Good point. Again.

"I never lied, Vika."

The grifter in me had to applaud his smoothness; it could be argued I simply hadn't been asking the right questions. I would try to now. "Is there anything else you haven't told us that I would like to know? Are there any more secrets?"

"*Da.* Since I first learned your address, I've had one of my men watching over you. When I wasn't."

I knew it! I couldn't decide what level of creepy that was.

"You are the most precious thing to me in the world; how could I not protect you?"

When he put it that way, *creepy* seemed a bit extreme.

"In fact, each of you had a detail until I was satisfied the cartel danger had passed completely."

I gazed over all of my family, lingering on little Cash. Dmitri had safeguarded each of us when we'd needed it most.

As if he was already a member of our pack.

He parted his lips to say more, then hesitated.

I shook my head warningly. "Spit it out."

"The cartel was embarrassed to have been swindled. They wanted to make an example of your father."

My gaze shifted to my parents. Mom's nails dug into Dad's arm. How close she'd come to losing him . . . He covered her hand, expression grave.

My lips moved wordlessly. Instead of having this conversation, I could be putting flowers by a tombstone right now, sick with the knowledge of how much my Dad had been tortured.

That was the checkmate.

Dmitri turned to Karin. "You should know the father of your child spies on you. Every Tuesday and Friday when you take Cash to the park."

Karin clutched her son closer, her face lighting up.

Dmitri added, "But also outside of the, uh, camera house."

Her face fell. To Walker, it would look like she'd slept with tons of lechers.

We would deal with that in time.

Dmitri turned back to me. "Now you know everything. Vika, I have no secrets left."

The anxiety I'd struggled with disappeared, because there was nothing left to ping my radar. He'd laid all his cards on the table.

My grift sense was finally at ease.

He took another step closer, his eyes solemn amber. "This past year was torture—I heard your voice and saw you, but I wasn't able to talk to you or touch you. Every day I tormented myself wondering if you could love me back. Yet I would do it all over again." His voice broke lower when he said, "Understand me, *moya zhena*, I would do the whole thirty-two years over again."

My breath left me. The magnitude of what he was saying . . .

I glanced around. Gram and Al raised glasses in approval. Karin nodded emphatically. Benji gave me a thumbs-up, and Pete mouthed, *Duh.*

Mom and Dad held hands, looking so in love, a shining example that fairy tales did in fact exist. Well, when they were so perfectly matched. . . .

It fully sank in that Dmitri Sevastyan hadn't just pulled a single con. He hadn't merely utilized tricks of confidence artistry. Grifting was a life choice, and he'd lived it for a year, learning our lingo and our ways to become a master. An aristocrat grifter. The con who played cons.

Getting played never felt so good.

I crossed the short distance to my husband. "Dmitri, you're not a gull." Hadn't I called him a thrall from night one?

"I . . . no, I don't suppose I am." Hope flared in his eyes. "Perhaps I'm starting to read people better. Because I think you're about to kiss me." He murmured, "Do it, Vika."

Two tears in a bucket. Right now I didn't feel as if I'd be reaching for the stars; I felt as if I'd be claiming what was mine. My *due*. I clasped him close and rose up on my toes. Then I kissed my husband.

A grifter for a grifter. . . .

EPILOGUE

One wedding dress later . . .

You would think I'd given Dmitri the moon.

From our bedroom balcony, I watched him showing off his ring to his groomsmen—Maksim, Aleks, Pete, and Benji—at our reception.

Glorious did not begin to describe my husband in a tux.

In fact, the five of them made quite a picture, all of them formally dressed, lit by the brilliant fire-red and gold sunset over the Pacific.

Karin, my maid of honor, and bridesmaids Lucía and Nat had just helped me gather the train of my gown into a pleated bustle. Then they'd returned downstairs to give me a minute to decompress.

Our home was inundated with family, all of our bungalows filled. Guests laughed on the dance floor, drank fine wines, and polished off sumptuous delicacies. Hey, free food awakened any grifter's appetite. My little cousins ran around on the beach with the dogs Maksim and Lucía had brought with them.

How Jess—part bridesmaid, part coordinator—had planned the elaborate ceremony and reception in such a short time was beyond my comprehension.

She'd even made all the arrangements for Dmitri and me to go to Paris for our honeymoon, advising me cryptically that there was one club in particular we'd want to visit. . . .

Champagne glass in hand, I leaned on the balcony rail and watched Dmitri laughing with the others. Seeing him this happy made my heart feel too big for my chest. Over the last three weeks, he'd relaxed so much, radiating contentment now that he had nothing to hide.

The day we'd cleared the air at my parents', I'd introduced him to in-laws who already adored him as my "hero husband," the man who'd saved Gentleman Joe's life. Dmitri had been less discomfited than usual, probably because he'd already bared his soul in front of everyone.

That night, he'd taken me back to the Caly. After he'd made love to me until my toes curled and I'd promised him *everything*, he'd told me one last secret:

"If I hadn't hit rock bottom, I never would have been in Las Vegas. I never would have found you. The pain of the past is so much easier to bear now that I feel it had purpose. It led me to you. *Moya zhena*, you are my reward for enduring. . . ."

Today I'd pledged myself to Dmitri Sevastyan with no pressure and for only one reason: I loved him.

As if he'd sensed my thoughts, he glanced up at me. His vivid eyes brightened even more, and his smile widened. He started for me at once.

Judging by Pete and Benji's puzzled looks, I figured Dmitri

had left the conversation midsentence. His brothers just appeared amused.

Footsteps boomed as Dmitri bounded up the stairs to reach me. How fitting. Two months ago to the day, I'd climbed the stairs to reach his lair, hoping I could tempt a beast.

I had. Then I'd made him part of my pack.

And Lady Luck smiled. . . .

Catching his breath, Dmitri joined me on the balcony. A healthy flush tinged his chiseled cheekbones, highlighting his golden eyes.

The color always brought to mind blazing sunsets and new beginnings.

"I've been waiting for you to come down," he said, as if I'd been gone ages. "How much time does it take to do a bustle? You *made* the dress quicker than this." The first garment created in my new studio.

The strapless silk gown was a modified A-line with a straight-cut neckline, classic seams and no embellishment. The traditional-white skirt had a sweep train and ballroom bustle. So incredibly simple.

Except the bodice was black.

I called the look "edgy angelic." It'd turned out pretty snazzy, if I did say so myself. Like any great idea, the process of making it had been inspired, fast and furious.

Dmitri had been there for every step. He'd made sure I ate and slept, and we'd nearly broken that poor couch.

Well, he'd been there *almost* every step of the way. I'd surprised him with the final reveal, loving his brows-drawn expression when he'd first seen me on my dad's arm. As Dad had murmured, "He's bewildered by his good fortune.

A man like that will never take it for granted. He'll never take *you* for granted. . . ."

Now I gazed up at Dmitri. "I was just savoring the sunset and the music—and my husband showing off his ring."

"You saw that, did you?" He held it up, unable to stop another grin. "At last, it's mine. Which means I'm yours."

I'd had the band engraved on the inside with the words: *Because I know you'll never take it off. Love, V.S.*

We'd decided to go with traditional vows today—his voice had been rumbling and proud as he'd repeated his—but last night, I'd asked him what he would say on the fly.

He'd answered, "I want to protect you. I want to spoil you. I want to have children with you and spoil them too. I want to grow old with you. And at the end of our lives, you will have no doubt you were loved and adored by me for every second."

Yep, I'd jumped him all the way up till midnight. . . .

He put his arm around my shoulders, enveloping me with his heat and tantalizing scent. Together we watched our families celebrate.

Among all the other things Dmitri had brought into my life, I'd gotten two new brothers and three sisters (with a long-suffering sigh, he'd finally claimed Jess as family). All of them were thrilled by this marriage.

Before the ceremony, Lucía had teased me, "Make sure Vice has something old, something new, something stolen, and something blue."

With no secrets, our families could be themselves and meld. We already saw signs of it.

By the pool, Vasili and Al were deep in a game of chess, Gram spectating. When Al had first broken out the board, I'd murmured to Dmitri, "It's like Iceman versus Maverick, huh?"

Zero recognition. *"Top Gun?"* My husband and I had a decade of movies to get through.

And then there was melding with Benji and Jess.

Reading my mind, Dmitri waved in their direction. "I never saw that coming."

They were sitting together, both laughing at something Jess was saying. When they'd first met earlier, zany, ballsy Jess had gazed up at his face and *blushed.* And then she'd grown tongue-tied. As for Benji, he couldn't seem to take his eyes—or his camera lens—off her.

I nodded. "I'd worried how Karin might take it, but she's happy for him. She admitted she's still lost for Cash's father." The fact that Walker was watching his son grow up, every Tuesday and Friday, was huge for her.

Until she figured out what to do about their relationship, she'd decided to continue going to the park—without letting on that the ruse was up—so he could have that time.

Down on the dance floor, she laughed with Cash in her arms, while he gurgled his delight. He looked very dapper in the tuxedo romper Mom had made him and seemed determined to flash everyone his pair of teeth.

"I have an idea about Karin and Walker," Dmitri said, his eyes lively. "I think we should run a little con."

"You grifter!" I said in mock indignation, before murmuring, *"Tell."*

"We buy the remains of his company—in Karin's name. Yet then they'll learn they only have so much time to right the ship before it goes down. Perhaps a fake loan coming due?"

My eyes widened. "Forcing them to work together! You brilliant man."

He took my hand and pressed a kiss to my palm. "Con artistry is what I do."

I sighed. Being married to Dmitri trumped a royal flush.

He was still a dream man; he remained too good to be true. But when we reached for the stars *together*, they became ours.

And he was right; why did dreams have to end?

Laughter sounded from below, drawing our gazes.

Maksim escorted Lucía to the dance floor, twirling her around. Natalie was even coaxing Aleks to dance.

That Sevastyan devotion shone bright.

Mom and Dad were already out on the floor, as flirtatious and excited as if this were their first date. They were *living* a happily-ever-after.

I turned to Dmitri. "Do you think we'll be as happy together as my parents in thirty years?"

He cradled my face in his hands, and our gazes locked. His eyes no longer held secrets, only promise. "Victoria Sevastyan, I will make sure of it."

I laid my hand over his strong heart. "I'm going to want this for a lot longer than three decades. I'll want you forever."

He leaned down to graze his lips over mine. "What my wife wants, she gets."

Below us, cheers and wolf whistles sounded, and we grinned as we kissed.

Dmitri Sevastyan had told me he would free me and give me the entire world.

He does both, every single day. . . .

CPSIA information can be obtained at www.ICGtesting.com
Printed in the USA
LVOW11s1922230616

493837LV00008B/554/P